The Gathering

THE PROPHECY SERIES
BOOK THREE

DINAH MCCALL

Editing by Sharyn Cerniglia
scerniglia@gmail.com

Cover Design and Interior format by The Killion Group
http://thekilliongroupinc.com

DEDICATION

The Gathering marks the third book of the Prophecy series and as the Dove stated, "the end of one thing and the beginning of another", which could also be an analogy for life.

As long as we live, we are changing. We grow in one aspect until it is no longer valuable to us and then begin anew, looking for a better way to spend our lives.

I dedicate this book to the people who aren't afraid to peek around corners, to push the envelope, to jump into the tide of change. They are the adventurers who pave the way for those less brave.

I dedicate this book to the People who first belonged in this, our world. Your names may have been forgotten, but the memory of your tragedy lives on.

FROM THE AUTHOR

The Gathering was to be the last book in the Prophecy stories.

These stories were given to me through dreams with the understanding that I tell them in a way that honors The People who are native to the two continents we call North and South America. It was first theirs, and while history was not kind to them, in my dreams they were given a way to change their fate and so I am telling it to you now, as it was told to me.

However, as this story unfolds, it became apparent that this story would not be the end – that the Old Ones had more they wanted known. So I continue as I am led with the full assurance that when it is finished, you will understand the depths of what was lost in the beginning and what is still possible before it ends.

PROLOGUE

The Old Ones knew. They'd always known.

They told of a prophecy.

They said a storm was coming.

They said a Windwalker would bring it and leave his child to end it.

They said the storm would spread quietly and unnoticed, like roots beneath the ground growing stronger and farther and linking one thing to another until what was above the ground could never be undone. So it was told, and so it would be.

The vast land of an untamed continent, which in the time of the New Ones had been called North America, was still a world in the making. The wealth of it was not measured by gold or jewels, but in the richness of a horizon that went on forever, rife with a race of people in perfect harmony with the universe.

But there was a plague in the making. A plague that, in the centuries to come, would decimate their people, destroy the ecosystem, annihilate the wildlife, and forever rock the balance of their lives. And the only thing standing between them and the end of everything were the people scattered out across the vast valley below.

The people in that valley called themselves the New Ones, although the time in which they were living was not the time in which they'd been born. It was difficult to explain to people native to this land that the New Ones were not only from the future, but they were all that was left of the Native American race.

Their quest was an urgent one that began in their time when a burning meteor appeared in the sky. Within the space of a few days it became evident to all that Earth was going to die with no way to stop it. People went mad. Some killed themselves. Others tried to buy their way to salvation.

For the majority of the population, hope was lost, except for the Native Americans. White men called it a meteor, but the People knew different. A prophecy had been handed down among the tribes for many generations that this day would come. They knew the death in the sky was not a meteor but an ancient spirit called Firewalker, and they knew why it was coming.

It had become angry with them for losing their sense of pride and foregoing the Native way of life. They lost their faith and lost their culture and in doing so, lost their pride. They had destroyed who they were meant to be. Even their young were committing suicide rather than face the sadness of a hopeless future. And because of all that, Firewalker had come to end the suffering in a fiery blast of annihilation.

But as the Old Ones had warned of Firewalker's coming, they had also foretold that a woman of The People would appear, and with the help of an ancient spirit called the Windwalker, would be given all the knowledge and power she would need to lead the thousands who awaited her to safety.

And so it came to be.

A woman called Layla Birdsong let the Windwalker teach her, and then she let him love her. When his task was done, he left her with his baby in her belly and disappeared as mysteriously as he had appeared, and it broke her heart.

Still grieving his loss, she did what she'd been born to do. As Firewalker's journey was coming to a fiery end, she led The People through a portal back in time to the place where everything first began to go wrong – back to the jungles, to a city of the ancient Mayans called Naaki Chava, ruled by a chief called Cayetano.

The survivors came into the city into another way of life, broken by what they'd lost and horribly burned from the Firewalker's blast.

With time they healed and found a rhythm to their lives,

existing in peace and happiness for seventeen years while waiting for the Windwalker's baby daughter, Tyhen, to come of age. And just as she reached her seventeenth year, the city of Naaki Chava died in a fiery blast of ash and lava.

The natives of Naaki Chava escaped to the south with the Chief and Layla, who had taken the name of Singing Bird, while what was left of the New Ones followed Tyhen, the Windwalker's daughter in the opposite direction. Once again, the New Ones were on a march to finish what they'd come to do.

CHAPTER ONE

Tyhen stood motionless on a ridge above the valley where the New Ones had stopped to rest. She had called a halt knowing there would be protection from the wind between the two hills. As she did, the people dropped where they stood, some sitting, others stretching out to catch a quick nap.

Now the wind slapped her in the face like a jealous lover, stinging her skin and making her eyes burn. She turned her back to the blast and pulled the hood on her coat up closer around her face. The coat was made from bearskin and her leggings were made of deer skin. If she had been down on all fours, she would have blended easily into the background as an animal.

Although she stood lookout for unseen dangers, she stole a few moments to look for sight of Yuma, the man who held her heart. The New Ones called her The Dove, because she had been born to unite the native race, but it was Yuma, the Eagle, who loved and protected her.

Tyhen was young, barely seventeen when her journey had begun, and although the experiences had been harsh and they'd all lost weight and sleep over the months on the march, nothing could mar the beauty that came from within her.

As the daughter of such a powerful spirit she had been given all of the abilities she would need, all of the magic that a Windwalker possessed, but today she was feeling most human, grieving the loss of the family she'd left behind.

She would never see her mother or Cayetano again, and the twins Adam and Evan, who saw both the future and the past and who were like her brothers, had stayed behind as well. In the midst of thousands, she stood alone but for one man.

Pushing aside the sadness, she swept the horizon with one last glance and then began walking back down to join the others. As she did a harsh wind ruffled the brown fur lining the hood of her coat, tickling her cheeks and reminding her of the winter to come.

Once she reached the edge of the gathering she shoved the hood from her head, letting her long hair fall free as she sat down.

Grateful to be off her feet, she began watching a young boy of about ten years playing a few feet away. He was a handsome little man with skin as brown as hers and dark hair almost as long. He called himself Gecko. The name fit. He was skinny and as quick with his movements as the lizards that used to crawl on the walls inside the palace at Naaki Chava.

At the moment he was playing intently with something he'd found in the grass, and she wondered what it was that held his interest. When she realized he'd caught her staring she smiled. As she did, he quickly looked away.

She combed her fingers through her hair and then frowned as she glanced up. Storm clouds were gathering quickly – too quickly. Yesterday they'd found a marker tree pointing the way to water. The trunk had been bent when the tree was young to let travelers know which direction to go, and from the carving on the rock beneath the tree, it appeared to be a river. Now the tree was older and the trunk had formed an unnatural bend that would, for the life of the tree, point the way. However, from the looks of the sky, it was likely it would rain before they reached the river, so the riverbank would have to be their campground for the night. In the morning they would cross, bringing them one day closer to the great gathering of tribes. The Gathering would be the end of one thing and the beginning of another and while she was ready for this march to be over, for now she had other concerns.

With one last look at the sky, she pulled the pack off her back, dug out a piece of Montford Nantay's deer jerky and took a big bite. She eyed the people as she chewed and then glanced up at the sky again. The clouds were building, growing taller in the sky and turning dark. Soon they would have to leave.

She looked back at the little boy called Gecko as he continued to play, unaware that he'd been casting looks of longing her way. As she took another bite of her jerky, she caught Gecko watching, and laughed out loud at the startled expression on his face. When he grinned, she waved him over. As he approached, she offered him the other half of her jerky. As he took it from her hand, he dropped something in her palm in return and then ran.

Tyhen looked down at what he'd given her and frowned. She was still frowning when she felt a hand on the back of her shoulder and then Yuma was kneeling behind her. When he leaned forward to whisper in her ear, a swath of his long dark hair swung away from his face and slid down across her shoulder onto her breast, making her wish it was his hand and not his hair touching her there.

"You, my little Dove, are most beautiful when you laugh."

Just the sound of his voice made her ache for him. Some day they would have a life of their own again. It was enough to keep her focused on all of the dangers that still existed between them and that day.

"Thank you, my Yuma," she said, but in truth, she was silently admiring his wide shoulders and long legs as he knelt down beside her.

Yuma studied the dark circles beneath her eyes. She looked as weary as he felt. They had all been pushed to both physical and emotional limits, but none as much as Tyhen.

He traced the shape of her cheek with his thumb and then ran it lightly beneath the edge of her lower lip, remembering how soft it was and how crazy she made him when they made love.

"Did you eat?" he asked.

"Yes, a piece of Montford Nantay's fine jerky. I gave the last bit of it to Gecko."

Yuma shook his head. "That little one is never far from you. I will have to watch out for him. He is in love with you, I think."

Tyhen shrugged. "He is too young to know love."

Yuma's smile faded. He reached for her then and kissed her, leaving the imprint of his lips and his love on her heart.

"I was his age when I killed the man who would have ended your mother's life, and with you still in her belly. I knew I would love you before you were born. I knew you would be mine and you would love me forever."

The ache grew within her to lie with him again, but there was never any place or time to make that happen.

"Yes, I remember the story."

His dark eyes flashed. "I wasn't any older than Gecko, so I have no doubt what he feels is real to him." He started to say more when he saw what she was holding. "Where did you get that?"

She dropped it in Yuma's hand. "Gecko gave it to me. It's something I think he found in the grass."

"So, they were already here, too," Yuma muttered as his gut knotted. Yet another sign of how urgent this journey was becoming.

Tyhen frowned. "Who was here? What is this called?"

Yuma turned it over and over in his hand, studying the size and style of the hammered silver.

"It is called a buckle. It comes from a white man's belt to hold up his pants. It looks Spanish, which means the explorers – the men who were part of the ruin of our people - have already been here. Most likely this one died here since this would have been part of his clothing, but that won't stop more from coming."

The burden of what lay on Tyhen's shoulders felt even heavier.

"Are we too late to stop them?"

"No, no, but this just makes our journey more urgent," Yuma said.

Before she could answer, a hard gust of wind came over the rise, sweeping down the hill and bringing with it the faintest tinge of a scent that did not belong.

Yuma saw her frown.

"What's wrong?" he asked.

She shrugged. "Probably nothing. I think I'll walk around a few minutes before we leave just to make sure everyone is okay."

"Don't forget your gift," Yuma said, and held out the

buckle.

She didn't want anything that would remind her of intruders into their world, but Gecko had given it to her innocent of its origin, and so she dropped it in her pouch.

Yuma brushed a last kiss across her lips, then stood and helped her up.

"Soon, we need to start moving," Tyhen said.

Yuma nodded. "I will see to it, but first I need to find Stanley Bluejacket. He wasn't feeling well this morning."

Stanley was the oldest man living from the ones who'd come through the portal with her mother, and they all went out of their way trying to keep him healthy and on his feet.

"Find a healer if he needs one," she said.

"I will," Yuma said, and walked away as Tyhen ran back up the rise for a better view.

The wind was changing. It was coming out of the southwest now, moving the gathering storm clouds above them at a fast pace. She was trying to judge how long it would be before it caught up with them when she felt movement around her feet. Just as she looked down, a half-dozen rabbits came out of the tall grass, moving at a frantic pace. Startled by the unusual behavior, she turned to watch as they disappeared and missed seeing the deer that came over the rise behind them.

She jumped as it leaped past her. At that point she then turned and ran the rest of the way up to the highest ground. Yuma had the people up and moving now, strung out across the landscape as far as the eye could see and walking at a steady, plodding pace. The wind, which was part of the storm front, was pushing hard at their backs, giving them a sense of unspoken urgency and subconsciously hastening their steps.

She watched them a few moments longer then turned and faced the wind and heard screams coming from within. Her skin crawled. The Old Ones were talking.

Something bad was coming!

She began looking for Yuma and when she didn't see him, had to trust the spirits to send him her thoughts.

Yuma! Where are you? Can you see me?

Yes, I see you. I always know where you are. Look down. Both my arms are in the air.

She saw him and quickly shared her concerns.

Something is wrong. The New Ones must get to the river as fast as they can. I will give the warning, but you must lead them and see to the crossing. They have to get on the other side of the river to be safe.

She saw Yuma's reaction to her warning as he turned in place, searching the horizons.

I see nothing. What is it you fear? Is it the buffalo? Do you fear a stampede?

No, not the buffalo. Fire. I think the land is going to burn.

Yuma had long since learned not to question the Windwalker's daughter. She might be young in years, but she was ancient in power and wisdom. He was already shifting his pack for a swifter pace when he heard her voice on the wind, carrying her warning for all the New Ones to hear.

"Danger comes! Follow Yuma! Run with the wind at your back and don't stop until you have crossed the river! The prairie is on fire!"

The New Ones had been moving in groups, staying together in families, walking without looking up and, when needed, leaning on the younger and stronger, determined to see this walk through to the bitter end. But when they began hearing Tyhen's voice they immediately stopped. Her warnings had saved them too many times before to ignore one now.

The message was frightening, but there was no time to lose focus. Like Yuma, they shifted the loads they carried, grabbed the hands of the young and the old and started moving – first at a trot, and then a little faster, and then lengthened their strides to an all-out race.

Yuma purposefully moved part-way up the slope on the opposite side of the valley so that he was easily visible then set a pace. Their numbers were in the thousands and the river was still at least an hour away. He didn't know if they could outrun a fire and get across the water before they burned, but they were about to find out.

Tyhen watched until the people were in motion before she walked down the other side of the rise and out of sight. She had to go higher to see what they were facing, and since she had been standing on the highest point in the area and still saw nothing, she had to go to the air.

Lifting her arms above her head, she began to chant, summoning the wind to do her bidding. The air above her began spinning, going faster and faster, gathering in size and power until it grew into a giant whirlwind and took her up, carrying her high above the ground.

From that height she could see for many miles in all directions and it didn't take long to find the source of her concern. The storm clouds far behind them were dark and low to the ground, and every few seconds a quick flash of the long fire would come down from the clouds and strike the earth and the dry grass upon it.

In the jungles of Naaki Chava where she'd been born, rain came quietly and without warning, falling from the sky like tears from the eyes. But in this land, the fingers of fire that came down from the storm clouds made noise like the mountain that had burned up Naaki Chava, popping and cracking in horrifying explosions before it would let go of the rain. She didn't like cold and frozen, and she didn't understand how fire and rain could come from the same clouds, but in this land they did.

She rode the wind a little higher, going farther away from Yuma and closer to the gathering storm. When she finally saw the wide swath of smoke many miles behind and how fast it was growing in power and speed with every bite the fire took of the long grass, her heart sank.

She rode the whirlwind back down to the ridge and looked toward the east, to the frantic exodus of the New Ones. There was a knot in her belly as she watched them run. She had to stop a wind-fed fire before her people burned.

To the New Ones, the horror of Tyhen's warning was like a bad dream. They'd run from a landslide after leaving Naaki Chava. They'd survived so much since that it was difficult to accept that they were running for their life again.

Tyhen was still on the rise when she heard Yuma's voice in her head.

Run with me. I cannot keep you safe if I cannot see you.

She felt his fear for her and understood because she felt the same for him.

But I cannot keep all of you safe if I hide from what comes. I am the Windwalker's daughter. I cannot die.

Yuma wouldn't look back. It took everything in him to lead the people away from her and certain danger. She'd made the right call. He just didn't like it.

And so the New Ones ran until their sides were aching and their lungs were burning. When someone stumbled and fell, others paused long enough to gather up the dropped belongings and pull the runner back to his feet. They'd come too far together to abandon anyone now.

Yuma was young and strong, yet even he felt the strain of keeping up the speed. Running in cold-weather clothing was confining, but there were no other choices. Even after they reached the river, getting everyone safely across would take longer than the race to get there.

He did not panic until the animals came up from behind them and ran into their midst as if the people were not there.

The first to appear were antelope. They came over the ridge beside him in a thundering herd and enveloped him. Before he knew it he was running with them, caught up in a life and death situation completely separate from the fire. If he stumbled or fell they would trample him before he had a chance to regain his footing.

He could feel the heat from their bodies, hear the grunts and the squeals as they jostled each other to get away, and when he caught a glimpse of their wild-eyed panic, the flared nostrils, and the flecks of bloody foam coming from their gaping mouths, he knew they had been running for a very long time.

When the last of the herd finally ran past him and up and over the next rise, his legs were shaking and his gut was in knots.

After that, he began seeing rabbits coming out of their burrows and running in circles, as if unsure of which way to go. Flocks of birds that should have been going to roost were, instead, taking to the skies.

When a small herd of buffalo appeared on the horizon ahead of them and running at an angle the New Ones would eventually intercept, he groaned. They had to stop and let them pass or be trampled.

Luckily, the herd was small and the time loss was brief. It allowed the New Ones pause to catch their breath. When they began to run again, they moved faster, lengthening their steps to make up for lost time.

The smoke was getting stronger. Already it was making Tyhen's eyes water and burn even though she had come to what felt like an impossible conclusion. She had to stop the fire. But how? Her power came from the wind, but it was wind fueling the fire that threatened their lives. She looked up at the clouds. If only it would rain here – now – but the wind-driven storm front was ahead of the rain.

She wouldn't let herself think of Yuma. She couldn't think of what they might lose if she didn't succeed. She stood up and began to chant, once again creating the whirlwind that took her up into the air. Now she was flying above the smoke and below the storm – a dangerous place to be, even for a Windwalker's daughter.

Never before had Tyhen doubted her ability to do what must be done, but she'd never before been faced with an enemy that did not have feet.

When the thick black smoke enveloped the whirlwind, it began pulling sparks from the fire into it until she was part of the blazing inferno. The heat enveloped her, and the smoke blinded her, but still she flew until she'd reached the backside of the fire - until she saw the vast landscape of blackened earth behind it, and the still smoking bodies of animals that had not been able to outrun it, and felt sick.

Off in the distance the thunderstorm was in full force. Rain was falling from the clouds like water spilling over the waterfalls back in Naaki Chava. It was what Yuma called a deluge. Tyhen needed that rain. If only there was a way to move the rain forward like she moved through the sky. And then a thought occurred. She didn't know what would happen, but she was willing to give it a try.

She flew into the rain, chanting as she went, wrapping the rain up in the whirlwind like the smoke and fire had done before, pulling more and spinning faster until the whirlwind became the eye of a rain-wrapped tornado. She aimed the storm to the East and began barreling across the prairie, pushing the tornado toward the fire and then through the fire until she outran it.

Then she threw back her head, held up her arms and closed her eyes. Remembering the feel of her father's arms around her as he gave her all of his wisdom and power, she called upon the Old Ones and pulled the breath from the sky into the storm front, turning it into a maelstrom.

Seen from below, it was a mile-wide monster of rain and hail sweeping across the prairie ahead of the fire, so big and so powerful that it was pulling up grass and earth within the funnel as it went.

Inside the storm, the long fire ebbed and flowed around Tyhen, growing and waning as the power continued to build, swirling all around her as it popped and cracked until suddenly it exploded and shot down through the tornado, cutting through the rain and the clouds all the way to the ground.

The hood of Tyhen's coat had long since slipped from her head. She had become part of the storm and the rain and she was so charged by the power from the long fire that the mass of dark hair normally hanging halfway down her back was fanned out around her face like shiny black feathers on a warrior's headdress.

She rode the storm until the flames were gone and the valley was rain-soaked for miles, too wet to catch fire. The New Ones were safe, but the funnel of the tornado had become too dense for her to see. She didn't know how far away she was from Yuma, but her strength was almost gone. It was time to let go of the wind.

She began decreasing the power until the tornado she had created was gone, and all that was left was the small, rain-wrapped whirlwind around her.

Unaware of where she was and was too weak to focus, she went down, landing on the slope of a hill. The moment her feet touched earth, she staggered, dropped to her knees, and passed out.

The thunderstorm finally caught up, pounding the land and

the smoking remnants of the fire and soaking the body of the unconscious girl lying on the side of a hill.

CHAPTER TWO

By the time they finally reached the river, the New Ones collapsed where they stood. Some were too tired to be afraid, while others dropped to their knees sobbing, praying to the Old Ones to save them.

Yuma looked back, but all he could see was a wall of black smoke rising higher, coming closer. If he didn't get them across the water, this race would have been for nothing.

His legs were shaking and he was trying to catch his breath when Montford and Johnson Nantay came stumbling toward him. They looked as exhausted as he felt, and yet the first words out of their mouths were offers of help.

"Yuma, what do you need of us?"

"We need to find a safe place to ford. The river is wide. I am hoping it is not so very deep."

"We can both swim. We will search," they said, and hurried back to get their gear.

Yuma called out to those around him, telling them to rest until they could find a safe place to cross and to spread the word. And so they did, repeating the order until every person there knew what came next. After a brief rest they began coming to the river to quench their thirst and refill water bags.

Yuma walked down to the shore, dropped to his belly and drank water until his teeth hurt from the cold. When he got up, he turned around to look at the wide swath of towering smoke and closed his eyes against the horror of what he saw.

Tyhen... I cannot fly with you. You have to fly back to me.

Then he dropped to his knees, swung the pack from his back to his lap and dug out a piece of jerky. He ate without tasting, eating only for nourishment while watching the sky, wondering how long they had before the fire caught up with them.

Montford and Johnston came back, but not with good news. The river was over their heads a mile in either direction. Either they swam across, or started walking downriver to find a crossing, or waited for a miracle.

Yuma felt sick. He didn't want to believe they had come this far only to die in some random prairie fire.

"There has to be another way," he muttered, but before he could offer up a suggestion, Johnston grabbed him by the arm.

"Look! Look at that!"

Someone screamed while others groaned in disbelief. A massive tornado had just come out of the smoke. It was many miles away but because of its size, easily seen. After a few minutes, it became evident that, with no place to run and no place to hide, unless that tornado turned or dissipated they would not burn, but they would still die.

They watched the rain come down from the massive cloud, falling so heavily that at times the tornado almost disappeared.

The little boy who called himself Gecko walked up beside Yuma and pointed at the sky.

"The fire is dying," he said.

Yuma flinched, and then his eyes narrowed as he put a hand on the young boy's head.

"I think you are right," he said.

Satisfied that he'd said what he came to say, Gecko walked away.

Yuma glanced at the boy and then back at the storm. It did appear as if the smoke was less, but he'd thought it was just hidden. And then it hit him. A tornado was made of wind and the rain wrapped tornado was putting out the fire.

Yuma's heart skipped a beat.

It was Tyhen!

He looked out across the land where the New Ones had stopped. He could see their fear but no one seemed ready to quit. Some were praying. Others were talking about running out of the tornado's path, when Yuma began running through the crowd, shouting aloud to be heard.

"That is not a tornado. It is Tyhen. She is bringing the rain to the fire to save us," he yelled, and word began to spread.

The New Ones turned, staring in disbelief at the monster of rain and wind, trying to imagine the tall, slender girl being capable of such a feat.

But then one of the New Ones noticed the tornado was beginning to dissipate, which caused great elation among those stopped along the river. The funnel got smaller and smaller until it ended as abruptly as it had appeared. When they realized the fire was out, they knew that Yuma had been right.

She'd saved them! The Windwalker's daughter had saved them once again!

Shouts of happiness and the laughter of relief rang out as the people began recounting their luck. Even if the rain came later and drenched their camp, being alive to get wet was a good thing.

Yuma was in awe. His pride in what she'd done was beyond words. He began setting up their camp, expecting her to show up at any time.

Back in the jungles far south of the ruined city of Naaki Chava, the survivors who'd gone with Chief Cayetano and Singing Bird were building a new place to live, laying it out like they had in Naaki Chava, with streets that intersected and dwellings built within in a small square plot of cleared land. They named this city Boomerang. They were the same people, but in a new place with new ways.

Word was already spreading throughout the nearby tribes about the new way of life and that other languages were being taught in the new city. The People had been told if they learned these things, they would know how to protect themselves from the strange white men who came in from the water, who ravaged their people, stole their food, and left babies in their women's bellies.

Meanwhile, Adam and Evan, the adopted sons who'd grown up to be the shamans of Naaki Chava and who had followed Cayetano and Singing Bird to help them get safely settled, were making plans to rejoin Yuma and Tyhen.

Two new shamans had been chosen to serve the Chief once they were gone, and despite their initial fears that Cayetano would not accept them, the past few weeks he had proved them wrong.

The morning had been spent discussing the wisdom of putting guards at strategic places along the shoreline. They would be the warning system for the city should any long boats reappear. They were deep in discussion about the project when the meeting was interrupted by a long, high-pitched scream. Before the twins could react, Cayetano was on his feet.

"Singing Bird!" he shouted, and ran out of the throne room toward his sleeping quarters with the others close behind him.

Guards ran into the palace, thinking someone was attacking the queen, and for a few frantic moments, chaos reigned.

Cayetano found Singing Bird face down on the floor, sobbing so hard she could barely breathe.

"What's wrong? Who has hurt you?" Cayetano shouted, but she couldn't answer.

As he picked her up in his arms, she fainted.

"Look and see if she was bitten," Evan said, and started to examine her arms and legs for sign of snakebite.

But the moment he touched her, he saw what had made Singing Bird scream. He gasped and jumped back as if he'd seen a ghost.

"Dark clouds. A firestorm! Tyhen flew into it and disappeared."

Adam's heart sank. If this vision from daughter to mother was so strong that it crossed the thousands of miles between them, then Tyhen was in trouble.

"It is time, brother!" he said quickly.

Cayetano was torn between concern for the love of his life, losing the two men he'd raised as his own sons, and the daughter of his heart in another country in dire need. And much as he regretted the need, they'd all known this day would come.

"Go! Do what you must! Better my children live away from me than not at all!" Cayetano cried.

"But what about Singing Bird?" Adam asked.

The tallest shaman, a young man named Moki who bore the

scars of a jaguar on his face and chest, quickly stepped into the conversation.

"We are here and will not betray your trust," he said, and with that, Adam and Evan took off at a lope, heading for their lodging.

They had packed for this day many weeks ago, and now all they had to do was grab their things, take the crystal cube from their childhood that had saved them from Firewalker, and find Tyhen.

Adam was digging through his pack for Tyhen's silver necklace with the little bird charm. It was the link they needed to find her when they stepped into the portal. He dropped it over his head while Evan was stripping off his clothes and issuing orders.

"We have to dress for colder weather like we see the New Ones in our dreams, and we need to hurry. I can't get a fix on Tyhen and she's not answering my messages," he said,

"What did you see?" Adam asked, as he also began to change.

"All I saw was her flying into fire," Evan said.

Adam paled. "Windwalkers don't die, remember? Surely she is alright."

Evan shrugged. "She may not die, but she can suffer great harm. If she is alone, many things could happen that might hinder the process."

Within minutes they were ready to leave. The pants they were wearing were long and made of animal skin which they wore tucked into the fur moccasins that laced up to their knees. Their shirts were also animal hide, scraped and cured to soft, supple leather, and their long, hooded coats were spotted jaguar skins lined with Alpaca wool procured from the traders who passed through their city. It was clothing for cold and frozen, not here in the sweltering heat.

"I feel like I am cooking in a stew," Evan said.

"But not for long," Adam said, as he took the crystal cube from his pocket, balanced it on one point and then started it spinning like a top.

At first it wobbled, but he spun it again, and the second time it caught. It began to spin in front of them, faster and faster until a light appeared behind it. A humming sound came from it as the light grew brighter and larger until the energy pull from one dimension to the next opened the portal in a blinding flash.

Adam was holding onto the bird necklace with one hand, and Evan with the other.

"Grab the cube!" he yelled, and between one heartbeat and the next, they leaped into the light and disappeared.

The next thing they knew they were flat on their backs in the dark. The air smelled of rain, although the sky was clearing in one direction enough they could see a few stars. A bolt of lightning streaked across the sky in the other direction, and as it did, momentarily lit the land around them.

That's when they saw a body a few yards down, lying motionless on the side of the hill.

"There! She's there!" Adam yelled, and then the light was gone.

But he'd seen where she was and began crawling on his hands and knees with Evan right beside him until they reached her body.

Evan thrust his fingers along the base of her neck, feeling for a pulse.

"She's alive!" he cried.

"But something's wrong with her!" Adam said. "Concentrate! Where is Yuma? Where are the others?"

Evan closed his eyes and saw the encampment spread out along a riverbank and saw smoldering fires built with wet wood, making more smoke than heat.

"That way," he said, pointing east.

"How far?" Adam asked.

"I can't tell, but we need to get her there. Healers will know what to do."

Adam touched her and then froze. She had grown more powerful than she'd been when she left Naaki Chava, beyond anything he could ever have imagined. He'd seen the storm and the fire and he'd seen her in the tornado, and despite the fact that they'd grown up together, for a few frantic moments he was afraid of her.

"She doesn't need a healer," Adam said. "Remember when

she was younger and fought the spirit of the evil shaman that died on the swinging bridge? Remember how exhausted she was when it was over?"

Evan nodded. "Yes. Cayetano carried her all the way back to the palace."

"That's what's wrong with her now. She fought something today that was so powerful it sapped all of her energy."

Evan took the backpack off of Tyhen's shoulders and handed it to Adam.

"Here, you carry this," he said.

"What are you going to do?" Adam asked as Evan began shifting the straps on his pack higher up on his shoulders.

"I'm going to carry her," he said, and scooped her up in his arms.

As another flash of lightning momentarily lit their way Evan glanced down, frowning at how light she felt despite her height, and how thin her face.

"Hey, little sister. It's good to see you," he said softly, and then started walking.

"Be careful where you step," Adam said. "I can't see anything and you don't want to fall with her in your arms."

Evan shook his head. "You forget yourself, brother. You can see. Just use your magic."

Adam chuckled. "Oh, right. I forgot."

They hadn't gone far when Evan had a vision of people.

"I don't know how far away they are, but I see men coming this way carrying torches," Evan said.

Adam focused and nodded. "It's Yuma. He's coming after Tyhen."

"He must be frantic," Evan said.

"Do you think we should tell him we're coming," Adam asked.

Evan shook his head.

"No, let's just surprise him."

So they kept walking East, slogging through the thick wet grass and mud and getting wetter and colder by the minute.

"I've never been cold before," Adam muttered, thinking back to the tropical island on which they'd been born and the heat of the jungles.

"It's worse than being too hot, for sure," Evan said.

Tyhen moaned.

"Is she waking up?" Adam asked.

Evan was connected to her thoughts by the simple act of carrying her, and all he saw was the fire and the storm.

"No, just remembering," he said.

The night sky continued to clear until stars began to appear, and then a half-moon glow bathed the land around them.

Evan's arms were aching and his feet were so cold he couldn't feel them when he began seeing lights bobbing up and down in front of them.

"I see torches!"

"It is Yuma," Adam said. "He's found us."

It was getting dark.

The storm had passed, but when Tyhen still had not returned, Yuma's worry turned to panic. Obviously she had succeeded in keeping them alive, but at what cost? Where was she? Why wasn't she back? He hadn't wanted to leave her behind. He hadn't wanted her out of his sight. And because he had done it anyway, this was the result.

Montford Nantay knew Yuma was worried, and when he saw him making a torch to go look for her, he motioned for his brother, Johnston, and then headed toward Yuma.

"We'll go with you," he said.

Yuma nodded and started off at a trot. Johnston picked up a couple of unlit torches from their campsite as they passed and then they were gone.

They walked without conversation, putting one foot in front of the other, feeling the chill of the wind on their faces and hearing the howl of a wolf pack somewhere off in the distance. Thinking of her unconscious and at the mercy of wild animals made Yuma crazy and he increased his stride.

The first torch was beginning to burn out when Montford lit a new one from it and kept on moving. The sky was clearing and the faint glow of the half-moon was casting blue shadows on a black velvet night.

When Yuma began feeling a tightening across his chest, he knew they must be close. But how would they find her in the dark?

"The light! Bring the light forward," Yuma ordered, and Montford moved into the lead a few steps, holding the burning torch high above his head.

When Yuma first saw her emerge from the darkness, it looked like she was on her back and floating waist high above the ground. Her legs were bent at the knee and dangling downward, with one long graceful arm swinging back and forth in front of her like the pendulum on the grandfather clock he remembered from his childhood.

He stumbled, certain he was hallucinating, and then realized she was being carried. And then he saw the face and the smile of the man who was carrying her and shot past the Nantay brothers as if they were standing still.

"My brothers! I don't know how you got here or knew Tyhen was in need, but I am so grateful that you found her!" he cried, thumping both of them on their backs.

Then as quickly as he greeted his brothers, his focus shifted to Tyhen. He believed she couldn't die, but she could be hurt and that was something he could not bear. He lifted her from Evan's arms and laid her down on the ground. His hands were trembling as he thrust his fingers beneath the hood to feel her head then felt the length of her arms and legs. He knew that she could heal herself. He'd seen it happen, and nothing seemed out of place or injured.

"Tyhen, can you hear my voice?"

Montford and Johnston caught up, shocked by the sight of the twins.

"How did you get here?" Montford asked.

"Magic!" Adam said, grinning.

Yuma picked Tyhen up in his arms.

"What's wrong with her? How did you know she was in trouble? Where did you find her?" he asked.

Evan put a hand on Yuma's shoulder in reassurance.

"Nothing is wrong with her. She's just exhausted. She rode a very powerful storm today and saved your lives, didn't she?" Adam said.

"How do you know that?" Montford asked.

"Remember who you are talking to," Yuma said. "They know everything."

Evan pulled the hood a little closer around Tyhen's face as he added his reassurance.

"Remember when she fought the evil shaman on the swinging bridge and Cayetano had to carry her back to Naaki Chava? She is tired like that."

Yuma felt of her hand, willing the fingers to curl around his hand as they always did, but they were limp against her belly.

"Yes, I remember. She saved my life that night. You swear she has come to no harm."

Adam nodded. "I swear, my brother. She just needs rest."

"And food," Evan added. "She's very thin."

"We all are," Yuma said. "Come. We will talk as we walk back to camp. This has been a very long day. Twice today we thought we would die, but she saved us."

Evan took the pack off Yuma's shoulder to lessen his burden as Yuma cradled her like a baby, walking with her head tucked beneath his chin and her body close against his chest.

He could hear the men talking behind him, sharing stories about the new city of Boomerang that was being built, and how Singing Bird was already teaching others the new languages and math. He heard them bragging how Cayetano was turning the shoreline into a fortress and felt a new sense of urgency. They were already creating what the New Ones had yet to begin.

When Tyhen moaned, he shifted her to a more comfortable position and lengthened his stride. The sooner he got her into their tent and under warm robes, the better.

CHAPTER THREE

The twins were stunned as they walked into the camp. Although the number of tents was great, they were noticeably less than when they left Naaki Chava.

When Montford and Johnson parted ways to go to their camps, Evan caught up with Yuma, whispering so as not to disturb the people sleeping among them.

"Is this all that's left of the New Ones?" he asked.

Yuma nodded.

"That is so sad. What happened?" Evan asked

Yuma shrugged wearily as he wound his way between campfires and tents.

"An earthquake. A landslide. Many things. Many sad days," he said softly.

Evan understood. They, too, had lost many when they'd run from the mountain that blew fire into the sky, but he had no memory of it. He would have died then but for Tyhen. He glanced at the sleeping woman in Yuma's arms and said no more.

Yuma's arms were aching by the time he reached their campsite. The fire he'd built before they left was still burning, which surprised him, and then he saw Gecko wrapped up in a blanket a few feet away and the small pile of wood beside him and guessed he'd been feeding the fire for Tyhen. Grateful for the heat, he said nothing as he laid Tyhen down.

The little boy's eyes flew open and Yuma saw relief on his face.

"She is well?" he asked.

"Yes, she is well," Yuma said. "Thank you for the fire. Go

back to your tent and be warm."

He was up and gone in moments.

"Who was that?" Adam asked, as he dropped his pack at his feet.

"My competition," Yuma said. "He fancies himself in love with Tyhen."

Adam watched the little boy disappearing among the tents and then shook his head.

"They have a connection, but it's nothing like that."

Yuma heard, but was too busy trying to get everyone down to rest, and didn't ask more.

"You and Adam can set up your tents close to ours and share our fire for the night."

"Can we help you in any way?" Evan asked.

Yuma glanced down. She was so still. He just needed to hold her to reassure himself that she still breathed.

"No. I'm going to get her into the tent under a warm buffalo robe and feed her tomorrow. Did you bring warm covers for your beds?"

"Yes, Singing Bird prepared us well," Adam said.

"Then good night," Yuma said, and opened up a flap in the tent so he could get her inside. As soon as she was settled, he tied down the flap to keep out the wind, straightened the bedding and lay down beside her. Subconsciously she curled into the shape of his body as he pulled the wooly buffalo hide over them.

"I am in awe of the woman in my arms," he whispered, then put his arm around her and closed his eyes.

Captain Diego DeVille sat his horse with the casual grace of a man born to the saddle. He was a muscular man of average height with black curly hair and a black scruffy beard. In another place, clean and in decent clothing, he would have been considered a fine figure of a man. Here, he was one of fifty-two filthy, exhausted, and bad-tempered Spanish soldiers who had been turned into explorers and all in the name of their King.

He had been given a map to an outpost built two years earlier, and was to leave the men who rode with him and bring back the ones who'd been manning it. But he was beginning to get concerned. They should have already reached it and yet they had not, which in his mind did not bode well. Either he was lost, which was going to make finding their way back to where their ship was anchored difficult, or the fort and men were no more, which would likely not please the King.

He was thinking about roasted chicken, a fine red wine, and a buxom woman to warm his bed when his lieutenant, Luis Estevez, called out.

"Captain DeVille. We need to stop. One of the horses is pulling up lame."

Diego cursed beneath his breath as held up a hand to halt the line.

"Tell them ten minute break. Do what they need to do and do it quick," he ordered.

Lieutenant Luis Estevez gave the order and the riders came to a halt and dismounted. Some headed to the bushes to relieve themselves while others poured water into their metal helmets to give their horses a drink. Two staggered off to the side and threw up.

Diego saw them and frowned. He had already lost four men to sickness. He couldn't afford to lose any more, but the ship's doctor had been the first to die and he had no notion of what was ailing them.

Diego took a drink from his water bag as he watched the soldier with the lame horse trying to dig a good-size pebble from the horse's hoof.

He watched for a few moments more and then turned and faced the north wind. It was cold, damn cold. He took a long, deep breath and then closed his eyes, wishing he could wake up and discover this was all just a bad dream. Ten minutes later they were back in the saddle, still in search of the outpost.

It was mid-morning of the next day when they rode up on a few broken poles still sticking out of the ground and a part of a roof with long grass growing up between hand-hewn shingles.

They'd found the outpost.

Diego DeVille stared mutely at the sight before them as he reined in his horse.

"Captain, is this it?" Lieutenant Estevez asked.

Diego felt sick. This did not bode well for the rest of their expedition.

"What's left of it," he said.

"So what do we do now?" Estevez asked.

Deville looked up past the broken poles. In the distance he could see conical structures rising above the long grass and saw signs of habitation from the smoke of scattered fires rising into the sky.

"There!" he cried, pointing toward the rising smoke. "The men must be there! We ride!" he shouted, and actually kicked his horse into a trot with the others following suit, anxious to come face to face with the men and find out what had happened.

DeVille was already formulating what needed to be done. The first thing, of course, was to rescue the men. He would see that they were commended for not abandoning their post, regardless of what had befallen them. His expedition to the frontier outpost had become an extraction. His job now was to get the survivors back to Spain.

For the first time in days DeVille felt optimistic. And then they rode into the camp. The tent-like dwellings were made of some kind of animal skin and the smoke he'd seen was coming out of the smoke holes at the top.

"Hello the camp!" Diego called out, expecting to see some of his people emerge.

When dark-skinned savages wearing skins and furs came out of the dwellings, he was shocked. They came out without fear, staring curiously at the men and coming close to touch the horses they rode.

"Habla Espanol?" he asked.

One of the old men stepped forward. As he did, Lieutenant Estevez saw the jacket the man was wearing beneath an animal skin robe and started shouting.

"He's wearing part of a uniform! He's by God wearing a

uniform! They killed them. That's what happened to the men!"

DeVille frowned.

"With what? Their fists? They're old. Do you see any weapons?"

The old man motioned toward where the outpost once stood and began saying the same thing over and over in Spanish.

"Many Tatanka. Some die."

"Some? Where are the others?"

The old man shrugged and then pointed west.

"What is Tatanka?" Diego asked.

The old man pointed to one of the images painted on the skins of their dwelling. It looked something like a large wooly bull. They had seen animals similar to this already. Was he saying the men died because of these animals? That was ridiculous. It would take many thousands of large animals to stampede through that outpost and knock it to the ground.

"Where are these animals?" Diego asked.

The old man shrugged, then pointed toward the prairie and waved his arm as if indicating they were anywhere and everywhere.

"Why are you here alone? Where are your people?" Diego asked, but evidently the old man had exhausted the few words he'd learned from the soldiers and just stood there.

"Lieutenant, take some men and search these dwellings."

Estevez dismounted and gave the order. Men came off the horses and ran toward the dwellings with their swords drawn.

The old men started shouting and running after the soldiers as the old women came running out, shrieking in fear and dismay at the destruction of their belongings.

One elderly woman swung a stone axe at a soldier, and the act triggered a melee. The soldier shouted, cursing at the woman as he ran her through with a sword. The sound of her shriek sent birds in a nearby tree in flight, and brought the old men running to her aide.

When the woman dropped to the ground, an old man jumped toward the soldier. The soldier slashed the old man's throat and he died between one breath and the next.

It triggered the rage of the other soldiers still astride. They piled off their horses and came at the savages with weapons

drawn. Some wore armor of padded leather while other had
chain mail beneath their winter coats. The clubs and stone
weapons the savages had were useless against the weapons of
steel.

Diego cursed. He had no intention of this happening, but
when his soldiers began killing the savages and the females
started running, it heightened their lust, and now they were out
of control.

One woman with long gray braids shed the animal skin she
had held around her for warmth and chose to stand her ground,
wearing nothing more than a shift-like dress that hung down
past her knees. Armed only with a club, she waited as four of
the soldiers surrounded her, laughing and poking at her with
the points of their swords, drawing blood from her arms and
the backs of her hands.

Estevez already had a woman stripped naked on the ground
and was humping her in unbridled lust. She was screaming as
he pounded himself into her body, and when the climax
overtook him, the next soldier in line was already undoing his
clothing, ready to take a turn.

The act of lust swept through Diego so fast that he was hard
just from watching. He looked back at the woman still
surrounded by the four soldiers and was taken by her defiance.
Just the act of resistance heightened his lust and he began
shouting as he dismounted.

"Leave her! Leave her! That one is mine!"

The four soldiers turned heel and took off in pursuit after the
other old women who were running away.

One of the dwellings had caught fire during the turmoil and
the smoke was burning his eyes as he walked toward her. It
never occurred to him that she was old enough to be his
mother, maybe older. Like all the others, he'd been without a
woman too long to consider some savage's feelings.

He walked up to her smiling, and when she swung the stone
axe at him, he dodged it then knocked it out of her hand. The
woman screamed at him and lunged for his throat. He side-
stepped her move and as he grabbed her from behind was
assailed by the scent of wood smoke and dirt. Wrapping one
arm around her neck to hold her still, he cut the loose animal-

skin shift from her body with one slash of his knife, then threw her to the ground.

She was dazed and bleeding as he loosened his clothing, straddled her body and began pinching and pulling at her sagging breasts. Their continuing struggles stirred the dust in which they were lying until the air around them was saturated with it so thick that he could taste it on his teeth.

The woman was screaming and writhing beneath him, hitting him with her fists and trying to blind him with her nails and he'd had enough. He doubled up his fist and hit her hard. Her head snapped as her eyes rolled back. Now she was unconscious beneath him, which heightened his excitement.

He shoved a knee between her legs and rammed his rock-hard erection into her body without care that she was tearing. It had been a very long time since Diego had been inside a woman's body and the sensation was too heady to control.

One thrust into the warmth and he was gritting his teeth to keep from coming.

His second thrust was so hard that her body moved upward in the dirt a good three inches.

And the third thrust ended it. Blinded by the blood-rush of the climax, it washed him over the edge of reason. He fell forward, grabbing her by both breasts and humping erratically as his seed gushed into her barren womb.

When he was finished, he rocked back on his heels and looked up. It appeared his soldiers were pleasuring themselves accordingly, passing around the dozen or so women they had caught. At first the women's screams were loud and then they were not, and then the only sounds that could be heard were guttural grunts and male cries of satisfaction.

The sounds stirred the Captain's blood to the point that he took the old woman two more times before he was done. He did not know until he pulled away from her body that sometime during the act, she had regained consciousness and had been watching him with eyes as dark as night. The fact that she had not uttered a sound was unnerving and he pulled a hand back and slapped her just to hear her cry, only she disappointed him by her silence. Instead, she turned her head and spit out the blood gathering in her mouth then looked back at him again as if nothing had happened.

Something about the look on her face made him nervous, and he yanked the bone necklace from around her neck for a souvenir and then kicked the bottom of her foot as he stood.

She received the kick as silently as she'd received his seed. Shrugging it off, he put the necklace around his neck, letting it hang over the padded leather armor covering his chest, and then began rearranging his clothing.

He picked up his weapons, slipped his knife back in the scabbard, and then stood, staring at her. The act of sex had linked them, whether he liked it or not. It was then that he also noticed the blood all over her belly and realized when he'd cut away her clothes, he'd cut skin as well. He looked down at his hands, somewhat shocked that he hadn't noticed the blood on them before, then looked back at her. She was the oldest woman he had ever had and while she was nothing to look at, it had still felt good to be inside of her.

Thinking he would calm her rage with a trinket, he dug into his pack, feeling around for some of the trade goods that they carried, and pulled out a necklace made of blue glass beads. He dangled it in the air above her head and then dropped it on her breasts and walked away to reclaim his mount.

By the time his men were finished with the women, the scent of dust and blood was thick within the air as they rode into the west, still in search of the remaining soldiers they'd come to find.

The smoke from the dying cook fire spiraled up through the small opening in the tipi while the people inside still slept.

The camp consisted of misfits and outcasts, renegades from several tribes of the Plains.

They were led by a Comanche called Crow Walks, a warrior who had slept with Red Deer, a woman who was his brother's wife, then lied about the deed. Before that day was out, he had fought and killed his own brother for a woman he did not want.

His family had denounced him and the chief had followed up by exiling him from the tribe, and all the while Crow Walks could not believe it was happening. He was the strongest warrior in camp and the one most favored by the Chief. He could run farther and faster than any other warrior and was, by all their standards, a man of great stature. His long black braids were wrapped in the whitest of rabbit fur, his spear held many notches for killing enemies in battle. He had driven many bison over a precipice to fall to their death below, thereby furnishing much food for the tribe. And it had all come down around him for taking his brother's woman.

Angry beyond words, he left the tribe with a pack on his back and a spear in his hand and never looked back. Red Deer did not escape her own brand of punishment. She had been held down by her own people and cut on both cheeks to make her ugly, then cast out as the tribe packed up and moved on, leaving her alone on the prairie without food or shelter and winter coming on.

She walked for days until she found Crow Walks' camp, found him trying to scrape the flesh from a deer hide, which was woman's work, and took her place in his life without asking.

Crow Walks said nothing to her in the way of welcome and daily viewed her scars as a reminder of what he'd lost. He had fallen so far from grace that his resentment began to fester. Before long he was making raids on different camps, stealing what he wanted until he had what he needed to survive. Word spread from tribe to tribe about Crow Walks' daring feats, and other warriors who had left their tribes soon joined him. The numbers slowly grew within his camp until he and his band of renegades had become feared by their own people on the plains.

Crow Walks had heard the stories of a woman with great magic coming into their midst. The People called her the Dove and claimed she came with much knowledge and a message that would save the People from future ruin.

He knew about the Gathering and rejected it outright. Even if he wanted to go he would not be accepted. He'd seen the white birds. He knew the signs. But he didn't accept the reason she was coming or the need. He had not seen any sign of these strange men who would come into their land and take it from them. Even though he'd been driven out of his own tribe, he did not believe the People could ever be driven out of their lands. The People were many and the lands were vast. Such a thing was impossible.

But on this night as a rainstorm moved over the land, he and his band huddled close inside their dwellings, satisfying their bellies with food and their sexual desires with their women until they were sated in every way. Finally the fires burned low, the coals were banked, and they fell asleep.

As Crow Walks slept, he began to dream, and in his dream he saw a woman of great height leading a large tribe of the People into his land. In the dream there were white birds flying ahead of her and circling the sky around her, and he knew it was the Dove. He saw the people who came behind her and saw their numbers and in the dream the people turned into a herd of the great wooly beasts and ran his camp over.

He woke up in a sweat, imagining he would hear the thundering hooves of a stampede. Instead, he heard the soft snores of his woman's sleep. Still rattled by the dream, he got up, pushed aside the flap of his tipi and walked out away from the camp to relieve himself.

As he looked out across his camp he saw a faint light on the horizon. The Great Spirit was pulling back the flap on His tipi to let out the sun.

Crow Walks remembered the dream and turned to the East, waiting for the first rays of sunlight to strike his face. Dew was heavy on the long grass from last night's rain. The air smelled fresh. The silence enveloped him.

A short while later he heard his woman come out and walk away to relieve herself. When she came back she was carrying a basket back inside the tipi.

Crow Walks did not greet her and she did not acknowledge his presence. They were where they were, not because of any affection toward one another, but because of their respective falls from grace.

Red Deer shivered slightly in the chill of the early morning as she carried out a turtle shell full of smoking embers from the fire inside their tipi then rolled the embers out onto a handful of twisted grass she'd taken from the basket. After it caught and flared, she added dry buffalo chips until she had a small fire going, then went down to the creek to pick up more wood for the fire. It would all be wet from last night's rain and it would smoke for a while, but it would burn and that was all that mattered.

Crow Walks heard her walking away, but paid her no attention. He was still waiting for sunrise.

Other members of the camp began to emerge from their tipis and before long everyone was up and about. Voices filled the empty space, laughter and jeers were traded. Two of the men in the camp had no woman of their own and woke up surly.

Crow Walks was still staring at the horizon, watching it become lighter and brighter as Red Deer returned. Soon the fire began to smoke.

"Stupid woman," he muttered. "She does not even know how to build a good fire."

"Stupid man does not remember that rain makes wood wet and wet wood makes smoke," Red Deer fired back.

Crow Walks sighed, not for the first time wishing she had never been born and then he would not have been tempted. Frowning, he refocused his attention on the arrival of a new day.

When the first slice of the white light rose above the horizon his pulse accelerated. He continued to wait, seeing it emerge bit by tiny bit until it was almost whole.

He took a deep breath, holding it, holding it, holding –

One moment he could see sky and the creek and the trees along the bank, and then he saw nothing but a painful blast of blinding light. Before he could look away, a vision came out of the light and began moving toward him.

It was a tall figure of what he took to be a man wearing a dark jacket with dark fur lining the hood over his head. The stride was long, arms swinging with every step. The man came closer and closer and then all of a sudden the hood fell back and long black hair tumbled out around a face of such beauty it made him gasp.

The only thing that registered was that it was a woman and not a man and that he never seen a woman that tall. And in the vision she raised her arms up over her head and flew up into the sky, then while he was watching her ascent, and eagle came out of nowhere, slicing Crow Walks eyes from his face with razor-sharp talons.

Crow Walks cried out and covered his face to stop the vision, staggering backward and moaning with every step.

Red Deer heard him and stood up from the fire.

"Crow Walks! What is wrong?" she asked.

He dropped to his knees, which brought the rest of the camp running toward them.

Red Deer walked over to where he was kneeling and tapped him on the shoulder.

"Are you sick?" she asked.

He shuddered. "No," he said, and dropped his hands in his lap. "I had a vision," he said, as the others all gathered around him.

A small wiry warrior called Two Rabbits squatted down in front of Crow Walks.

"What did you see?" he asked.

"The Dove. She comes."

A warrior called Black Hand laughed.

"I do not believe there is such a person. The Old Ones would not give their power to a woman."

"How do you know it was the Dove?" Two Rabbits asked.

"She lifted her arms and flew up into the sky like a bird," Crow Walks muttered, neglecting to mention what happened afterward. He stood up. In his world, when he was threatened, he fought back. "I, Crow Walks, will kill this witch, myself," he said, and then he walked away.

Red Deer frowned. If Crow Walks got himself killed, then where did that leave her? She glanced up and caught Black Hand watching her and relaxed. He had no woman. She would be fine.

CHAPTER FOUR

Tyhen was dreaming of a sky full of black birds that were trying to peck out her eyes when she heard someone cough. Thinking it was Yuma, she reached for his hand then realized he was gone. She rolled over onto her back and stretched, then sat up. Her hair was in tangles and her clothes smelled like smoke.

Her belly growled as she crawled out of the tent and stood up. She was finger-combing her hair when someone tugged it from behind. She turned around, thinking it was Yuma, and came face to face with Adam and Evan. A big smile spread across her face as she threw her arms around their necks and hugged them.

"My brothers! You are here! When did you come?"

They were laughing, very happy to see her back to normal instead of the unconscious woman they'd found on the plains.

Adam removed the silver chain with the bird charm from around his neck and dropped it over her head.

"Time to return your property, I think," he said.

Tyhen thought of her mother as she fingered the little bird charm and then dropped it around her neck where it fell beneath her clothing.

"How are they? Are they well?" she asked.

The twins didn't have to ask who she was talking about. They knew she missed her parents, but she didn't know how much they missed her.

"It is because of your mother that we are here," Evan said.

Tyhen frowned. "I do not understand."

"She had a vision. She saw you flying into a fire and when

you didn't come out, she fainted. We had been planning to join you for several weeks but when that happened, Cayetano sent us early."

Tyhen groaned. "Oh no. My poor mother still doesn't understand that I cannot die."

"It is difficult for us to accept that, too," Adam muttered. "You are an anomaly."

She frowned. "What does that mean?"

"It means there isn't another person like you," Evan said. "You are one of a kind."

She shrugged. "I don't know any other way to be but how I am."

"That's why we love you," Evan added.

She smiled and in her excitement hugged them again, and then felt a hand slide beneath her hair and squeeze the back of her neck. She didn't have to look to know. She knew his touch.

"Yuma! Did you know our brothers were here?"

Yuma kissed the side of her cheek and then glanced at the twins.

"You didn't tell her?" he said.

"Tell me what?" Tyhen asked.

"You didn't come back. The Nantay brothers and I went looking for you, but the twins found you first. You had passed out on the prairie and they were bringing you to the camp when we met up with them." His eyes darkened as he cupped the side of her face. "I was very glad to see you safe in their arms."

Tyhen sighed. "I was too tired to go any farther."

Yuma dropped his hands and stood quietly before her, remembering the power of that massive tornado, in awe of what she was becoming.

"If I didn't know that you would love me forever, I would be afraid of you," he finally said.

"You have grown so much in strength and power," Adam said. "You are becoming as powerful as the Windwalker."

Tears suddenly spiked her lashes but she blinked them away. Sometimes the burden of her existence was overwhelming.

"Enough about me. Is there anything to eat?" she asked.

"I heated up the rabbit stew," Yuma said.

"Did you eat?" she asked.

"Yes, we ate. What's left is yours. Eat it all. Soon we'll have to find a place to ford this river or many will drown as we try to cross."

Adam frowned.

"You forget. You have us now. We will find the safe crossing and won't have to get our feet wet to do it."

"And we are so glad that you are here," Tyhen said, and took the small cooking pot of stew Yuma handed her and sat down to eat as he and the twins walked away.

Gecko slipped up beside her, handed her a spoon he'd made from a dry gourd many weeks ago, and then sat, intending to watch her eat.

"Thank you, Gecko," Tyhen said, and took a big bite of the stew.

As she chewed, she scooped up a second bite and handed it to him. He popped the bite in his mouth and then handed back the spoon and so it went until the stew was gone. When she was finished, she leaned over and held out the spoon. He took it, then sat without moving.

Tyhen could tell he wanted to talk but she had yet to hear his voice.

"What is it, Gecko?"

He fidgeted for a few moments and then stood abruptly. They were now so close Tyhen saw her reflection in his eyes.

"My name is Dakotah," he said, and then lifted his chin and walked away.

Tyhen was so taken aback she didn't know how to respond. Even though he was just a boy, she'd just seen the man he would become. She didn't know what would happen in the years ahead, but there was a link between them that had yet to be named.

The men were down at the river, staring at the dark moving water. Adam and Evan were side by side, quietly conversing, while Yuma stood behind them. It wasn't the first time he was seeing differences between the twins, but they were much more noticeable now than when they'd left Naaki Chava.

Adam used to be the one who stepped up first, the one who spoke first. Now Yuma was seeing a new side of Evan, but the most noticeable thing were the weapons. Before, they would never have considered being armed. They were nonviolent in every aspect of their lives, and the only power they wielded came in their psychic abilities. Now Evan had a big knife strapped to his leg and at any time would have a bow and a quiver of arrows on his back or be carrying a spear.

Yuma glanced back at the camp. People were packing up and getting ready to leave.

"So, what can you tell me?" Yuma asked,

Adam pointed up river.

"There is one place we can safely cross, but it's a long walk upriver."

Evan pointed down river.

"That way," he said.

Yuma eyed the confident expression on Evan's face and then grinned.

"Who *are* you, my brother? Not the same twin that I left back in Naaki Chava."

Evan shrugged. "I nearly died when the mountain blew fire. Tyhen saved my life. I had no memory for a while and who I am now is how I came back."

Adam grinned. "I'm still the smartest one."

"But I'm the strongest," Evan said.

Yuma grinned.

"So, my brothers, just so you know, the Nantay brothers scouted the river about a mile in either direction yesterday and said it was too deep to cross. Is the crossing you see a safe one, Evan?"

"There is a place. I will walk it and show you, then we'll mark the boundaries," Evan said.

"I'll tell Tyhen to get them started. You two will lead the way and we'll mark the crossing after we get there."

"We need to get our packs," Adam said, and started to walk away then stopped. "I don't know exactly what it is yet, but there will be danger ahead for Tyhen. Someone wants her dead."

The hair crawled on the back of Yuma's neck. Just because she couldn't die, didn't mean she couldn't be hurt.

"Is it someone at The Gathering?"

"No. This person is what you would call a renegade. He is an outcast from his tribe."

"Is he alone?" Yuma asked.

"He has men who follow him," Evan said.

Yuma sighed. They had already been that route when they ran into the warriors who had captured Little Mouse. They did not fare well with the Windwalker's daughter and he had no doubt these would suffer a similar fate. The problem was how Tyhen had suffered afterward. She had been born to unite a nation, not bury its people, and yet when it came down to fulfilling her destiny there could be no mercy for those who got in her way.

"I will talk to her. She needs to be aware," Yuma said.

The news was sobering.

The twins went to get their packs.

Yuma went to find Tyhen. When he got to their camp he saw that their tent was down and their packs ready to go, but she wasn't there.

Tyhen. We are ready to leave. Where are you?

Stanley Bluejacket is dead.

Yuma felt like he'd been sucker-punched. He'd been so sure the old man would make it all the way to the Gathering. He'd tried so hard to get there. This hurt his heart.

What do we need to do?

Oh Yuma, he asked to be left on the highest point of land.

Yuma heard her pain.

I will help you. Just tell me where you are.

Only I can get him to the highest place. It won't take long.

Yuma waved the twins down.

"Wait!" he yelled.

They stopped, and when they turned around noticed the people were all looking in the other direction. They came running back.

"What's wrong?" Evan asked.

"Stanley Bluejacket died. Tyhen just told me. She also said he wanted his body left on the highest point."

Adam frowned. "There are no high points on this prairie. Just rolling hills.

Yuma pointed at the line of mountains far to the north just as a whirlwind came up over a ridge. It hovered among a group of people for a few seconds, and then it was gone.

A drum beat broke the silence. The mournful, repetitive yi-yi-yi cry of singers picked up the drummer's rhythm.

The New Ones stared transfixed at the whirlwind as it went farther and farther away until it was completely out of sight, and all the while the voices rang out, singing to the Old Ones, letting them know Stanley Bluejacket was making his journey to the Great Spirit.

Tyhen held Stanley within the eye of the whirlwind as if they were in an embrace. Even though the New Ones were far behind her, she heard the drums and the singers and knew the song was for him. Hot tears that she could not stop began rolling down her cheeks. She couldn't remember when she'd last cried, but it had been pent up so long that it felt like she was drowning.

Stanley's small stature was not a burden to hold. His body had withered to little more than skin and bones from the arduous trek. His long gray braids brushed the backs of her hands and the deerskin jacket lined with rabbit fur his daughter had made to keep him warm had not held the magic to also keep him alive.

Tyhen remembered him from when she'd played the New Ones' game in Naaki Chava. He had been the man who stood behind home plate and called himself the umpire. She'd had no notion as a child that this end would come their way, but they were here and the mountains were there and they still had a ways to go.

Stanley slipped a little bit in her arms and she shifted position for a better grip, as she did the sadness of this trip overwhelmed her. The farther they went, the harder she cried until she was blind with tears and didn't understand why. She'd lost other people she knew better and had not come undone like this. Maybe it was the suddenness of the discovery of his body, or maybe her endurance had reached some kind of limit.

"I am sorry your people could not come, Stanley Bluejacket. I am sorry you will not see the Gathering. I know you wanted to rejoin your mother's people, the Absaroka. I will tell them of your walk. I will tell them how far you came. I will tell them that you lived."

Stanley had no comment, but since she was fulfilling his final wish, his approval was understood.

And so they flew until the blue mountain turned grey, and the black crevices and sun-kissed ridges came into view - closer yet until she could see the changing colors of the trees on the south side of the slope. She rode the whirlwind up to the snow-covered peak and when she began to come down, sent a blizzard of icy shards flying into the air. Moments later she was, for the first time in her life, standing in snow.

She looked down and remembered a vision she'd had once back in Naaki Chava of wearing clothes like this and walking in snow, but she had not known that Stanley Bluejacket would be with her.

She took a deep breath and then gasped as the cold air burned her lungs. Now it was time to make Stanley's final wish come true.

She looked at where she'd landed and then turned with Stanley's body in her arms so they were facing the east and with a clear view vista before him.

"Do you see this, Stanley? You are on the highest point. You are as close to the Great Spirit as a warrior can be."

Then she carried him a few yards forward to large boulder sticking out of the snow and laid him down upon the surface. The tears began to freeze on her cheeks as she straightened up his clothing, laid his braids down across his shoulders and then brushed the hair back away from his face.

A few flakes of snow began to fall in Stanley's eyes but he didn't seem to mind. She reached down to close them and then stopped. If she closed them, he could not see, so she walked away, looking back at how far she'd come. This was the farthest she had been on her own. And except for an old man's body, was as alone as she would ever be.

Her heart started thumping and the urge to be gone was so strong she started shaking. She needed Yuma. She needed to see his face. No sooner had she thought his name than she heard his voice.

Come back to me, Tyhen. Come back to me now.

She lifted her arms above her head and began to chant, and as the wind began to turn, so did the snow. It turned with the wind until the peak was in a white-out and Tyhen was in the air.

She looked back once.

Stanley's body was slowly being covered by the settling snow, but he was still on the rock and looking up.

The drummer was still drumming. The high-pitched cry of the singers echoed the rhythm of Yuma's heartbeat. He had watched the whirlwind until it was out of sight and he was still standing in the same place, waiting for her return. When his chest began growing tighter, he knew she was on her way.

He couldn't imagine what this had been like for her, holding that small withered body in her arms all that way alone. And he was only going to add to the emotional beginning to her day by having to warn her that sometime in the near future someone was going to try and kill her.

Tyhen was high above the earth, cocooned within the spinning wind, when she heard the drumming and the singers. They were calling her to them, just as they'd sung Stanley Bluejacket home. She pushed the whirlwind to its limit, ready to be back among the living, and flew through the sky without hesitation until she could see the encampment. The drumbeat was loud in her ears. The singers' cries were a balm to her aching heart. Yuma was somewhere nearby. She could feel him.

She landed on the backside of the hill and paused a moment

to wipe the tears from her face and straighten her clothing. It would not do for the Windwalker's daughter to show emotional weakness. With that river yet to cross they were still not out of trouble.

She looked up. The sky was clear and the sunshine was a welcome sight after the cold wind and storms of the day before. Still, there was no amount of sunshine that was going to make crossing a river of dangerously cold water a simple task.

Her head was up and her stride was long as she came over the hill. The drumbeat stopped the moment the people saw her and the singers stopped with it. They acknowledged her presence with reverence, whispering softly to each other as she passed. She was searching the faces looking for Yuma when she heard his voice.

I am here, on your left.

She turned, walking blindly in that direction until he came into view and the moment they were face to face, he wrapped his arms around her.

"You did a wonderful thing," he said softly as she went limp against him.

For a few precious seconds Tyhen pretended she was just a woman being held by the man she loved. She hugged him back and then kissed him quickly before letting go. By the time she looked up to face him again, she had all of her emotions under control.

"Do we have a safe place to cross the river?" she asked.

Yuma held out his hand and she took it.

"Evan says yes. Tell everyone to follow the twins."

She nodded, and with the innate power of her voice let the wind carry her words and gave the order that all could hear.

"For those who do not yet know, my brothers Adam and Evan joined us last night. We are most fortunate now to have Chief Cayetano's two wisest shamans to guide us the rest of the way. We will leave now. Follow the ones who follow the twins."

A cheer went up throughout the camp that made Yuma smile.

"That will go to their heads," he said, and led her through the encampment to join up with the twins.

Tyhen and Yuma soon caught up and as they began walking downriver the three men began talking. Tyhen let the conversation go on without her input, satisfied just to be back with Yuma and her brothers.

As she walked, she thought of her mother and wondered if Singing Bird was sad that the twins were gone, too.

Mother? Can you hear me?

The silence after her question was telling. Singing Bird was either too upset to tune in, or had lost the ability to hear her daughter's voice.

Tyhen lowered her head and hid the sadness. It was one more thing she had to accept.

After all the concern, the crossing was anti-climactic. Evan led them almost two miles downriver to the widest part, which because of its breadth had also lowered the depths. At the deepest, it was only waist high on an adult and because it was so wide, allowed for more people to cross at one time.

Most of the riverbed consisted of gravel-sized pebbles, so the danger of sinking into sandy depths was also averted. Yuma and Tyhen had gone across with the first wave while the twins and one of the Nantay brothers stayed on the other side to help.

It took hours for the last of them to get to the other side. By the time it was done it was past mid-day and their numbers were strung out for a good three miles with the stragglers at the rear.

Montford Nantay and Evan had stayed behind on purpose, following the oldest and the slowest. Adam had walked ahead with Johnston and Susie Nantay, then jogged for a while until he reached the front where Yuma was leading.

"Hey, brother, where is Tyhen?" Adam asked, as he slowed his pace to a walk.

Yuma pointed to a rise a few hundred yards ahead, to the lone figure silhouetted against the sky.

Adam saw her, and was once again struck by how she had changed.

"Is she this way all the time?" he asked.

Yuma frowned. "What way?"

"Alone. She holds herself apart from the rest."

Yuma shrugged. "Emotionally, this is difficult for her. The more her power grows, the more distant the people become who were once her friends. They love her, but they also fear her. We are all stretched to our limits daily, but she is not allowed to be gentle. There is no place in her life to be a woman now. She is just the Windwalker's daughter fulfilling what she was born to do."

Adam sighed. "I feel her sadness."

"As do I," Yuma said. "It will be different once we reach the Gathering. Most of her responsibility will end once the New Ones are assimilated into their old tribes and return to the lands of their people."

Adam hadn't thought past the Gathering and it occurred to him that he didn't know where he and Evan would belong.

"Where do you go, my brother?" Adam asked.

Yuma glanced at Tyhen one last time and then focused on the land before them.

"My people were in Oklahoma when Firewalker came, but the original tribal lands were in what was the state of Georgia on the East Coast. I think we will go there. We need to build up all of the coastal tribes first so that the white men do not get inland easily. You and Evan are our family. You will come with us."

Adam nodded. It made sense, and it was good to have a stopping point in mind.

"Where is Evan?" Yuma asked.

"He and Montford stayed behind with the old ones. They will be the last to make camp tonight. On another note, have you talked to Tyhen about the danger?"

"Not yet. She was so sad when she came back without Stanley Bluejacket that I waited, and then before I knew it she was gone."

Adam frowned again. "You can't wait to tell her something like that. I don't know when it will happen. She could be attacked while unaware of the threat."

Yuma glanced toward Tyhen as Adam dropped back to talk

to one of the young men he'd grown up with.

Hey, little whirlwind, I need to tell you something.

I heard Adam talking about me. Why am I in danger?

Yuma sighed. *I forgot you heard their words, too. All I know is what he told me. There is a band of renegades. The leader plans to kill you.*

Does he say where this will happen? Tyhen asked.

No, only that it will happen before the Gathering.

So I have been warned. It is enough.

Yuma frowned. He felt like she'd just brushed him aside with full intention of taking care of this on her own. What she didn't realize was she couldn't go around dropping the bad men like flies if she was going to sell the idea of bringing peace into a land of people who were often at war with each other.

Don't do this, Tyhen.

Do what?

Don't shut me out.

There was a long moment of silence. He was guessing she was trying to figure out what to say, and when she finally began denying it, he didn't answer back. Despite what she thought, this was not okay with him. If she was going to shut him out, then he was going to have to depend on the twins to keep him abreast of what she was doing.

When Yuma didn't answer her, Tyhen was crushed. She could not bear for him to be angry with her. He was her only support system – the only person she could relax around – the only person who made her feel like a woman and not a God.

She kept watching him, willing him to turn and look up, but when he did not, her shoulders slumped. This day had started off sad and seemed to be getting worse. They needed to find time to be together as man and woman. Too many weary days had passed since they had made love. They needed to rebuild that magic that was between them and soon.

After giving Yuma one last regretful glance, she turned to the east, imagining she could see the cooking fires– imagining how it would be to walk into the midst of an entire nation of people who were gathered in one place for the sole purpose of hearing the message she would bring. She could still hear the drums. They were always in her head. It was how she led the New Ones and how she knew where to go. After one last glance back, she started walking east again along the rise, knowing they would follow.

CHAPTER FIVE

Crow Walks was stomping through camp and gathering up what he intended to take with him to kill the witch. He already had two spears and his tomahawk lying beside his pack. He had split more than one head with it and had no doubt it would serve him the same way when he used it again. He also had dried meat and a deerskin pouch to carry water. He wasn't sure how far he would have to go to find them and didn't want to be concerned with food in the process.

He had chosen Two Rabbits to go with him, and Black Hand to stay behind and keep order in the camp until he returned.

Two Rabbits wasn't convinced it was even possible to kill a witch and didn't want to go, but arguing with Crow Walks was not something a man did and lived.

It never occurred to Crow Walks that Red Deer was being too helpful in seeing him off. In his mind, she was just making sure he had what he would need like any woman should do.

The sun had been up less than an hour when he shouldered his pack. His tomahawk was tucked beneath a strip of rawhide he'd tied around his waist and his winter clothing bulked up the appearance of his size.

"Two Rabbits! We go!" he yelled, and without a word to anyone else they walked out of camp heading west.

Black Hand was puffed up by the importance of being in charge, however briefly, and was eyeing Red Deer as he strode through camp. She was still young and slender and her long hair was thick and shiny. The scars on her face could easily be overlooked in a dark tipi at night. It would be good to have a woman to ease his needs and cook his food. He was planning his future as Crow Walks left to end a witch's life.

For a while, Crow Walks and Two Rabbits walked without speaking. It wasn't until Two Rabbits stopped hours later to relieve himself that he brought up a subject he'd been hesitant to mention.

"Crow Walks, how do we find this woman you seek?"

Crow Walks frowned. "She walks with many. We will see them coming and they will not see us."

Two Rabbits' eyes widened. "There are many with her?"

Crow Walks nodded.

"Do you know what she looks like?" Two Rabbits asked.

"I have seen her in a vision. She is very tall and most beautiful."

"What if they keep her protected among them? If they are many we will never -"

Crow Walks shouted.

"Stop talking! You talk like a scared girl! We will find our moment. We go now!"

Two Rabbits grabbed his pack and spear, and ran to catch up.

They walked west until the birds began going to roost, then stopped for the night within a small grove of trees and set up camp beside the thin stream of water that ran through it.

Two Rabbits caught three small fish with his hands, and pulled a turtle out of the mud bank while Crow Walks built a fire. They ate fish and turtle and made their beds close to the fire.

A pack of wolves was already on the hunt. The warriors could hear them howling as they gathered in extra wood to keep the fire burning throughout the night. Their howls made Two Rabbits nervous. As he lay down, he turned his back to the fire and grabbed his spear, holding it tight against his chest. If the wolves came into their camp, he would be ready.

Crow Walks heard the wolves, too, but he was not afraid. He'd seen plenty of deer tracks and rabbit burrows as they walked. The wolves weren't starving. They would stick to their usual prey and stay away from humans and fire.

After a walk around the perimeter of their camp, Crow

Walks laid a couple more sticks onto the fire then crawled in beneath his buffalo robe, felt for his spear, then pulled it close and closed his eyes.

Tyhen finally came into camp long after they'd stopped for the night and began searching until she found where Yuma was standing, talking to the twins.

Adam saw her coming and pointed.

Yuma turned around and without hesitation went to meet her. She came toward him with that long, lanky stride, her hair swinging from side to side with the sway of her body. Her face wore a look of desolation. It seems his silence earlier had hurt her and he had not meant for her to take it that way.

They met with a touch of foreheads and without speaking Yuma took her by the hand and began leading her through camp.

Tyhen's heart was thumping and the ache in her belly was growing with every step they took away from the others. When he led her over a rise and then down to the backside of the hill, her pulse leaped. He had dug what amounted to a small alcove into the hill, pushed the backside of their tent into the shelter and had a fire burning in front of it with rabbit roasting on a spit.

Tyhen sighed. "Oh, Yuma."

"There is water to bathe," he said, pointing to the hammered metal bowl they had carried from Naaki Chava so many months ago.

Tyhen eyes welled. She turned to him, but he put a finger on her lips and shook his head.

"I will wash your back," he offered.

Despite the chill of encroaching nightfall, she shed her clothes within seconds and then stood before him, so shaken by this unexpected luxury that she couldn't think.

Yuma slid a hand beneath her hair, gave the back of her neck a quick squeeze, and then motioned for her to sit on the matted grass.

As she knelt she pulled her hair over her shoulder and bent

her head. When she felt the scrap of cloth and the water on her skin, she shuddered. By the time he was through washing her back she was crying.

"Don't cry, little whirlwind," he whispered, and gently wiped the cloth across her face.

She shook her head, too moved to speak as he finished her bath, and when he handed her the only clean shift she still owned, she dropped it over her head, then put the leggings and moccasins back on.

"Do you want me to wash your back?" she asked.

"I washed near the spring after I cleaned the rabbit," he said, and pointed to the tent. "Get inside out of the wind. I will bring the food."

She crawled inside the tent, saw the soft robes he'd thrown out for them to lie on and began to cry again.

Yuma crawled in carrying the cooked rabbit and tore off part of the meat and handed it to her.

Her first bite tasted so good she almost forgot to chew as she went in for the second. Yuma ran his thumb down the side of her cheek and smiled, satisfied that his surprise was so well received.

"This is so good. Thank you. Thank you for all of this," Tyhen said.

"You were long overdue for a treat," he said.

Her hands were shaking as she continued to tear into the meat and when she was finished with the first piece, Yuma tore off another and put it in her hand. They ate in silence, savoring the warmth in their bellies and the luxury of being alone.

When they had finished eating, they drank from the water pouch then Tyhen cleaned her hands while Yuma went back outside to add wood to the fire.

It was completely dark now but for the light of a full moon and a star-studded sky. Yuma knew there was a slight risk in being away from all the others, but he'd offset their vulnerability by digging into the hillside to pitch the tent. It was enough. He stood beneath the moonlight and shed his clothing. Tonight there would be nothing between them but love.

When he crawled back into the tent and dropped his

clothing near the entrance, he also felt her clothing beneath his hands. She was without her clothes as well. When the wind began to stir within the tent and he felt her hands upon him, he knew what was coming.

"Don't forget, my Yuma. Only you can control this storm," she whispered, as her hair began to lift from the back of her neck.

He put a knee between her legs then slid into her body. She gasped and then moaned, and as she did the spinning wind inside the tent was gone. She was tight, hot, and wet, and she was his. He began to move then, taking her hard and fast, knowing she would come within seconds of their joining, and she did, arching up to meet him, digging her nails into his back, whispering his name over and over against his ear. Before she had time to breathe, he took her again, and this time the loving was sweet and slow.

For the first time in months, Tyhen felt whole. Loving Yuma was her anchor to reality. Greedily, she took everything he gave her, coming over and over until she was shaking. Finally, she felt his control begin to slip. She could feel the blood rushing through his body and even the tension as his muscles tightened. When she heard the rhythm of his breathing change, she knew he was ready to let go.

She wrapped her legs around his waist, pulled him close and pushed him deep, then closed her eyes as he emptied his seed. They were good together. So good, she thought, and fell asleep.

They slept wrapped in each other's arms and woke just before sunrise.

Tyhen put her hands on Yuma's face, tracing the shape of his cheeks, the strong jut of his chin, and the arched eyebrows above eyes so dark they looked black.

"Yuma, I am sorry I made you mad yesterday."

He stopped her apology with a frown.

"I was not mad. I was concerned. You can't do this all by yourself, and if some are trying to hurt you, bringing peace to all is going to be more difficult if you're forced into killing them, too."

Her eyes widened.

"I never thought of it like that. I just did what I had to do to keep all of you safe."

"And you will most likely have to do it again, but you have to remember you're not alone. Trust me to take care of you. I did it before you were born. I have done it countless times since. You may not die, but you can be harmed, badly. Remember Evan. He still had all of his skills but he had been hurt so seriously that he didn't remember them. That could happen to you. Don't shut me out. Trust me."

She hid her face against his chest.

"Sometimes I am so tired I think I can't walk another step, and I think I am too young and I don't know what I'm doing, and then somehow instinct takes over and I do the right thing."

Yuma was shocked that she'd been feeling all this and kept it from him. He held her close, rocking her back and forth in his arms.

"I am sorry, Tyhen, I'm sorry. I did not know."

Just hearing her name said in the first language of her mother made her weepy. Tyhen meant whirlwind in the Muscokee language. When Singing Bird had given her the name, it had seemed fitting for a Windwalker's child. But she was no longer a child and was bravely trying to pull herself together. It was time to get up, not fall apart.

"As long as I have you, I can do this," she said.

And in that moment, Yuma knew he would never lose patience with her again.

"You are doing an amazing job. You are not failing anything. I am in awe of you. I honor you and I am so proud that you are mine to love," he said.

She raised up on one elbow.

"I love you, my Yuma, and I must thank you for last night. It was what I needed. I'm going to get dressed now. It's time to make some food and pack up our camp."

Yuma stroked the curve of her body, then the curve of her breast as he pulled her down for one last kiss.

They got up then without talking, doing what they had to do. It made it easier to get busy than to think about what lay ahead.

Yuma dressed quickly then pulled the meat off what was left of the rabbit and laid it out on some leaves. He scattered the ashes and made sure there were no burning coals, then rolled up their tent before sitting down to eat a few bites.

Tyhen dressed quickly, took the meat that Yuma gave her, and hurried back up onto the rise to make sure all was well, eating as she went.

The camp was just waking. A few fires were being rebuilt. She could see smoke rising about the encampment. Someone's child was crying and there were people walking out away from the tents to relieve themselves. It was a day like any other.

She was on her way back down to get her pack when she heard Adam's voice in her head.

I had a vision. There are two men coming for you. They slept by a small creek last night and are already up and moving. Be aware of everything around you today.

She sighed. And so it began.

I will be aware. Thank you.

Tell Yuma or I will, although it would be better coming from you.

She rolled her eyes. She'd forgotten how bossy big brothers could be.

Don't threaten me, big brother. I tell him everything.

She heard Adam laugh and then plopped down beside Yuma.

"What's wrong?" he asked.

"Adam just told me that the two men who are coming after me are on the way. He told me to tell you."

Yuma nodded. "And I thank you. You are the Dove. You look out for the people but I am the Eagle who looks out for you."

She was about to argue and then stopped. In nature, the eagle is stronger than the dove, and so it will be with them.

She put the last bite of rabbit into her mouth as she stood. Yuma helped settle her pack on her back and then cupped her cheek.

"I will ask Montford Nantay to lead today. If you do not see me, you are not to worry," Yuma said. "Just say my name and I will hear you."

She frowned. "Where are you going to be?"

"Today I am your shadow. Don't look for me. Just know I

won't be far."

"I will know," she said, and slid her hand beneath his hair and pulled him to her.

"Thank you again for last night," she said.

He pulled her close, letting her feel all that he was.

"No, little whirlwind. I am the one who is grateful."

She threw back her head and laughed.

Yuma was still grinning when she disappeared over the rise. Then he shouldered his pack, picked up his spear, and made sure that Warrior's Heart, the knife Cayetano had given him, was within reach.

Crow Walks was dreaming that he and Two Rabbits found the tall witch. She was standing on a hill watching the people walking across the prairie. They spilled out across the land like ants coming out of the ground, so many – too many.

In the dream, he left Two Rabbits behind and slipped through the tall grass unseen, coming up behind her on the ridge. He was only a few feet from her when she suddenly turned. Before she could utter a word, he thrust his spear into her chest and let out a war cry as she fell lifelessly to the ground.

In the dream he stood over her, gloating about how easy it had been to kill this witch. But when he pulled his spear out of her chest and went to leave, instead of blood, white doves began coming out of her body. When they saw him holding the spear, they began flying toward him, pecking at his face and his arms and his head.

Crow Walks began to run but the white doves followed, and no matter which way he ran or how fast, they kept growing in numbers. And then he fell, and in the dream, they pecked out his eyes and then flew away, leaving him blind and bleeding. In a panic, he began crawling and screaming for Two Rabbits.

"I am here! I am here! Stop shouting my name!" Two Rabbits yelled, as he shook Crow Walks awake.

Crow Walks sat up with a gasp and grabbed his face. His eyes were still there and there was no blood and no doves. He got up, stirred the coals and then laid a couple of sticks on the fire before walking away from his bedroll to relieve himself.

The moonlit night was clear and the tiny lights were many in the sky. The dream had rattled Crow Walks. Twice he had dreamed that he'd been blinded, but the more time that passed, the more he convinced himself that it was just the witch trying to scare him away.

He looked out into the night and thought he saw the gleam of an animal's eyes, but it was gone so fast he decided he had imagined it. He looked up at the hunter's moon and took it as a good sign. When he was finished, he walked back into camp and sat down in front of the small blaze.

Two Rabbits was sitting up on the other side of the fire, frowning.

"Why were you calling me in your sleep? I heard fear in your voice."

"It was dream sleep. It means nothing," Crow Walks muttered, and laid another stick on the fire and dug a piece of jerky from his pouch.

"Maybe it is a sign that you should go back," Two Rabbits offered.

Crow Walks leaped across the fire and shoved Two Rabbits down onto his back, gripping his throat in a choke-hold.

"Stop talking! It was not a sign!" he yelled.

Two Rabbits pushed Crow Walks off and then grabbed his buffalo robe and spear and stalked out away from the camp.

"Where are you going?" Crow Walks yelled.

"You are a crazy man. I do not wish to sleep beside you."

"You sleep away from fire and wolves will get you!" Crow Walks said.

"You will scare them away with your yelling," Two Rabbits shouted, and disappeared into the trees.

Crow Walks frowned. In the dream he could not find Two Rabbits and now he was gone and would not talk to him. He had not wanted to admit it to Two Rabbits, but the dream sleep had frightened him. If he had not already bragged about killing the witch, he would make up some reason and go back. But if he went back now, Two Rabbits would tell that he'd been crying out in his sleep and run away. He had created his own problem and did not know how to correct it and save face.

Angry at the man and the situation, he took another bite of jerky, pulled his robe up around his shoulders, and leaned toward the fire as he chewed.

He sat that way until the fire died and the sun was coming up and he was still sitting there when Two Rabbits came out of the woods carrying his pack.

"I will go with you," Two Rabbits said. "But I will not take part in trying to kill a witch. I do not think it can be done. I do not think it should be done. The medicine man I heard talking about her said she was a strong and powerful woman. He said she'd been born to save our People and I do not see a need to kill her if she's come to do good."

Crow Walks was furious. "Then I do not want you if you will be useless to me! Go! Run and hide! I do not need you. I, Crow Walks, will kill the witch alone."

Two Rabbits shrugged. "Why do you even care? We are not a part of the people she comes to meet."

Crow Walks couldn't bring himself to confess his fear – that twice he'd dreamed he'd been blinded because of her.

"She is a witch. She has no place here," he muttered, and began packing up camp.

"We don't belong to the People anymore. She is no threat to us."

"She is a threat to me!" Crow Walks screamed. "She has shown me that! I do not hide from my enemies! I attack first! I am Crow Walks! I do not hide!"

Two Rabbits took a step back, fearing Crow Walks would kill him where he stood, but when he didn't come at him, Two Rabbits took advantage of the warrior's hesitation and turned and ran.

Crow Walks was in shock. No one had ever refused to obey his orders before. The knot in his belly grew tighter as he turned to stare into the west. Many things were going through his mind, all of which revolved around maintaining his image.

He had been shamed and thrown out of his own tribe, but he'd regained pride in becoming feared, even though it was as a renegade. If he turned around and went back without killing the witch, they would make fun of him. He would sooner die that suffer that.

Still angry, he packed up camp and started walking. He would find her and cut out *her* eyes. If she couldn't see him, she couldn't hurt him.

He walked with the new sun at his back and his own shadow for company and when he accidentally flushed a prairie chicken from its hiding place, he considered it a good omen.

The soft fluttering whirr of wings as the bird frantically flew across his line of vision startled him, but he reacted instinctively. He swung the spear like a club and was surprised when he actually hit it. Stunned, the bird dropped into the tall grass and Crow Walks leaped forward and caught it before it could escape. He calmly broke its neck with a twist and then began plucking feathers from the carcass as he walked, scattering them along his trail. When he came to a small creek, he stopped long enough to gut and clean the bird and then slipped it into his pack to cook later. The simple act of providing his food was calming, and the further he walked, the better he felt. In fact, he had almost convinced himself that the witch sent him those dreams because she viewed him as a threat. And then he came over a ridge and froze. He drew a slow, shaky breath as the knot in his belly tightened.

There was a long dark snake weaving its way across the prairie – so big and so long that he had yet to see the beginning or the end. That it was made up of people walking together made it even more horrifying. Never in his life had he seen that many people in one place – not even when a tribe would gather up several camps to go on raids against their enemies.

They were still a long walk away, which was good. It would give him time to get in a safe position to see if he could spot the tall witch. He might have to trail them for a day or two before he got his chance to catch her alone, but he didn't mind. Now that he'd found them, he was getting excited. It felt good to have purpose.

He began to backtrack along the back of the ridge until he could see the actual front of the line. At the same time he saw the people in the lead, he saw a lone figure walking the ridge on the other side of the valley. Just like in his dream! It was her! He got so excited he laughed out loud. There she was, all by herself. This would be an easy kill.

He backtracked farther to where the tall grass had not been eaten down by the moving herds and dropped into a crouch. With one last look at the people in the distance, he began crossing the valley to get to the other side. He paused once to look for the tall witch and saw her on the ridge. Reassured, he kept moving, sometimes in a crouch, and a few times crawling on his belly when the grass was too short.

He was almost there when he crawled up on a covey of quail. The moment they saw him they exploded out of the grass, flying up into the air. He frowned. That was bad luck to have the birds fly up and pinpoint his location. All he could do was hope if they saw it that they would take no notice, and quickly made his way over the hill. As soon as he found himself a good hiding place, he settled in to wait for their approach.

He was belly down in the tall grass a short distance away from a small pile of fresh dirt. He recognized it as the diggings of a small animal that lived in tunnels underground. Every so often the soft pile of earth would move slightly, proof that the animal was directly beneath. He'd caught one once when he was younger and brought it home to show his mother. She was the one who showed him it had no eyes. The moment he thought it, he thought of his dream of being blinded and frowned. Again, it felt as if he was being warned of what was coming.

He thought again about running away – not going back to the camp and finding a new place to live. He already knew he could live on his own. If he had to he could do it again.

His heart was beating hard against his chest. Sweat was running out of his hair and into his face. He was not good at waiting. After a short time, he began hearing a low rumble and realized it was the sound of voices – so many voices. The strangers must be close which meant the tall witch would be close as well. He raised up just enough to get a glimpse of the ridge in front of him but didn't see her. He glanced up at the sun. It was directly overhead. Even his shadow was gone. He was definitely on his own.

CHAPTER SIX

Yuma had stayed out of sight all morning, using brush and tall grass as a means of concealment but staying within shouting distance of Tyhen. If she knew where he was, she had not given him away. He had watched her walk with that same lanky stride, her head up and gaze forward, always looking to make sure there was no danger ahead or behind.

He was crouched within the tall grass on the valley side of the slope when he saw a large covey of quail suddenly take to the sky. When they did, he flashed on a memory from his childhood of hunting with his father in the pasture outside of Tahlequah, Oklahoma. Their bird dog had flushed a covey just like that, and in his mind he was waiting for the sound of gunshots when he remembered where he was and that guns had yet to be invented.

That was when the skin crawled on the back of his neck. Something had flushed those birds and he immediately thought of the two men after Tyhen. He took off through the grass, going over the ridge and down the backside of the hill, moving fast to get ahead of her.

Montford Nantay was in the lead today.

Adam was about a hundred yards behind and walking with the New Ones when he had a vision of a warrior crawling through the grass. No sooner had he thought it than Evan's voice popped into his head.

Brother, Tyhen is in danger. Where's Yuma?

Guarding her.
I do not see him.
You are not supposed to.
Ah. Should one of us go tell him?

About that time Adam saw the birds fly up into the sky and smiled. No way would Yuma miss that.

See those birds? He already knows.

Although Evan accepted his brother's opinion, he sent a quick warning to Tyhen as well.

Tyhen had been looking in the wrong direction when the birds were flushed, and by the time she turned around they were just birds in flight. Still, she sensed something was wrong. When she caught part of the twins' private conversation and then Evan's warning she knew her instincts were right. After that, her first thought was Yuma.

Yuma, Evan said someone is hidden and waiting for me.
Don't look for me. I already know where he is.

Her heart skipped a beat. So the threat was real! It was troubling to know that while she was coming with a message of peace, someone wanted her dead. Even though she wasn't afraid for her life, she was concerned about Yuma. It was all she could do to keep walking.

Crow Walks was so intent on watching the tall witch that he didn't see the slight ripple of movement in the grass downwind. She was close to him now. So close that he could almost hear the inhale and exhale of her breath. He couldn't resist looking up, but when he did, her height and the length of her legs were exaggerated by his angle of sight, giving him the notion that she was too tall to be human. And once again, he second-guessed his plan to kill a witch.

He was still giving it consideration when she paused, and when she turned, giving him a clear view of her back, he took it as a sign that she was his. He leaped to his feet with the spear in his hand and was adjusting for an upward throw when he heard the sudden rustle of something running through the grass. He spun toward the sound, and after that, everything seemed to happen in slow motion.

He saw the tall witch turn at the same moment he saw the man running toward him. The man was big – even bigger than the witch, and he was carrying weapons unlike anything he'd ever seen. He saw the warrior pull a stick from his back and fit it into what he was carrying. He was so taken aback by the strange weapon that he forgot to protect himself. Before he could think what to do, something was flying toward him.

One second he was standing and then it felt like he'd been punched in the chest. The next thing he knew his knees were buckling and a hot, searing pain was spreading throughout his body so fast his legs went numb.

Crow Walks was flat on his back and looking up at the sky when the man's face blocked his dimming view. Anger mixed with regret that he had failed and even then, he was defiant.

"I am Crow Walks," he whispered.

Yuma reached down and pulled the arrow from the man's chest then wiped it on the dying man's clothes. Rage was still thick in his voice as he leaned down to make sure the man heard every word.

"And I am Yuma. I am the Eagle who protects The Dove."

Crow Walks exhaled slowly.

The vision was coming true. He'd tried to kill the tall witch and an eagle had blinded him.

The sky turned black and then he died.

Tyhen sensed danger even before she turned around, and was startled by the man running toward her. Then she saw Yuma coming at him with a look of cold determination on his face. Transfixed by the life and death moment playing out before her, she did not move as the arrow left Yuma's bow.

It was over as quickly as it began and when Yuma started walking up the slope toward her, she took a slow, shaky breath.

"I didn't hear him," she said.

Yuma slipped an arm around her waist.

"Do you still hear the drums?" he asked.

She nodded.

"Then lead us, Tyhen. We are all ready to reach the Gathering."

She leaned into his body as he pulled her close. The wind encircled them as his mouth centered on her lips, and when she moaned the wind spun harder. As he pulled away he heard a sigh and did not know if it was part of the wind or if it came from her.

When she lifted her chin, he met her gaze.

"Thank you, my Yuma."

Quick tears blurred her vision. No one down in the valley knew what had happened, and she had no intention of revealing it and causing them to fear what lay ahead.

"I will protect you with my life and you will love me forever," he said softly, then waited until she turned and walked away. Yuma watched, seeing her first steps as hesitant, but she quickly picked up her normal stride. His eyes narrowed as he looked out at the vast landscape of the country before them, wondering how many more dangers they would face before they were done.

Adam and Evan watched Yuma and Tyhen's brief embrace from the valley below and knew that the danger was over. They also knew the man had acted alone and that he was no longer of this earth.

Two Rabbits ran most of the way back, returning only to find them breaking camp and packing up to leave.

"What's happening?" Two Rabbits said, as he ran to where Black Hand was standing.

Black Hand pointed at Red Deer, who was busy turning the poles of a tipi into a travois to carry the owner's belongings.

"She had a vision. She saw Crow Walks die. She said an eagle killed him and she did not want to be blamed again for something he had done. We decided to go to the mountains with her. Winter on the prairie is hard."

"I would go, too," Two Rabbits said.

Black hand pointed at Two Rabbit's tipi.

"Red Deer is taking it down for you. She said you would be back."

Two Rabbits looked nervous.

"How does she know all this? Is she a medicine woman?"

Black Hand shrugged.

"Crow Walks left me in charge. He is dead and I am taking his woman."

Two Rabbits frowned.

Leaving with Crow Walks had left him absent when the woman came up for grabs. He slumped. Maybe he would find a woman on their travel to the mountains. He did not want to winter in his tipi alone.

"I will go pack up my things," Two Rabbits said.

"We are leaving soon. You should hurry if you wish to travel with us."

Two Rabbits punched Black Hand on the shoulder.

"Do not order me around. Even if you took his woman and his tipi, you are not Crow Walks."

Black Hand frowned. "I am in charge."

"I think your woman is the one in charge," Two Rabbits muttered, and then went to reclaim his things.

Night came none too quickly for Captain DeVille and his men. They were exhausted, hungry, and in need of water. The fact that they'd found a river solved one problem, and a good night's sleep would solve another. But they needed food – fresh meat in particular.

He'd sent a half dozen of his men out hours ago to hunt and they had yet to show up. He was beginning to believe they were either lost or dead when he heard one horse whinny and then others answer from outside the camp. He didn't let on but the relief was huge. The men were coming back. Hopefully they'd had good luck on their hunt.

As soon as the hunters rode into camp, he began issuing

orders. Soon, the scent of cooking meat was in the air and the knowledge that they would sleep with a full belly tonight made all of them jovial.

The two ailing soldiers were still sick and stayed in their bedrolls instead of getting up and eating. Diego didn't know what to do for them, and was beginning to worry that whatever was wrong with them might be catching. Later, as they were getting ready to bed down the camp grew quieter, and it was then he heard the wolves.

Their yips and howls sounded close. But there were many men in camp and he had no fear that they would be attacked. The danger lay in losing horses to them. He moved through the camp until he found where Estevez was sleeping and kicked the bottom of his boot.

"Lieutenant! The wild animals are coming in too close. The horses are drawing them. We need to pull the horses into the camp, not tether them outside of it."

Estevez was already up and fastening his clothing.

"But Captain, if something spooks them, they might trample us."

"Then make sure you tether them well. Hobble them if you must, but we cannot afford to lose a mount."

"Yes sir," Estevez said, grabbed a dozen men and began moving the horses inside their campground.

Once the horses were moved, the wolves disappeared, looking for easier prey. Everyone was bedded down for the night now, including the horses.

Diego couldn't get comfortable and kept turning from one side to the other until he gave up and laid flat on his back looking up at the stars.

Out here the sky seemed like it went on forever. The stars seemed closer. The world was bigger and unfamiliar and most times frightening. He didn't know why the King wanted to lay claim to this godforsaken place. There wasn't one facet of civilization, and so far he'd seen nothing of value. He watched some night bird fly between his line of sight and the moon, tracking it until it disappeared into the night.

He didn't know when he began hearing the drums, but when he did, he jumped up and turned toward the west to listen.

The sound was faint but constant. Sound carried a long distance out on a prairie, so he had no idea of where the natives were or how far away. He couldn't help but wonder if they would have answers to what happened to the soldiers from the outpost, then realized being unable to communicate would most likely leave the question unanswered.

He didn't know whether to circle their village and keep going, or if he should confront them. Then he decided to make that decision after they found them and saw the size of their camp. If he had a choice, he would turn around and go back to Spain with the bad news that all was lost and hope the King was disenchanted with the idea and give it up.

He was still listening to the drums when he fell asleep.

While Tyhen and the New Ones were anxious to reach their destination, the ones already there were also anxious for the arrival of The Dove. The first ones who'd left their tribe to begin the journey to the Gathering were people from the Ojibwe tribe.

Their medicine man had visions for days of a medicine woman coming among the People who carried a message for all of the tribes. In his vision, it was the white doves that would signal her arrival and when the doves appeared to them they were to pack up their entire camp and follow the birds.

At first the people were not agreeable. It was nearing winter, not a time to be traveling, and a medicine woman was unusual. They did not want to hear her message. But the medicine man persisted and the moment the white doves appeared in their camp they realized his predictions were coming true. If the birds were real, then his message must be important, too, so they packed up their entire village, except for those too old to make the trek, and began following the birds. Every night they would make camp near the trees where the doves stopped to roost, and every morning they would get up and follow the birds in flight.

Their journey was long and arduous and there were some who wanted to quit and go back, but the medicine man insisted and the chief gave the orders and so they kept walking until the morning when they woke up and the white birds were gone. That's when they knew they'd reached their destination.

Soon after the arrival of the Ojibwe, a group from the Tuscarora showed up, and after them were the Nez Perce, and then Osage and Iowa, and Tlingit from the north. Sauck and Fox tribal members arrived and added their numbers to the growing encampment, and then came the Navajo and Pueblo, along with the Seminole who arrived with their colorful feather headdresses and walk-weary feet.

Within another week, members of the Chickasaw, Abenaki and the Caddo, the Creek and the Crow, the Iowa and the Hidatsu, the Mandan and the Pequot were added to the mix as more came flooding in each day.

Cultures clashed. Old enemies were camped next to each other. When the Comanche came into the camp, they did a lot of strutting and glaring at tribes they had been at war with for generations until the Lakota arrived and the tribes began to realize this had nothing to do with who was best and who was right.

The Lakota came in a downpour, exhausted, sick and most without anything but the clothes on their backs. They'd lost everything in crossing the great river that, in the time of the New Ones, had been called the Mississippi.

That was when the meaning of the Gathering began to become real. Tribes that would have once fought them were now taking them into their tipis and giving them shelter. Healers came to minister to the sick, and the day the first one died was the day everything changed. It was no longer us and them, it was we.

When the Washo and Yuma tribes arrived within a couple of days of each other, the encampment had shifted to establish a kind of order. Pathways between camps and tribal dwellings were purposefully left open to point the way toward the river. Hunters went out daily on the vast plains and brought down deer and rabbits, while others hunted down many of the great wooly beasts to help feed the growing multitudes.

Those with visions continued to swear the Dove was coming, but they did not know how close she was until a cold fall morning after a two-day rain.

It was at least an hour before daybreak when a young boy from within the Comanche camp emerged from a tipi to relieve himself. Although the sky was turning lighter, the sun had yet to emerge from her blanket of sleep. The stream of the boy's urine was warmer than the air that he was breathing, causing a tiny cloud of steam as it hit the ground below his feet. He could see his breath as he inhaled and exhaled, and was wondering what his mother would have for them to eat when he heard what sounded like a deep grunt and then a bellow. The sound carried across the silent encampment, bringing more people out from their tipis.

When they heard it again, they looked to the east where the land made a slow upward sweep to the highest point around them. There, silhouetted against the approaching day stood a single buffalo.

At first, all they could see was a silhouette, but they could tell by size alone that it was a massive beast, and because this was unnatural behavior, some began to fear that they were about to be engulfed by a stampeding herd and ran back for weapons.

More and more people began to come out until the encampment was awash in people – so many that their breath in the cold morning air had formed a low-hanging cloud above their heads. They were still watching the solitary beast when the sun broke the horizon in a quick flash of light. Every minute afterward the light swept further across the land, across the river and then the camp, and finally illuminating the snow white coat on the solitary beast.

They gasped in unison and took a few steps back as the reality of what they were seeing began to spread.

It was a most sacred omen – a white buffalo, and an old medicine man was the first to speak.

"It is a sign! The Dove will be here soon. Make ready to receive those who come with her," he said, and his word spread throughout the camp.

And so it began.

While hunters began going after more food, others were gathering buffalo chips and making twists of the dry prairie grass to help them set up their cooking fires. As for the rest of them, the drumbeats grew louder - the singers' cries more strident. They were calling her to them.

Tyhen woke with a start, her heart beating in time to the drums she could hear pounding in her head. In a panic, she crawled over Yuma to get out of the tent, waking him in the process.

Thinking something was wrong, he grabbed his spear and followed her, but once he was outside and saw the still, watchful expression on her face, his anxiety eased.

It was almost daylight. The sky in the east was already lighter and the chill of the air made smoke where she breathed. She shook her head, uncertain of what was happening, and then felt a wind come sweeping down the valley, stirring the ashes of the dying fires and lifting the hair from the back of her neck. It was then she heard the voices of the Old Ones.

"What is it?" he asked.

"Something comes with the sun," she said.

Within moments, Adam and Evan were out of their tent. They'd had the same awakening and were also looking east.

And so they stood, all of them waiting for an unknown messenger while the sky turned pale, taking on a tinge of yellow followed by a wash of pink and purple like the orchids that had grown in the jungles of her childhood.

When the sun came over the horizon, she watched the landscape before her come alive, painting the surface of the tall grass with a light that turned the grass to a moving sea of molten gold, undulating with the wind, awash in ever-changing hues.

One moment there was nothing on the hill and then the next time she looked, it was there.

Yuma gasped. The white buffalo was a powerful messenger.

"It is white!" Tyhen said.

"The white buffalo is powerful medicine to the People and is considered holy," Yuma answered.

She stepped away from him then, and when he started to follow, she lifted her arms to the sky and let the wind carry her up the hill, leaving him behind.

The moment her feet touched earth in front of the bull, she felt the blood rushing through the animal's body and smelled the musky scent rising from the heat of its thick white wooly hump. The great white bull snorted softly as she looked into his eyes. Then she laid a hand on its head and heard the message from the Old Ones that it carried in its heart.

Yuma was watching intently, wondering what was transpiring between them when it suddenly disappeared before his eyes.

Tyhen was just as startled. One moment it was there, and then it was gone and all she could think was that at least she knew what came next.

She looked down into the valley at all of the New Ones who had followed her all this way, then turned south and closed her eyes. In her mind, she could see the city of Boomerang and her mother sleeping in Cayetano's arms. Just for a moment she wished for the comfort of Singing Bird's touch and then she heard Yuma's voice and turned around. Her heart skipped a beat at the sight of him coming up the hill – coming to her.

In that moment, she understood. Her mother was the past and Yuma was the future. Wherever this journey continued to take her, he would always be at her side. She went down the hill to meet him, and when he gave her a questioning look, she put her arms around him and hid her face in the curve of his neck.

"What happened? Are you okay?" he asked.

"I love you so very much," she said softly.

Something in her voice made him tighten his hold.

"Talk to me, love. What do you know that I do not?"

She sighed.

"I will have to pass some kind of test before the people at the Gathering will believe what we've come to tell them."

He frowned. "What kind of test?"

"I do not know anything but that it will happen there."

"Nothing is ever easy for you, is it, my love?"

She stepped back so she could see his face.

"Loving you is easy," she said.

Yuma's voice softened. "Every sad thing that has happened in my life has been worth it to be standing here with you today."

Tyhen knew what he'd lost and what he'd endured, and how much the New Ones had given up to do this. Her voice was shaking as she blinked back quick tears.

"My Yuma... please tell me there will come a time in our lives when we will live in one place again and make a life and a baby together."

He held her close, longing for that day as well.

"It will happen, but for now, it's time to eat some food and pack up camp."

All of the New Ones were weary and needing to replenish their food. They ate as they packed while thinking of the walk ahead, most of them planning to take advantage of whatever game they came across throughout the day.

Tyhen was putting the last of her things into her pack when she began to pick up on a disturbance somewhere within the camp. Within seconds, she got a message from Adam that confirmed it.

The little boy called Gecko is missing.

Her heart sank.

"No," she muttered, and shrugged out of her pack.

At the sound of her voice, Yuma turned.

"What's wrong?" he asked.

"Gecko is missing. We have to find him," she said.

"Where does he camp? Who are his parents?" Yuma asked.

"I don't know," she said. "He's just always around."

"There comes Evan. I think he's looking for you," Yuma said.

Evan came running, breathless and a little bit panicked because he felt trouble for the boy that he could not see.

"He wasn't in his bed when they woke up," Evan said.

"Who are his parents?" Yuma asked.

"He doesn't have any. They said his parents died months ago, just after we left Naaki Chava. They died after the earthquake, when the mountain came down. Montford and Johnston's sister, Lola, and her husband, Aaron, have been feeding him and seeing to his needs."

Tyhen saw the shock on Yuma's face. She knew exactly what he was thinking. This boy was walking alone with the New Ones just as Yuma had done when he was young, when they were running from Firewalker.

"We have to find him," Yuma said.

"I'm going up," Tyhen said. "You men fan out from where their camp was. He can't be far."

"Follow me," Evan said. "I know where they camp."

Yuma and Evan left on the run.

Tyhen wouldn't let herself think of all the things that could have happened as she lifted her arms and began to chant. Within moments she was surrounded by a whirlwind and flying above the encampment.

CHAPTER SEVEN

Dakotah woke needing to relieve himself. Lola was asleep and so was her husband Aaron. They always told him to let them know where he was going when he left their camp, but all he needed to do was pee.

He got up and slipped out of their tent, then quickly made his way to a less populated area of the camp to do his business.

The air was still and he could tell by the faint light in the east that the new day was not far away.

After he was finished, he paused a moment and glanced up at the sky, transfixed by a shooting star falling toward earth. When it burned out in mid-air, it looked to him like magic. It was there and then it was not. And then while he was still looking another star came into sight, hurtling down, down, down with the burning tail marking the way.

Dakotah gasped. This time the star did not disappear. It was still falling. Without thinking he took a few steps away and then a few more and a few more until he was running, still watching the star. When it finally burned out he groaned in disappointment. He'd been certain that one was going to fall right out here on the prairie.

He glanced toward the east again. The sky was getting lighter which meant the sun would be up soon and Lola would be waking and wondering where he was. He turned to walk back when he heard a growl, and then another on the other side of him and froze.

Wolves!

When he saw their yellow eyes watching him through the grass he began to shake. They were standing between him and safety and it was no accident. They'd cut him off – just like they did the very young and the very old buffalo that they separated from the herd. He was scared - as scared as he'd been when he'd run with his mother and father after the earthquake - as scared as he'd been when he saw part of the mountain bury his mother and father alive. The only thing that had kept him alive then was that he hadn't stopped running and he was guessing this was one of those times again. He wanted to cry and scream for help, but something told him they would jump him before help could come.

He thought of Tyhen. She was going to need him in the years to come, so he couldn't die. The Old Ones had told him his path in a dream. All he could do now was hope they helped him run fast enough to get to the small grove of trees a few yards behind him. But first, he needed something to put more distance between him and the wolves and the only thing he could think of was to jump up in the air with his arms held high and make a loud, angry noise. So he did it.

The noise was an abrupt and startling interruption into the darkness within which the trio was standing, and Dakotah was the only one who knew it was coming. As he'd hoped, the two wolves skittered sideways a good distance back and that was all the chance he needed. He pivoted on one heel and started running for those trees as fast as his long skinny legs would take him, running through the tall grass like it wasn't even there.

He knew when the wolves gave chase because he could hear them crashing through the grass. He knew they could outrun him, but the trees were close – so close. He thought of the landslide that crushed his mother and father and ran for his life.

He leaped as he reached the first tree, grabbing hold of the lowest branch and using his momentum to swing himself and his legs off the ground in one motion. He clamped his arms and legs around the limb only seconds before the wolves were beneath him, snarling and snapping and leaping into the air. One grabbed onto the tail of his shirt and the weight of the wolf's body almost made him lose his grasp.

"No!" he screamed, and frantically worked the loose deerskin shirt over his head.

The moment he was no longer in it, the wolf fell to the ground with the shirt in its mouth and Dakotah began climbing up as fast as the gecko for which he'd been named.

Now the wolves couldn't climb up, but he couldn't get down. He began yelling for help, expecting at any moment to see people come swarming over the hill, but when he looked up, he was stunned to see how far away he was. That's when he remembered chasing after the falling stars. He yelled again and again, and then in a panic, imagining the New Ones breaking camp and going off without him, he screamed.

Below, the wolves were still circling the tree, and to his horror, three more came out of the grass to join them.

As it began to get a little lighter, he saw something black dripping on the limbs and then he realized his back and arm were burning. When he realized the black dripping on limbs was his blood he panicked again. He'd been bitten, probably when they'd grabbed his shirt. Without knowing how bad he was wounded, he wondered if he would bleed to death. The horror of his situation kept growing. In desperation, he began calling for help again.

"Help me! Help me!" he cried, yelling it over and over until his throat was raw.

The frantic tone of his voice sent the wolves into a snarling frenzy. They began jumping up and then circling the tree, growling at him and then fighting among themselves. By now there were so many wolves he could not keep track of their number.

He gripped the tree a little tighter and held on while the sun came over the horizon, casting a horrific light onto the danger of his situation. He called out until his voice was gone and he was beginning to get dizzy.

To his horror, it felt as if the land was rolling all around him. Fearing he would roll out of the tree, he wrapped his arms and legs around the trunk and closed his eyes.

Evan and Yuma cleared the camp just a few yards ahead of a group of warriors. They saw Aaron in their midst and knew that he was heartsick that the boy was lost.

Yuma paused on the ridge to call out Dakotah's name, then waited a few moments, hoping he would hear an answer, but all he heard was Tyhen's voice in his head.

He's in the trees. Wolves beneath it. I'll get him. You get the wolves.

Yuma saw the small grove of trees about a quarter of a mile ahead and pointed.

"Tyhen said he's there! Wolves have him treed," he cried, and started running.

A dozen armed warriors followed Yuma, running through the tall grass as Tyhen flew above them. She could feel the boy's fear and rapid heartbeat, but she also felt his weakness and exhaustion.

Hold fast, Dakotah. I am coming.

Dakotah felt himself going in and out of consciousness and tried to wedge his body between the fork in two big limbs in case he passed out, hoping it would stop him from falling among the wolves.

In his mind he was still screaming for help, when in reality he had not uttered a word. He did not see the warriors coming for him or the whirlwind flying through the air above them, until out of nowhere, he heard Tyhen's voice in his head. He opened his eyes, thinking she was right behind him. When he didn't see her, he thought he'd been dreaming and looked out at the distance between him and safety. That's when he saw armed warriors running toward him, and a whirlwind of motion in the sky above them.

He was saved!

The relief he felt was so overwhelming that, for the first time since it happened, he began to cry.

All of a sudden the warriors were below him and in the midst of the wolves. He saw Yuma spear one and slash another one's throat with the big knife from his belt and in the back of his mind Dakotah wondered if he'd ever be that brave and strong. He watched Evan shoot an arrow into one that was running away, and then the other warriors waded into fight. The snarling soon changed to yelps of pain as two more wolves went down and then a third one fell. At that point, the remaining wolves made a run for it.

Evan ran after them, taking down one more with his spear just as Tyhen took the whirlwind into the trees.

One moment Dakotah was clinging to the branches and the next he was inside the whirlwind and cradled in her arms. The last time he'd seen that look on a woman's face was from his mother just before she disappeared beneath the mountain.

"I went too far," he said softly, and then passed out.

Tyhen felt the blood on his back and flew faster. When she reached the ridge, she set down and then ran the rest of the way into camp.

When Lola saw Tyhen come into camp carrying him and saw the blood all over his little body, she let out a wail of despair, certain he was dead.

"He's not dead," Tyhen said. "Bring water to clean him and find a healer."

Lola ran to get her water pouch as one of the men took off running through the camp.

Tyhen laid him down and then turned him over to inspect the wounds. When she realized the bite marks had not torn flesh and that part of the puncture wounds had already stopped bleeding, she breathed a sigh of relief. When Lola returned with the water and the cloths, they began washing the blood off his body and cleaning out the wounds.

Yuma and the warriors returned just before the healer. He dropped Dakotah's shirt down near his body and then got down on his knees to look at the wounds Tyhen was cleaning.

"Did he talk to you?" Yuma asked.

"All he said was that he went too far," she said.

Evan glanced at his brother who was standing within the crowd and arched an eyebrow questioningly.

Adam nodded.

Say nothing.

Adam nodded again, agreeing with his brother's judgment. Tyhen did not yet need to know the connection between her and the boy.

Tyhen was so involved in tending to the boy that she didn't tune into the cryptic conversation between the brothers, and then the healer arrived and Tyhen and Yuma were moved aside.

The healer, a woman named Myra Begay, checked the wounds they'd cleaned and then opened her medicine pouch and poured a powdered substance into the punctures. She laid the last of her medicine leaves from the jungle on top of each bite mark and wet them down to make them adhere to Dakotah's skin, and then she was done.

Tyhen laid a hand on the back of the little boy's leg and felt the weakness, then sent her voice out across the prairie so that all would hear.

"We do not travel today. Today we hunt for food to fill our bellies and our packs. Today we repair what is broken and will be thankful this boy is still with us."

Lola looked up at Tyhen with tears in her eyes.

"Thank you. Thank you for bringing him back."

"I did not do it alone," Tyhen said, and pointed to the warriors behind her. "They killed the wolves. If they had not, the beasts would have followed us daily, waiting for someone else to go too far."

She glanced at Yuma who was still on his knees beside Dakotah.

"I am going to set our camp back up," she said.

Yuma gave the child one last pat and then stood.

"I will hunt for food," he said.

"I will go with him," Evan added.

By the time she left, a large number of the men were gathering to make up several hunting parties and go in all four directions. She hoped they were able to bring down some of the larger game, like the buffalo and deer. She was heartily tired of rabbits and birds.

Adam stayed with the boy, leaving Lola to unpack her camp and set it back up. He could see what the child had endured through his pain-filled dreams and felt instant empathy. He and

Evan had suffered in similar ways until Singing Bird rescued them. But he also knew something that Tyhen and Yuma did not. One day, this young boy would be as vital to their daughter's future as Yuma had been to Tyhen, and a most remarkable thing – the boy already knew it.

For Adam, time was dragging and he was almost wishing he'd gone hunting with Evan. It was still disconcerting how Evan had changed after he'd lost his memory so many months ago. Before, the twins had been unemotional geniuses. Their psychic abilities and their bond to each other was all that mattered to them. They liked other people, but never got personally involved. It was like that part of humanity had been left out of them at birth.

And then Evan got lost and hurt during the race to escape the erupting volcano and nearly died. When he came to, he was an entirely different man. It had taken him weeks to remember everything and heal, but after he got well, he wasn't the same. Now, he laughed, he cried, he got angry and he got even, where Adam was still as he'd always been. Adam didn't mind, but there were times, like today, when he felt left out because in a way, he had also been left behind.

Lola returned, thanking Adam for sitting with the boy, and just like that, he was no longer needed. With nothing left to discern and no skills to add food to their cooking pots, he returned to their campsite and began setting it back up.

He had just put down the bedding inside their tent and was getting ready to go fill up their water bags when a most remarkable thing happened.

He picked up the water bags and when he turned around, he was confronted by a vision of a beautiful young woman staring at him. She was not one of the New Ones, and he guessed she was with one of the tribes already at the Gathering.

The startling part of seeing her was in knowing that wherever she was, she was seeing him, too. The shock on her face was real and then he saw her gaze shift to just over his shoulder, and her expression changed to one of fear.

He looked over his shoulder to see what she was seeing and saw Evan. That's when he knew that wherever Evan was, he was having the same vision of her.

An odd sensation rolled through him. He'd seen her first. She was his vision, not Evan's. He looked back at her. She was still standing there, staring at the both of them like she'd seen a ghost. He wanted her to acknowledge him, and so he spoke.

"My name is Adam."

And the moment he spoke she disappeared. Shaken by the feeling that she was no longer just *his* vision made him uncomfortable. He didn't know that what he was feeling was jealousy because he had never felt like that before.

He made his way to the spring to refill their water pouches and had to wait in line behind others who were there to do the same. He took a deep breath and closed his eyes for a moment, and as soon as he did her face popped back into his mind.

Dark eyes flashing – a full, sensuous mouth - long black braids. Her clothing consisted of a long shirt that fell way below her knees with fur-lined leggings to protect her from the cold. He had no way of knowing what she had on was all she owned, then someone tapped him on the shoulder, urging him forward. It was his turn at the spring.

Evan had been walking beside Yuma when the young woman materialized right in front of him. Before he could think to speak, he saw his brother standing between them. That's when he realized it was a vision and that what was happening was going to change their lives forever.

In the vision, he saw Adam turn and glare at him. He didn't understand what was happening, but Adam looked angry, which was, for him, strange and unexpected behavior.

Then all of a sudden she was gone and so was Adam. Evan tried to shake off a feeling of dread as he ran to catch up, and after a few more hours of successful hunting, it slipped to the back of his mind.

Suwanee, youngest daughter of Matto, Chief of the Lakota, was still standing by the water when she heard her mother's voice telling her to hurry. But how was a woman to hurry when she just had a vision of two of the most beautiful warriors she had ever seen?

Their faces were the same. Their hair was black like hers, but not straight. It had motion in it, like the ripples in water. Their skin was lighter and their winter clothing was made from the skins of some kind of animal with black and yellow markings on its pelt.

It wasn't until one of them spoke to her in a language she'd never heard that she lost her concentration, and when that happened, the vision disappeared.

"Suwanee! Bring the water now!" her mother shouted again.

Suwanee sighed as she knelt at the river to fill the cooking pot, then hurried back to the tipi.

They'd been at the Gathering for many sleeps now, and shamed that they were living in someone else's lodge.. The people of their village lost everything crossing a wide river. Some drowned in the crossing and her grandfather died just after their arrival.

She was sad about her grandfather, and tired of the noise and the crowd. At this point, she didn't care about any messenger and did not care if she ever saw the old woman they were calling the Dove.

Her steps were swift as she hurried back with the water, but her thoughts were still with the warriors from her vision.

Were they part of the people who were coming with the Dove, or were they spirits with a message she didn't understand? Only time would tell.

The hunters came straggling back into the encampment in far different numbers than when they'd left. Some had luck early and came back with the carcasses of their kills already field-dressed. Older men had automatically opted for smaller game, while the younger ones had gone after the larger game. Hunting in tandem with several others, they'd been able to run down and kill both deer and buffalo. So now they were all on their way back to camp, loaded down with meat and green skins.

Yuma was carrying more than his body weight in fresh meat and still had a distance to get back to camp. He was tired, concerned about Dakotah, and worried even more about this test Tyhen would be facing, so he had no breath left for talking.

As for Evan, who was also packing a large amount of fresh meat, he had no interest in talking, either. He was still trying to discern the meaning of the vision he'd had earlier and wondering what Adam would say about it.

The face of the young woman still haunted him. He doubted if she was any older than Tyhen. She'd worn her long dark hair in braids and the braids had been wrapped with some kind of white fur. Her eyes had flashed with obvious spirit and he had been holding his breath, waiting to hear the sound of her voice when she'd suddenly disappeared.

She seemed ill-equipped for the impending winter since she wore no outer garment over her dress, and had no leggings to go with her moccasins. Evan wondered if she'd come from a warmer climate and could not imagine how they would fare once the snow began, then wondered why he cared. She wasn't real to him. Just a vision, and for all he knew a vision from the past or the future.

They had more important things to focus on besides visions. The weather was holding. It was cold but not freezing and the sky was clear. At least there would be no rain tonight, he thought, and shifted his pack to keep it from rubbing a sore on his shoulder. Walking in rain and mud was miserable. He assumed walking in snow and ice would be worse and hoped after the Gathering that they found a place to wait winter out before going farther.

By the time the hunters reached camp they were exhausted. The New Ones had several large cooking fires in different locations to accommodate the number of people needing to be fed. Every time someone came in with fresh meat, it was immediately put on the fire to cook. There were many to feed, but their bellies had shrunk and it didn't take nearly as much to satisfy them now as it would have back in Naaki Chava.

Yuma dropped off his meat at one of the cooking fires then went to the spring to clean up. He was hungry, but too dirty and bloody to stop and eat. He stripped down near the spring, and by the time he had washed he was cold and shivering. He thought of the luxury of warmth and spare clothing he had enjoyed in Naaki Chava and then shrugged it off and got dressed.

The next thing on his mind was Tyhen.

Where are you, my love?

With Dakotah.

He smiled to himself. He should have known.

He went to Lola's camp and saw Tyhen sitting beside Dakotah. He walked up behind her, slid a hand beneath her hair, and squeezed the back of her neck.

Tyhen smiled as she looked up.

"I saw you come into the camp earlier. You had good luck hunting."

He nodded as he squatted down beside her and then touched Dakotah's leg.

"How do you feel, little warrior?"

Dakotah's eyes widened. Being considered a warrior by the Eagle was a great compliment.

"My back is sore. It is my fault. I went too far," he said softly, then looked away, embarrassed by the situation he'd put everyone in. They had not walked today because of him.

"We all make mistakes," Yuma said. "Were you in the trees when the wolves found you?"

"No. I was in the middle of the prairie between the trees and the camp."

Yuma frowned. "Where were the wolves when you saw them?"

Dakotah shuddered, remembering the yellow eyes and the low throaty growls.

"Right in front of me. I was watching pieces of the sky falling. When I turned around they were there."

Yuma leaned forward.

"What I want to know is how you ran that far and got up the tree before the wolves took you down."

"I jumped up in the air and made a loud scary noise. They ran backward and I ran for the trees."

Yuma rocked back on his heels, staring at the young boy in disbelief.

"How did you think to do that?"

"I just did," Dakotah said. "I will not go too far again."

"I am very glad you ran fast. You are a brave boy, Dakotah. I think you should not be Gecko anymore. You are a warrior. You faced an enemy and defeated them with your wisdom and your speed."

Tyhen smiled.

"That's what I told him," she said. "He was very brave."

"He is well?" Yuma asked.

She nodded. "No fever. The wounds are no longer bleeding. Myra Begay will be back later to put more medicine on his back before he sleeps."

Yuma nodded, pleased to learn he was doing well.

"Are you hungry, Dakotah?"

The boy sniffed the air and then nodded.

"The cooking fires make me hungry," Dakotah said.

"Here is a basket you can use to carry the food," Lola said, as she stepped out of her tent.

Tyhen took the basket. "I will go get it," she said, and brushed a hand across Yuma's shoulder as she walked away.

CHAPTER EIGHT

Like Yuma, Evan left the meat he'd brought at one of the cooking fires and stopped by their camp to get clean clothes, expecting to find Adam there. He was nowhere in sight.

He didn't think anything of it as he hurried to the spring. After he washed and dressed, he washed his bloody shirt and carried it back to camp and spread it across the top of their tent to dry out. When he still didn't see Adam, he did what they always did and thought the question he needed answered.

Brother, where are you?

The silence was startling and he was just about to become concerned when Adam finally answered.

"I am here."

Evan jumped. Adam was right behind him and he had not sensed his twin's presence. That had never happened before.

"How did you do that?" Even asked.

Adam frowned. "Do what?"

"I did not sense you. I always know when you are close."

Adam shrugged, unwilling to admit he'd purposefully blocked him.

"You are different. Maybe you do not discern as you once did."

Evan felt like he had just been slapped.

"Are you saying I am less than I was?"

Adam shrugged.

"Different is not less," Evan snapped. "What is wrong with you? Why are you talking to me like this?"

Adam's chest felt like it was swelling. There was a pain in his heart that was growing with every breath he took and his eyes were beginning to burn. He'd never felt this way before and had no understanding of what was happening. All he knew was to lash out. They did everything together and he wanted Evan to hurt, as well.

Adam doubled up his fists. His voice was shaking. He had never wanted anything in his life beyond the bond he and Evan had shared - from speaking their own secret language as children to surviving the monster who created them, to being the only two people who were not Native American to survive Firewalker. He had never wanted anything else but being Evan's twin until today – until the vision.

"I saw her first," he said, his voice shaking.

Evan was shocked. That sounded like jealousy. Jealousy was an emotion and Adam did not experience emotions. But then neither had he until he nearly died.

"So you saw her, too? I wasn't sure. She just appeared out of nowhere. What do you think it means?"

Adam was taken aback by Evan's calmness. When he looked into her eyes, had he not felt like he was dying?

"You saw me. You know I saw her because you were behind me."

Evan slowly shook his head.

"Brother, I do not understand your anger. What I had was a vision. I had no way of knowing we were having the same one."

"Well, we were," Adam snapped.

"So why are you angry with me? I can no more control a vision than you can. They just come. Right?"

"I saw the way she looked at you," Adam said. "She liked you better."

Evan felt like he'd just been punched.

"Liked me better? Have you lost your mind? We look the same. We had a ten second look at a total stranger and you are angry with me? I'll tell you what's happening to you. You have just had your first experience with an emotion. It's called jealousy, which makes you a fool. Brothers do not fight over the same girl, especially one they do not even know."

Adam took a deep breath, and then closed his eyes. He could still see her face and he wanted to die. They were going to meet her, and she was going to choose Evan. He shuddered, then lifted his head and looked away.

"You are right. I'm sorry, brother. I don't know why I said all of that."

Evan was so happy that this was over that he threw his arms around Adam's shoulders and gave him a hug.

"It's okay. Emotion is hard. Feeling it is worse. You'll figure it out as it happens more. I did."

Adam nodded as he pulled away.

"I am sure you are right. I over-reacted and I am sorry."

Evan was so relieved they were not fighting that he missed the less than sincere manner in which that was delivered.

"It's okay. Let's go get some food. I'm starving."

Adam let himself be led away, but the knot in his stomach was still there. This was far from over.

And he was right.

That night as they lay sleeping, the girl from the vision walked in their dreams.

Adam was dreaming of Naaki Chava when he saw her coming through the tall grass. He wanted to wake up and go to her, but his body wouldn't respond. Instead, he became an onlooker to her approach.

The prairie grass moved aside for her passage as if she was nothing more than wind, parting just enough to let the sylph move past. His heart started to pound and his body responded. His manhood grew hard, throbbing with every beat of his heart. He knew what he wanted. He wanted her. See me, he shouted, but she was on her own walk and did not hear him.

Back in Naaki Chava he and Evan spirit walked at will, but on this night his spirit was as trapped in his body as he was in this dream, and when he saw his brother's spirit suddenly standing beside her, he groaned. As she reached toward Evan they were enveloped by a white, bright light. When the light exploded, Adam couldn't control his ensuing climax, and when it was over, it left him sad and shaking. The vision slid away as he rolled over onto his side, but there were tears on his cheeks as he fell into a deeper dreamless sleep.

Evan was also dreaming of Naaki Chava. He was dreaming of Singing Bird and Cayetano and how they let him and Adam feed the monkeys in the trees outside the palace when they were little. He could hear Singing Bird's laugh as one of the monkeys stole the fruit right out of his hand and turned around to say something to her when the girl walked into his dream.

He was confused. She didn't belong here. She was not part of his past, and then he heard Singing Bird whispering in his ear... *but she is part of your future.*

He looked at her more fully as she came closer, noting the gentleness in her gaze and the slight tilt of a small smile at the corner of her lips. She was beautiful and when she touched him his body betrayed him. He grew hard beneath his clothing and his heart began to beat faster. All of a sudden he was no longer in Naaki Chava. He was standing in the tall grass beside her and when she touched him again, she leaned forward. He put his arms around her, but in the dream she was weightless. Then she moved forward and her spirit flowed through him like water while everything inside him exploded in a bright white light.

Suwanee woke within her tipi with her heart pounding and her breath coming in short, uneven gasps. The throb between her legs was ebbing and there was a part of her that believed she'd just died and was once again reborn.

She'd felt her spirit leave her body and didn't understand why she was suddenly out on the prairie alone beneath the stars. All she knew was that she was being drawn in that direction by a power greater than anything she'd ever known.

When she saw one of the brothers with the same face suddenly appear before her and open his arms, she knew this was her sign – this was the one destiny had chosen for her.

She touched him and then watched in disbelief as he began to glow. When she touched him again, he wrapped his arms around her and in that moment she felt her body begin to vibrate. Seconds later she fell into the light as a great heat was within her. Just when she thought she would burn up, the light exploded. Now she was awake, the warrior was gone, and she would never be the same.

When the sun rose the next day, Adam's mood was dark and Evan's mood was thoughtful. The twins had not shared their dreams with each other and so the secret only added to the growing distance between them.

As for the others, the mood for the New Ones was hopeful. They were near the end of their journey and ready to begin the next phase of their lives. The urgency of educating the tribes to the dangers of the strangers who would come to their land was immediate.

When Tyhen took to the high ridge and Yuma struck the trail East, everyone followed with renewed vigor.

Tyhen had the hood pulled up on her coat and walked at a brisk pace to stay warm. The sky was without clouds. The sun was weak and very far away which exacerbated the cold wind on the ridge.

Every now and then she would pause to look in all directions to make sure there was no imminent danger, and when she did the cold sliced across her face.

She glanced down at the New Ones, wondering where Dakotah was and if he was strong enough to walk all day. She made a mental note to check on him later and then looked for Yuma. Her heart skipped a beat when she saw him – a head taller than most of the people around him and walking with that long, rhythmic stride. The simple act of looking at him made her ache. She smiled to herself, thinking of how he made her feel when they made love, and as she did, the wind swirled around her so strong it almost lifted her off her feet. She laughed aloud and then made herself focus to the task at hand. When she was confident there was no danger, she listened again for the drumbeat and followed the sound.

Down below, Adam and Evan walked without speaking. They were not communicating with each other in any way.

Adam could not disguise his new-found emotion any more than he could control it. He was scared to the core that he was losing his brother and didn't know how to stop it.

Evan continued to ponder the message from Singing Bird while trying to reconcile the fact that he was becoming entirely too involved with a woman who might not even be real, and if she was, following his heart would destroy what was between him and his brother. It was a reality he didn't want to face.

Captain DeVille and most of his men were devoid of clothing and standing in the river up to their balls, scrubbing weeks of trail dust from their skin and leaving stark white bodies to bare the evidence of thick ropey scars and missing fingers from the violence of their lives. All of them needed a shave and a haircut and were far too thin.

Estevez was humped up like a toad on a rock, shaking from head to toe.

"Dios mio! The water she is cold!" he shrieked.

Diego glared at the little man.

"Because the weather is cold," he muttered.

Diego continued to whine.

"Then why are we in the river?"

"Because we all smell dreadful. Because we are human beings, not savages like those that came out of their hovels."

Estevez muttered beneath his breath.

"What? What did you say?" Diego shouted.

Estevez wanted to shout, but he was just afraid enough of the captain to test him, and so he answered in soft, hesitant voice.

"I said that savage was good enough to scratch your itch when you wanted her."

Diego glared a moment and then started to laugh.

"You are right, Lieutenant! You are right! And, because I am a much more satisfied man than I was before that happened,

I will not cut your head from your neck for subordination. Now wash your body and hurry up. We are losing time. I heard drums last night. I believe we are close to finding more savages. Maybe they will know where the rest of our men are."

The men didn't have to be told twice. They were washed and dressed in no time, and were still shivering as they saddled their horses.

Just as Diego was about to order them to mount up, one of the soldiers who'd been tending the horses came running.

"Captain DeVille! Ortega is dead and Castillo is missing."

DeVille's stomach rolled.

These were the two men who'd been throwing up for days. This made six men he'd lost to this ailment. There was no mistaking it was spreading, but without knowing what was wrong, he didn't know what to do about them.

"Lieutenant Estevez, pick five men and go find Castillo." Then he waved at the nearest six soldiers. "You six, dig two graves. Wherever Castillo is, he's most likely dead, too. The rest of you pack up their gear on their horses and ready them to take them with us."

The men were somber as they went about their assigned tasks. A while later, Estevez and his men came back with a body dangling over a horse.

"Where did you find him?" DeVille asked.

Estevez pointed to the west.

"Lying in the middle of the prairie. Probably out of his head with that fever when he wandered off."

DeVille nodded.

Estevez didn't move.

"Captain... that makes six men we've lost. What's wrong with them? Are we all going to get sick?"

DeVille frowned. "I am no doctor. I don't know was wrong and I don't know if we will get it, understand?"

Estevez's shoulders slumped.

"Yes, I understand."

DeVille wouldn't even look at the body.

"Now take him away. They are digging his grave."

Estevez walked away, leading the horse.

Diego DeVille looked out across the prairie and then back at

the way they'd come. It wouldn't take much for him to turn his
men around and go back. But he had his orders, and until he
knew for certain what happened to the men, he couldn't go
anywhere but forward.

Suwanee was scraping bits of flesh from one of the buffalo
hides with the sharp side of a flat rock, cleaning it up to cure. It
was stretched out on a rack beside the lodge where they were
sleeping and was a mindless task to keep her busy.

Today the sun was hiding its face, which made the air
colder. It cut through her clothing as if she was naked, making
her shiver as she worked. The cooking fire was nearby, giving
off some heat but not nearly enough, so she kept her head bent
to her task knowing the sooner the hide was cleaned and cured,
the quicker she would have a new winter robe.

Chata, her mother, was nearby doing the same to rabbit
skins. They would become leggings, something they both
needed desperately.

Matto saw their discomfort and was sorry for it, but there
was nothing he could do but provide the hides and the food.
The rest was women's work.

When Suwanee looked up from the buffalo hide and caught
his eye, he smiled, knowing she would smile back. And she
did. It was enough for him to take with him as he walked away.

Suwanee sighed. Her father was concerned about the tribe's
well-being. The other morning she'd looked to the far
mountains and seen snow on the tops. It would not be long
before snow would be here as well. She wanted to go home.
And at the same time she thought about leaving, she thought of
the two warriors with the same face. She didn't know if they
were real but the dream she'd had about one of them was
locked in her heart. She wanted to feel that again. She wanted
him.

Her shoulders slumped as she returned to her task. She
worked without thought, ignoring the chill of the wind until it
brought the sound of a high-pitched shriek above her head. She
glanced up, saw the eagle circling the sky above them and at

the same time she saw a white dove in flight. When the eagle suddenly dived toward it, she thought the eagle would kill it, but then the eagle slipped in beneath the dove, like it was protecting it from danger below and as it did, the birds began to fade and she was looking into a waking vision.

Suwanee saw a tall, dark-haired girl in a bearskin coat walking through the tall grass. The hood on the coat framed a sad face of great beauty. A very tall warrior, also dressed for the cold, was walking in front of her carrying weapons unlike any she had seen. All this time she'd thought the Dove would be an old woman, but the moment she'd seen her face she knew she was the Dove they waited for, and the warrior protecting her was the eagle she'd seen up in the sky.

What surprised her even more were the two men walking behind the Dove. It was the two warriors from her vision – the ones with light skin and the same face. Now she knew for sure that they were real. They were coming with the Dove and they were near. Her heart began to pound as it had in her dream last night and she could almost feel his arms around her again. Then all of a sudden the vision was gone.

She glanced down at the buffalo hide and began scraping harder. Time was shorter than she had supposed.

Dakotah did not feel like his usual self, but his back did not hurt as much as it had the day before. Lola and Aaron kept him close by them as well and he did not mind. As long as he could see Tyhen he felt safe.

He had dreamed of wolves all night - large, oversized animals strong enough to bite into his flesh and carry him off. In the dream he had called out first for his mother and then for his father but they did not come. He kept seeing the wolves' yellow eyes in the darkness and feeling their hot breath against his flesh. He didn't understand why his mother couldn't hear him or why his father did not rescue him, and then he saw a great bird coming down from the sky, diving toward the wolves at breakneck speed.

All of a sudden the wolves were yelping out in pain as the

bird flogged them and pecked at their faces until they could not see. When all the wolves were blind, the bird swept past him in the dark. He had only a brief glimpse of it but it made him think of Tyhen.

In the dream, he turned and ran away.

Now today was like all others. Walking, walking - always walking. He had almost forgotten about play. He would like to play again - maybe when their journey was done.

He glanced up at the ridge.

Tyhen was taking long steps. He looked down at his legs and feet and tried to match her stride but could not.

"I will have to grow more," he muttered.

Lola heard his voice and turned around.

"What did you say? Are you in pain?"

"No. I said I need to grow."

Lola slowed down a step so that she could walk beside him and put a hand on the top of his head.

"You are already growing every day. What is your hurry?"

He pointed to the ridge.

"I need to be tall like Tyhen."

Lola shook her head.

"I'm not going to ask why," she said. "Knowing you, I'm sure you have your reasons."

He shrugged. His reasons were still not for sharing.

"Are you hungry? I have food."

He nodded, anticipating the cooked meat she took out of her pack.

"Thank you," he said, as she handed him a large piece from last night's feast.

Lola smiled again. "You are a good boy, Dakotah. Stay close today, okay?"

He nodded as he chewed, thankful to fill the ache in his empty belly.

Yuma knew something was wrong between the twins. They were not looking at each other and were walking with just enough distance between them so that their bodies never touched – not even so much as a shoulder bump. He had known them for most of his life and had never seen this. He feared they were hiding some terrible secret from him regarding Tyhen. Maybe it had to do with this test she would have to face. He wanted to ask them but there was no privacy in a crowd.

He glanced up at Tyhen and when he did, caught her looking down at them.

Are you all right?

He sighed. How did she always know when something was bothering him?

Yes, but something is wrong between Adam and Evan.

When she didn't immediately answer him, he suspected it was because she was trying to tune into them. Whatever was going on, she would get to the bottom of it he thought and then lengthened his stride.

Tyhen thought of the twins which usually had one or both of them tuning in and talking to her, but the silence was telling.

She tried for several minutes to listen in until it dawned on her that it wasn't because she could no longer hear them. What was happening was that they were blocking their thoughts from each other. Now *she* was concerned.

Adam! Evan! What is going on?

Adam answered first.

Nothing.

Evan's answer was immediate, as well.

I'm fine, too.

Then both of you come walk with me.

Evan gave her the first excuse.

I am helping an old man carry his pack.

When Adam stayed silent, she frowned.

Adam?

When he finally spoke, it was the last thing she expected him to say.

There are strangers in the east riding on horses toward the Gathering.

What do you mean, strangers?

Their skin is white. They wear metal coats and hats.

A rush of shock ran through her.

The explorers? The ones who threaten our land and way of life? Here now?

Now Evan was adding to the warning.

I see them, too, Tyhen. Forty, maybe fifty and there is something wrong with them. I think they carry a disease. If they reach the Gathering before we do it will be a disaster. They will infect the entire population waiting for you.

Tyhen was trying not to panic.

How much time do we have? Can we reach the Gathering before them?

Adam spoke first.

If we walk all night we will be there by morning.

And what of the strangers? How far away are they?

Evan added more information.

They are not walking, they are riding. If we make camp tonight they will get there ahead of us and then it will be too late.

Now Tyhen understood the white buffalo's message. This was how she would be tested. She glanced up at the sky. It was already past mid-day. The New Ones would be tired and looking forward to a night's rest. She could go ahead, bypass the Gathering and deal with the strangers on her own, but it wouldn't solve the other problem. Until those already at the Gathering saw for themselves that she was truly a messenger with the power to change their fate, they wouldn't all follow what they needed to do.

There was only one option.

She raised her arm and then raised her voice. The wind carried her words across the wide valley and stopped the New Ones in their tracks as they all turned to face her.

"There is danger coming toward the Gathering. Strangers are riding in on the animals you call horses. They carry a disease that will destroy us all and there will be no way to stop it from spreading."

The cries of dismay echoed from one side of the valley to the other, giving Tyhen the opportunity she needed.

"Once more I am asking something of you that will cause you suffering. Once more you will be asked to sacrifice yourself and your well-being to help me stop it."

Again, their voices rose, but this time loudly and chanting only one word.

"Yes. Yes. Yes."

The land before her began to blur from unshed tears.

She held up her hand and the chanting stopped.

"The twins have told me if we walk all night without stopping to rest, we will reach the Gathering by sunrise, before their arrival."

"Then we walk!" they shouted, immediately agreeing to the obvious danger to the young and the old, as well of the obvious discomfort.

Yuma sent her a message.

Tell the people they need to walk closer together. Tell the hunters to take up positions of defense around us as we walk. There will be wild animals hiding in the tall grass in the dark, waiting to pick off easy prey.

And so she did, repeating his words exactly so that the New Ones understood the need and the reasons, then she watched as the stragglers quickly gathered up their packs and began jogging toward the front while the younger and stronger hunters pulled their weapons and moved away from their families to take up positions on the perimeter of their march.

It took nearly thirty minutes for the group to gather and for the guards to get in place. She watched, waiting for the signal that they were ready, and when they all finally turned to face her, their fists were in the air.

"We go!" she shouted, and once again led the way east, lengthening her stride with every step.

The drums in her head were louder. There could be no failure – not now - not when they were so close.

As the hours passed, Tyhen watched the sky, frowning when she saw clouds beginning to gather.

"Not now. Please not now," she muttered.

The sun continued its downward slide. The sky turned darker and long shadows came upon the land. She heard the soft flutter of wings from an owl in flight and somewhere far off in the distance she heard a howl and shuddered. Wolves!

The next time she looked down in the valley she saw Yuma coming up the slope toward her on the run. He was carrying

three torches, one of which was lit. She saw the flare of light as
more torches were being lit down in the valley and sighed with
relief. Something she had not thought of. Walking in the dark,
they would have had no way to see her or know which way to
go.

When Yuma reached the ridge where she was walking, he
handed her the lit torch and then fell into step beside her.

"Don't argue," he said softly. "Just taking care of what's
mine."

Choked by a swell of emotion, she leaned over and kissed
him quickly on the cheek.

"Thank you, my Yuma."

She saw a flash of teeth as he smiled and then all of a
sudden the light was gone and the world went dark.

"There is no moon," she said.

"Very little of this trip has been made easy for us. And so it
continues," he said.

Without light by which to see, the New Ones' footing was
less certain. More than one took a tumble, either stepping into
hole made by any number of the burrowing animals that
abounded or stumbling over uneven ground.

The cries of children too weary to go on were quickly
silenced as someone picked them up and carried them. The
clouds continued to gather to the point that the sky was as
black as the land in front of them. There was no demarcation
line – no sight of a horizon. Tyhen knew they were walking on
faith, following only the light of her torch.

Yuma was focusing so intently on keeping her on safe
footing and the night hunters away from her that they had not
shared a dozen sentences.

When the wind began to rise it blew away the cloud cover,
revealing the vast array of twinkling stars and giving the night
a new panorama to fill the sky. All of a sudden the things that
had been frightening minutes ago were rendered harmless. The
wind also carried the howl of a wolf pack, but tonight the pack
was far away and hunting elsewhere.

Even though the torch lit only the contours of their faces,
Yuma watched her when she wasn't looking. He kept looking
for a breaking point and never saw it. She had to be afraid of

what lay ahead and yet she did not speak of it.

He reached for her hand, threading his fingers between hers and giving it a gentle squeeze.

"Should we call a momentary halt?" he asked.

"Did Singing Bird give you time to rest as Firewalker fell to earth?"

"At first yes, and then the last day, no."

"Is this time as important to our existence as it was then?"

He sighed. "Yes, maybe more so. If we fail this before we even start, it will have all been for nothing."

She squeezed his hand back.

"If we let them stop, they will have to go faster to catch up. Understand?"

"Yes, and you are right, my little whirlwind."

She smiled slightly.

"You pretended you were concerned for the New Ones, but I know you. You were thinking I needed to rest. We all need rest, but when we do, we will rest together. We have to be close. The drums are so loud in my head it's hard to think."

Yuma looked toward the east, hoping for that first faint sight of sunrise and then glanced at his torch. It was their last one. When it was gone they would have to walk in the dark.

"If that happens, I will go down and walk with them," Tyhen said.

Yuma flinched.

"I didn't say that aloud. You just read my mind."

"Oh. Sorry," Tyhen said. "I didn't know. I just heard it and -"

"No apology. I was just surprised and I don't know why. I've witnessed far more amazing things from you."

"But they did not involve you, right? You felt a little bit like I had walked into your body without permission."

Yuma laughed softly.

"Oh, my love, you have eternal permission to walk inside my head, to lie with me, to let me grow old with you. I will ask for nothing more."

All of a sudden Tyhen was weeping.

Yuma heard the soft, choking sound of a sob and felt like he'd been stabbed in the heart.

"I'm sorry, I'm sorry. What did I say?"

She moved closer to him and then pulled his hand to her cheek, feeling the scar on the back of his left hand beneath her lips and trying to remember if she knew why it was there. Their whole lives were ahead of them and there were times, like now, when she felt like happy would never happen again.

"You said nothing bad. Your words are so beautiful that they make me ache. I want this over. I want to find a place to call home and be able to go to sleep and wake up with the same sense of safety that I feel in your arms."

Yuma frowned.

"I want the same thing, my love, and I wish this trip was over as much as you do."

After that, they were both silent, lost in dreams of what things may come. The wind grew colder and Yuma thought he could feel the sting of tiny pellets of ice.

Sleet!

Just what they didn't need.

CHAPTER NINE

The sleet didn't last, but left the wind far colder than it had been before.

Tyhen was miserable to the point that she couldn't quit shaking. She tried walking faster but could not keep up the pace. There was a pain in her side and the muscles in her legs were burning. She could only imagine what this was doing to the old ones and the people with children.

Once she slipped and would have fallen down the backside of the ridge but for Yuma, who caught her by the arm as she slid past him.

One second she was upright and the next thing she knew her backpack came off. Without knowing what awaited her in the dark below, she was scrambling to stop the slide when Yuma yanked her to a full stop. Seconds later he was on his knee beside her, moving the torch above her for a better view.

"Are you hurt?"

"I don't think so. Help me up," she asked, and held out a hand.

With the torch in one hand, he braced his feet and pulled her up and into an embrace.

Tyhen wrapped her arms around him.

"Thank you," she said, her voice sounding as weary as she felt.

He sighed and then slid his mouth across her lips.

She felt his tension fading as passion replaced panic. His lips were cold but soon warmed against her mouth as he deepened the kiss. When the wind began to whirl around them it was all the warning Tyhen was going to get that their passion was getting out of hand. Their feet were already partway off the ground when she pulled away.

"Sorry. I have no control over what your love does to me," she said softly.

"I know the feeling," he said, and ran a finger down the side of her cheek and then looked down into the valley. No one had noticed they were stopped. It was time to start moving before they thought something was wrong.

Reluctantly, she turned away to pick up her pack and then slipped her arms into the straps and settled it on her back. She had been cold for so long she couldn't feel her feet and it took a few moments of walking before that sensation went away. Cold and frozen hurt.

Are you all right?

She smiled to herself. Evan must have sensed her shock when she began to slide.

I just slipped. I am fine.

The Eagle takes good care of the Dove.

Evan was right. Yuma's every thought was always of her first. She put away the longing to be with him for another time and place and kept the New Ones moving, unaware that at least one other had noticed something was wrong.

When Dakotah saw the torch on the ridge above suddenly disappear from view, he stumbled.

Lola quickly grabbed her arm, steadying him on his feet before he could fall.

"Are you alright?" she asked, as her hand automatically moved to smooth down the hair on the top of his head.

He nodded, his gaze already moving back to the ridge where Tyhen would walk. When he saw the torchlight reappear, he breathed a quiet sigh of relief and, without thinking, reached for Lola's hand.

She felt his fingers against her palm and smiled to herself as she clasped his hand. He had been such a sad and quiet little boy since his parents' death. She was grateful he felt comfortable enough with her now to seek out her presence when he felt the need.

The longer the night went on, the colder it became. Along with that misery, the last torch in Yuma's hand was growing dimmer.

Tyhen also noticed the dying flicker of flames and gave Yuma an anxious glance. He did not seem fazed by the fact that it was about to go out. If he wasn't concerned she wouldn't be either. His strength and courage seemed endless and his faith in her kept her moving.

She glanced down at the New Ones. Very few had torches still burning. She frowned and looked up toward the east, willing the arrival of sunrise. The drums were so loud in her head now that she could feel the vibration all the way through her body. She had a vision of watching the sunrise over the Gathering and knew they must be close. What she didn't know was how close the strangers were. How much time would she have before that confrontation?

An hour, maybe more.

She sighed. This time it was Adam who answered.

Thank you, my brother.

When he didn't respond, she thought nothing of it. She had no idea that his gut was in knots from what he knew was going to happen.

What Adam knew that Evan didn't was that this night walk would be the last time they were together as they had been born. One thought - one mind - one heart – for each other. Sunrise would be the death of that bond and he was trying so hard not to weep.

$\sim$

Tyhen was looking toward the horizon when their last torch went out.

"I'm sorry," Yuma said. "Just hold onto me. I won't let you fall."

She was still holding on to the love in his voice when she saw the first glimmer of hope.

"Just in time," she said. "Look in the east."

Yuma saw it and breathed a quiet sigh of relief. Sunrise was on the horizon.

The sky continued to lighten as the landscape came out of hiding, revealing the trees and the tall, dry grass.

Tyhen heard a child's plaintive cry and looked back down at the New Ones for signs of trouble when all of a sudden Yuma stumbled, then grabbed Tyhen's hand and yanked her to a stop.

"What's wrong?" she asked.

He pointed.

Breath caught in the back of her throat. Even though true light had yet to break the horizon, there was enough for them to see the long snaking river and the shadowy outlines of the dwellings of more people than she had ever seen in her life.

"We have arrived," she said softly, and then turned toward the New Ones down in the valley. "Up here!" she called out, motioning for them to join her.

They moved as one toward the ridge, sensing her excitement, eager to see what they knew must be the Gathering.

Tyhen kept walking forward, making room for the others who fell into step behind her until the New Ones were strung out along the ridgeline as far as the eye could see. When they stopped, they were seeing the vast numbers of dwellings in the same way they'd seen their first sight of the buffalo. What a mighty people they had been, and oh, how far they had fallen.

Their faces burned from the cold. Their bodies were weary to the point of giving out, and yet not a word of complaint was uttered. They were in complete silence when the first rays of sunlight reached them, sweeping across their legs, then their faces, and all the way down the length of the hillside until they were all bathed in the light of a new day.

And with sunrise, came the doves. They appeared out of nowhere and immediately began circling the skies above them.

Tyhen watched the massive campground as people began emerging from their dwellings, some stretching, others beginning to rebuild a cooking fire, while elders came out for morning prayers. She saw a warrior turn and look up. She could not see the expression on his face, but she heard him let out a cry that brought everyone running.

Adam was shocked by the sight. He had never seen so many

people in one place before and although he knew they meant no harm, their sheer numbers made him uneasy.

"What do we do?" he asked.

Yuma glanced at the twins, glad they were here to enter the Gathering beside them. If there were any dangerous undercurrents, they would know it before it happened.

"We go meet the People," Tyhen said, and spoke to the New Ones, letting the wind carry her words yet again. "Wait here. Rest," she added, then shoved the hood from her head and started walking down the hillside.

Yuma was at her side and a step ahead.

The twins were right behind her, walking side by side.

The New Ones watched from the hillside, grateful to be off their feet.

The trip down was silent, and when Tyhen reached the edge of the vast crowd awaiting them below, they had already parted to make way for them to enter.

She saw fear on their faces as well as confusion. They didn't understand who she was and were still looking for the Dove. It was time to take flight.

Adam and Evan were on edge. They could hear the people's thoughts. They could feel the fear and distrust. Evan clutched his spear a little tighter while Adam scanned the faces for sign of the girl from his vision. He did not know she had already seen them and was hiding behind her father, too rattled by the sight of the two men who would love her to let herself be known.

Yuma was trying not to be shocked by the crude weapons and clothing. For some reason he had expected the people of this continent to be as advanced as the Mayans, but it was obvious they were not. The New Ones were going to have to influence far more than language and lifestyle.

He was still processing the scope of things the People were going to face when he caught movement from the corner of his eye. Before he could utter a word of warning, Tyhen lifted off the ground and sailed up into the air.

The cry from the People sent the doves into a frenzy. Within moments they had disappeared.

Warriors didn't know whether to go for their weapons or

run.

Women fell to the ground.

Children ran back into the lodges to hide.

Yuma groaned as Evan stepped up on one side of him and Adam moved to the other.

"It will be fine," Adam said.

Once Tyhen left the ground, the bird's eye view she now had of the Gathering was overwhelming. She had never imagined there were this many people in the world and for the first time realized what a task they were facing. She knew the people below were afraid, but she had their attention and now they would hear her voice, as well. She didn't know what language to use because there were so many dialects here, so she used the language of the Muscogee – the tribe from which Layla Birdsong belonged, before she became Singing Bird of the Mayan people.

"You have been waiting for the Dove and she is here. I am Tyhen... the Windwalker's daughter."

Another gasp went up, but this time it was one of awe. They had only heard of Windwalkers in the stories told by the elders around the campfires late at night. They had not believed that they could really exist, but it must be true. How else could a young girl command the wind to lift her into the air and fly?

Tyhen's voice was strong - her manner queenly. Seeing her beautiful face and her long black hair billowing out around her like a dark halo was staggering enough, but to see her floating so high above their heads was surely proof of her magic.

Tyhen continued to move as she spoke, circling the vast area of camps and people so that they not only heard her words, but saw her face.

"I was born for you. I have come with the New Ones to save you and this world in which you live."

Women began to weep and warriors looked upon her in awe.

"You see your way of life as something that will never end and never change. You see me, yes?"

"Yes!" they shouted, and the air vibrated with the energy of their voices.

"Now look to the hillside," she cried, pointing to the New

Ones. "Look upon the faces of the people who came with me. Know that the earth into which they were born is many, many lifetimes into the future."

The gasp was palpable, as if they'd momentarily sucked all of the oxygen from the air. They could not envision such a thing. They could not understand if it was true, how they came to be here? Did all of them have magic, too?

Tyhen swirled up higher, spinning through the air with her arms outstretched as if beseeching them to believe.

"The earth into which they were born and on which you now stand no longer exists. It was burned up by an angry Firewalker who came from the sky, killing every living thing upon it because of what our people let happen. Throughout time, we lost our way and then lost our land and our way of life. Firewalker destroyed everything because of that. Look upon their faces for they are all that is left of our magnificent race."

This time the gasp that went up was a moan. Faces turned to the hillside as they tried to imagine what disasters could have befallen the future of their People that would have caused that to happen.

And then Tyhen received a message from the twins that quickly brought her first meeting at the Gathering to an end.

Tyhen! Look to the east. The strangers come.

She turned in mid-air and in the distance saw a dark line of travelers approaching. Yuma had talked of horses, an animal she had never seen. He had spoken of how men rode them, but she had never seen this sight until now. She spun up even higher so that all could see her and pointed to the east.

"The beginning of our downfall started with the strangers who began coming to our land. Strangers like those who are approaching from the other side of the river. We did not know how to deal with them, and over time they took everything that was ours. Do you see them approaching?"

They turned, trying to see through the tree line on the shore and through the light of the sun still resting on the horizon, but they could not see and so they refocused on her voice.

"The two men with the same face who came with me are my brothers. They have the power to see the future and to hear people's thoughts. Nearly two days ago they told me the strangers were coming, and that they have a sickness. It is why we did not sleep. It is why we walked all day and all night without stopping to get to you. Again the New Ones have suffered on your behalf so that we would get here in time to save you. If the strangers come among us, we will all sicken and we will die."

Warriors jumped up and began brandishing weapons, shouting that they were ready to do battle.

Tyhen spun into a whirlwind, flew toward the river then turned back to the encampment and shouted so loud it knocked the warriors back to their knees.

"No! You cannot touch them. You cannot be close to them or you will carry their sickness back to your families. I will stop them. I do this for you now, and you will do something for us. When you leave this place, some of the New Ones will go with each tribe. They will live with you and teach *you* how to save our people and way of life. After they are gone, it will be your destiny and the destiny of all the generations who come to continue the changes and the languages and the skills that they will give you."

The people moaned at the thought of life as they knew it ending, then watched as she flew back to her people and quickly dropped out of sight.

Yuma was not happy, but saw no way out of what she had to do. When she landed beside him, he slid a hand beneath her hair and pulled her close.

"Stay in the air. Don't get close enough that they might touch you."

"I know, but do not worry. Windwalkers cannot -"

"I know, I know. Windwalkers cannot die. But if their disease gets on your clothing, it can harm others."

She laid a hand against his cheek, feeling a muscle jerking against her palm.

"I hear. I understand."

Adam pointed to the backpack that she'd dropped at their

feet.

"The silver buckle that Dakotah gave you. Take it with you," he said.

She didn't ask why. She just dug it out of her pack and took to the sky. A dark whirlwind formed around her and then she was gone, flying over the river into the sunlight, leaving the people of the Gathering on their knees.

Evan's eyes narrowed.

"When she turns away, one will throw a knife into her back."

"Tell her!" Yuma cried.

Evan shrugged.

"It will not stop her."

Yuma dropped his pack at Evan's feet.

A look of understanding passed between them and then he was gone. He ran to the river's edge and jumped into the icy waters without hesitation, knowing he would only have one chance to save Tyhen from terrible pain and the possibility of becoming infected by the disease running through the troops.

He swam frantically against the current and when his water-soaked clothing began pulling him down, he swam harder. By the time his feet finally touched bottom on the other side he was so cold he was almost numb. He crawled out of the water and then crouched down in the tall grass to get his bearings. He would have to stay hidden to save her but he needed to get closer, so he began moving toward the approaching soldiers, and the closer he got, the more anxious he became.

Diego DeVille was thinking about last night's dreams as he and his men rode west. He dreamed they were on a ship sailing home when a storm came up at sea. As sailors scrambled to lower the mainsails, a wall of dark water rose out of the ocean like a monster from the deep and swamped the ship.

Within moments they were sinking. The men who had washed overboard were either screaming or praying for mercy, but in his dream Diego did nothing. Instead, he was clinging to the mast with his eyes closed, remembering the lush green land of Iberia , imagining the smell of roasting meat coming from a turning spit outside the back door of the kitchen and baking bread coming out of the oven. He saw the new foals running through the meadows on long, spindly legs and his mother waving at him from a window, and in that moment he wished for the ability to turn back time.

It was his greed and desire for power that had driven him from such a paradise, and now it was sending him to a grave at sea. The water was washing over his feet, then up to his knees and when the ship began to list sideways, he knew they were sinking. Just as the water rolled over his head he woke up.

He had crawled out of his bedroll, drawing in long hungry breaths of air, and made a promise to himself that the trip home would be his last voyage. He would choose a life on the run before he'd come to this godforsaken place again.

It was because of the dream that he routed the men out of their bedrolls so early. In the midst of cold and darkness they had saddled up their mounts and struck camp while the stars were still visible. Now here they were with the new sun at their backs, elongating the shadows that rode ahead of them. From a long distance away they'd seen what appeared to be a line of trees running horizontal to the valley. DeVille guessed the trees were growing along a river and raised his arm to signal a halt.

"Lieutenant Estevez!"

Estevez spurred his mount forward.

DeVille pointed toward the faint line on the horizon.

"Send a man to scout that out. Tell him to ride fast, take the high side of the valley to see what's up ahead, then report back."

Estevez nodded, rode back down the line and picked out a soldier named Juarez who had a fast horse then sent him ahead.

"We ride," DeVille said, and set the pace at a walk, not wanting to get too close until he knew what they were riding into.

If there were any savages nearby, the likelihood that they would camp near water was almost certain, but the minutes passed into almost an hour and Juarez had yet to return. DeVille was getting anxious and now so was Estevez. He rode up beside the captain to voice his concern.

"Something is wrong," Estevez said. "Juarez should have been back long ago. Do you want me to send another scout?"

DeVille felt the same way, but hesitated to show it.

"No, we will see what we see for ourselves," he said, but straightened up in the saddle to stay alert and continued westward.

They were much closer to the trees when the horses began nickering back and forth. He guessed they smelled the water, and when he was within a half-mile of the location they began seeing spirals of smoke rising above the trees. As he guessed might be the case, there was a campground on the other side of those trees. He was hopeful it was his missing soldiers.

The day was cold, even though the sun was at their back. Their breath was visible, a visual reminder of the approaching winter. The creak of saddle leather, the slight jingle of metal against metal from parts of their tack and clothing sounded loud within the silence around them. The swish of the long grass as they rode through it made DeVille think of the sound of the handmade broom against the old stone floor in his mother's kitchen. The longing for home was so strong it actually brought tears to his eyes. He was still blinking to clear his vision when a small, funnel-shaped cloud suddenly appeared above the trees. When it began moving toward them, the horses began to rear and kick, nickering wildly as they began to buck.

It took several moments for them to get the horses under control and when they turned to look back toward the river, a young woman was standing in front of them, close enough that the new sun at their backs made her eyes look like they were glowing. The skin crawled on the back of DeVille's neck. Who was she? *What* was she?

The moment Tyhen's feet touched earth the flow of negative energy they brought with them was so strong she could smell it. It had to do with something they'd done but she didn't quite understand, and then she saw the bone necklace around the leader's neck and frowned. It seemed out of place.

He raped the old woman who wore it. They are Spaniards.
Speak the Spanish you were taught.

Evan's voice startled her, but not as much as what he said.
Now she understood what she'd been feeling and her anger
came through loud and clear through the tone of her voice.

"You stop here and go no further," Tyhen shouted, speaking
in perfect Castilian.

DeVille was stunned. She was speaking their language as
clearly as if it was her mother tongue. He shuddered. What
kind of witchcraft was this that she not only knew it, but could
be heard so easily from that distance? Still, they'd come a long
way for answers and one female was not going to stop them,
even if she was somewhat frightening.

"We are searching for the soldiers who manned our
outpost," he shouted, then watched the woman walk closer.
When he realized how young she was, he did not understand
why a tribe of savages would send one girl to speak for them.
He had yet to realize the spinning cloud and the woman were
the same.

"You want your soldiers?" she asked, then opened her hand
and flung the silver buckle Dakotah had given her through the
air. It landed a few feet away from his horse.

Deville dismounted, saw the buckle and grabbed it, yelling
out angrily as he turned her way.

"Where did you get this?"

"On the prairie. It is all that is left of your men. You are
trespassing on our land. You will leave now."

He reeled as if he'd been slapped. How dare she?

"We go where we choose! We claimed this land in the name
of Spain when we built our fort and raised the flag of our King.
It is now Spanish soil."

When she did not respond, he thought he'd made his point.
But then the wind began to blow as if from a storm front, only
the sky was clear. He was looking up when she lifted off the
ground and when he saw the funnel of air spinning around her,
breath caught in the back of his throat. She *was* a witch. His
heart started to pound as she swooped toward them, her voice
blasting at them from above.

"You are a thief. You are all thieves! You cannot claim

what already belongs to another! This place is called First Nation. It is the mother-land of the People. We are as many as the stars up in the sky and you will take nothing of ours, not now! Not ever!"

The horses were stomping as if begging their riders to leave. It was all the soldiers could do to hold them into a semblance of formation.

"I never heard of a land called First Nation!" DeVille shouted.

"Just because you are an ignorant man, does not change what is. Leave now! Go back to your people and tell them and all who would sail across the great water that they will lose their lives if they come onto our land with evil intent."

DeVille didn't know how to respond to an enemy who flew like a bird, but she was still just one woman. He mounted his horse, pulled his sword, and was about to order an attack when she sent a blast of wind across the troops that knocked him and his soldiers out of their saddles.

The moment the horses lost their riders they turned and galloped away, leaving the troops afoot. The soldiers pulled their weapons and then watched in disbelief as she rose even higher above them, spinning the air around her until it was a massive blast that ripped the swords from their hands and the helmets from their heads and then rolled their bodies across the prairie.

DeVille was flat on his back looking up at the sky as she swooped down toward him. All of a sudden the necklace he'd taken from the old woman was torn from his neck by the force of the wind, scattering the pieces within the grass. Certain he was going to die, he began to pray to God, asking forgiveness for his sins and wondering if he could go to heaven without last rites. Just when he thought he was done for, the force of the wind was gone. When the men realized they could move, they got up and started running without waiting for orders. Deville heard them screaming and crying as he got to his feet. He wanted to run away, too, but his fear of turning his back on this woman was greater.

"Run!" Tyhen shouted. "Run like our people ran when you killed them. Run like the women did when you caught and raped them. Run like the cowards you are and never come back!"

He wet himself as her voice slid through his mind, ripping through his conscience, holding him captive with the power of her words and making him feel what the old woman felt as he'd raped her – from the fear to the pain to the shame. When she finally let him go he turned and ran, sobbing with every step.

Tyhen wanted to destroy them all, but they needed to go back. The rest of the world needed to acknowledge what the People already knew. This continent was not up for grabs.

Yuma witnessed it all.

He heard her challenge their presence and heard the leader's angry reply. When the soldier jumped down from his horse and started to approach her it was all he could do to stay hidden. Even though he knew she'd come here to send them packing, he was not expecting what came next. When she began shouting, the side-wind from her anger flattened him as well as the soldiers. He rolled over onto his spear to keep it from flying out of his hand as they ran away. He was still on his belly when he felt a faint vibration beneath him and then heard the sound of a running horse. The soldiers' mounts were gone. What had he missed? What had she missed?

He raised up just in time to see a lone rider, a soldier, bearing down on Tyhen from behind. When he saw the dagger in the soldier's hand he thought of Adam's warning. He forgot the mind-numbing cold and the leaden feel of wet leather as he came up out of the grass and started running.

The ground was hard beneath his feet - the blood pumping through his body lent speed to his stride. The sun was high enough now to illuminate the soldier's metal helmet as well as the armor on his vest. He was aware of the horse's heavy breathing and the faint scent the animal's sweat and fear. After that it seemed as if everything began to happen in slow motion.

CHAPTER TEN

Juarez, the missing scout, was scared half out of his mind as he rode back toward the men, spurring his horse until blood was flying from the horse's belly, certain he'd been left behind. He was trapped between the savages at his back and the witch in the air ahead of him. He kept imagining being caught then tortured and killed, maybe even eaten like a side of beef. He was afraid of what the witch would do when she saw him and the only thing he could think to do was kill her before that happened.

She was coming down out of the sky as he drew closer. He leaned forward against the horse's neck, urging him on, urging him to go faster, bringing him within striking distance. She was less than twenty five yards ahead of him when he took the reins in his left hand and pulled a dagger with the other. He stood up in the stirrups, tightening his knees against the horse's belly and was about to throw his knife when he saw movement from the corner of his eye. As he turned his head, he saw a lone warrior coming toward him, running at what appeared to be a remarkable speed. There was a spear in his hand and the look on his face was one of great rage, and then he let out a war cry and Juarez froze.

Yuma was in a panic. There was no way the rider would miss her. He was too close and she was descending right into his line of sight. His heartbeat kicked with sudden panic.

Go up Tyhen! Go high! And then he let out a war cry.

Startled by the sound of Yuma's voice, Tyhen obeyed without question, shooting straight up into the air. The sudden movement of spinning air scared the horse and it began to kick and buck.

The dagger fell out of Juarez's hands as he grabbed onto the reins with both hands to keep from being thrown. By the time he had the horse under submission, Yuma had thrown his weapon. Juarez looked up just as Yuma's spear pierced his eye. He was dead before he hit the ground.

Tyhen saw everything from above – the frantic race Yuma ran to keep her from being knifed in the back, the New Ones watching from the ridge, and the People lining the riverbank. And then Yuma was on his hands and knees, his head down, his shoulders slumped forward as if he was too weary to look up.

Her heart skipped a beat.

Something was wrong with him!

She swooped down beside him and dropped to her knees.

"Yuma! What's wrong?"

Her hands were trembling as she ran them across his face and when she realized he was soaking wet and shaking, she knew he was in danger.

"Hold onto me," she begged as she put her arms beneath his shoulders and lifted him to his feet.

"I'm just cold," he said, as he wrapped his arms around her waist.

The wind began to turn around them and when he felt his feet leave the ground he looked up into her eyes.

"Finally, the Eagle is flying with the Dove."

Her voice was trembling as she moved the whirlwind back across the prairie toward the river a half mile away.

"You are a crazy man. You swam a river that is too cold. You clothing is wet and freezing against your skin. Are you trying to get sick?"

"Adam said someone would put a knife into your back."

She tightened her hold, telling herself not to cry, but she

was afraid for him.

"Did you not remind Adam I cannot die?" she muttered.

He answered with just as much aggravation in his voice.

"And did you think I would stand by and watch you bleed? Watch you suffer? See you in pain? Did you not think of the disease that man is carrying?"

She didn't answer, but held him tighter.

The trees loomed.

The people beneath them were staring up, transfixed by the sight. When she began coming down where the twins were standing, they ran backward to give her space.

She landed as lightly as a feather floating to the ground, but the moment her feet touched earth, Adam and Evan grabbed Yuma out of her arms.

"Is he hurt? What's wrong?" they asked.

"He's wet and cold," she muttered, and then turned to the people staring at them in disbelief. "This man is Yuma. He is the Eagle who watches over the Dove and he needs to get warm. Those people on the hillside are the New Ones. They need to set up their camps. Will someone give us shelter by their fire while others show the New Ones where to go?"

Several of the warriors nearby heard Tyhen's request and started up the hillside to escort the New Ones down into the campground. As they walked away, a young woman stepped out of the crowd. The twins stared. It was the girl from their vision.

"I am Suwanee of the Lakota Sioux. Come to our fire," she said, then led the way to their borrowed lodge without looking at the shocked expressions on her mother and father's faces.

Suwanee's heart was pounding. She knew her father was upset. He was Chief. It should have been his place to offer shelter, but he hadn't and she didn't want to lose her chance to meet the warrior brothers. Even though they were about to upset her world and everything she knew, it was her destiny.

It would be what it would be.

Adam was numb as he picked up Yuma's pack while Evan

grabbed Tyhen's. He was sick to his stomach and couldn't look at Evan without giving himself away. Everything in him was thinking 'don't do this, don't follow that girl,' but he couldn't turn away any more than Evan would.

Evan was so stunned to see the girl from his vision that he forgot about Adam's jealousy. He couldn't quit thinking about what had happened between them in the dream. Was his destiny linked with hers? He wanted to think so, and at the same time could not lose his brother over her.

Suwanee was afraid of her father's anger but it was too late to take back her invitation. Her steps were hurried as she led the way to their lodge. Once there, she stopped and pulled the flap aside for the others to enter.

Tyhen didn't hesitate. She had to bend down as she led Yuma inside and was slightly surprised by the amount of space and grateful for the sudden warmth.

The sage burning in the small fire scented the interior, while the smoke spiraled slowly up, disappearing through the opening above. Hides from the buffalo served as flooring as well as bedding and the moment Yuma stopped beside her she began pulling off his wet clothing, desperate to get him warm so he would not get sick.

"I can do that," Yuma said, but when his fingers were too cold to get a good grip, Tyhen pushed his hands aside.

She pulled at the half frozen clothing stuck to his body and didn't stop until he was completely nude, then pointed to a buffalo robe rolled up against the side of the tipi.

"May I use that to warm him?"

Suwanee ran to get it.

When Tyhen wrapped it around Yuma's shoulders his relief was evident.

"Sit by the fire," Tyhen said, and then glanced around to see if the twins had brought their packs.

"Adam, please find him dry clothes."

Adam dropped the pack and began sorting through the items while Yuma moved closer to the fire.

Tyhen slid an arm around Yuma's shoulders.

"Do you feel better? Do you want to lie down?"

"Yes, much better, and I will gladly lie with you anytime."

Her eyes narrowed as she struggled not to blush. What on earth made him say that in front of strangers? Then she realized he'd said that in the language of the English so that their hosts would not understand. When she saw the mischief in his eyes, she knew he was teasing her to make her stop worrying about him.

"So, now I know you are truly okay," she said, and then glanced at their hosts.

The two women seemed nervous and the older warrior standing by the entrance did not look happy about their presence, but she could certainly ease his concerns.

"We thank you for your kindness and will be leaving soon," she said.

The older man said nothing. Again, it was the young girl who spoke for all of them.

"It is our honor to give you shelter," Suwanee said, and laid more fuel upon the fire.

Chata, her mother, knelt beside her and pushed a rock with some roasting meat closer to the flames. She was afraid of this woman who flew like the birds, but she was also in awe of the fact that she was at her fire.

Matto stood near the doorway, watching Tyhen as a man might watch a beautiful but dangerous animal. He'd heard her words, but he didn't know what to make of her. He still didn't fully understand the urgency of the New Ones' appearance into their world, but he'd heard her words and knew it mattered. He'd seen the Dove and now he wanted to see these people who'd come with her – the ones who were going to change their world.

He was just about to leave when he caught his daughter looking at the young men. His heart sank. They were why she'd been so bold! What did she know about them that he did not?

His shoulders slumped as he turned and ducked out. He would know soon enough. For now he would see the New Ones. Some would come back to their lands with them. As Chief, it was his right to meet them first.

Chata watched her husband leave and considered it just as well. Maybe by the time he came back he would be over his disapproval of their daughter's behavior. She eyed the rabbit meat she had cooking and then pushed on the top of one piece with the tip of her finger to see if any blood ran out. When it did not she grunted with satisfaction and rocked back on her heels. As she did, she found herself looking straight into the face of the girl who flew with the wind.

Tyhen had seen the mother's concern and curiosity and immediately thought of her own mother, Singing Bird.

"Thank you for sharing your fire," Tyhen said.

"I am called Chata," the older woman said, then offered Yuma the meat.

Yuma took a piece and popped it into his mouth. Hot food tasted wonderful. He took another piece and gave it to Tyhen.

Suwanee watched the interaction between the young warrior and Tyhen. She could tell they were in love by the way they looked at each other and the tenderness in the way he saw to her needs. His bare body was nothing she had not seen before. Nudity was not a thing to be ashamed of in their world. He was obviously well-built and strong, but it was the two brothers with the same face who stirred her blood. She took two pieces of the rabbit to them.

They looked the same, but up close there were differences. One dressed like a warrior. One did not. She didn't know what that meant but she was shaking inside. There was an energy emanating from them that made her ache in the way a woman aches for a man. She remembered how good it felt to be with the one who dressed like a warrior – the one from her dream - and wondered if it would be like that in real life.

"You eat?" she said softly, offering each of them the food.

Evan took a piece of the meat.

"I am Evan," he said, and watched her dark eyes flash as her gaze continued to shift from one to the other. "This is my brother, Adam."

"You eat?" she asked, and offered food to Adam.

His hand was shaking as he put it in his mouth. She was even more beautiful up close, but she had eyes for no one but Evan. Knowing she would never return the feelings he had for her made him hurt in ways he could not express.

He glanced at Evan as he began to chew while wondering

what he was thinking about the girl. Without thinking he opened himself up to link to Evan's thoughts. He forgot that would leave him vulnerable to Evan reading everything he was thinking and feeling, too.

At that moment, Evan jerked as if he'd been slapped. He had felt Adam's hunger for her, but also the rage and jealousy toward him.

Adam flinched. There was a moment of regret that Evan knew how he was feeling and then his fingers curled into fists.

Evan shook his head in disbelief.

Don't be angry with me. I did not cause this.

Adam's chest hurt and his head was throbbing. He couldn't think. He'd never been out of control before and his first instinct was to fight back.

This is not fair. I saw her first.

Evan reached for his brother.

Adam, I won't touch her, I promise.

Adam pushed his brother's hand away.

It won't matter. She will choose you, whether you want her or not.

Evan felt crippled. He'd never been at odds with Adam and it felt as if part of his body had betrayed him. He felt Suwanee watching him, and even though he wanted to look at her, he wouldn't turn around.

But Adam wouldn't let up.

Look at her, damn it! Face your future, my brother. This is where we end and she begins.

Then Adam picked up his backpack and left without saying a word.

Evan grabbed his pack to go after him, and when he straightened up, the girl was standing between him and the exit. He felt her sadness, her fear and confusion – and to his dismay, so much more.

He didn't intend to give in, but when he moved toward her he automatically reached for her just as he had in the dream, and when his hand brushed the side of her shoulder, just like in the dream, his heart started to pound. How does such a small woman make a grown man weak?

These feelings were so new and so raw. He wanted to

explore them with her. He wanted her, but Adam was his brother. He dropped his hand and looked away.

"Tyhen, we go to help set up camp," he said, and then walked past Suwanee and ducked out of the lodge.

It wasn't until the twins were gone that Tyhen noticed the tears in Suwanee's eyes and realized something was going on. She'd been so focused on making sure Yuma was taken care of that she'd shut off the instincts that kept her rooted to the world around her. All she could tell was it had something to do with the twins.

"Why do you cry?" she asked.

Chata gasped. She had not seen her daughter's tears. Now she, too, wanted to know.

Suwanee was startled. She had no intention of revealing what was happening and had no way to explain it. She gave her mother a frantic look and then ran out.

Yuma frowned. He was fastening the ties on his leggings when he heard Tyhen's question, and when the girl left he stood up.

"What's going on?" he asked.

"It has something to do with the twins," Tyhen said, and glanced at the mother. "Have we done something wrong?"

"No, nothing," Chata said, wringing her hands. She was shocked that Suwanee had upset Tyhen. "I am sorry. Please forgive my daughter. She is young."

Tyhen shrugged. "As long as we have not offended you it is of no matter." She glanced at Yuma, and when she saw that he was ready to leave she picked up her pack. "Thank you again for the warmth of your fire."

Yuma led the way out, then held the flap open for her.

"What was that all about?" he asked.

"Something is going on with her and the twins," Tyhen muttered.

Yuma frowned. "How can that be? They are strangers to each other."

"I think not," she said.

"I don't understand," Yuma said.

"Neither do I, but I will," she said, and then shifted her pack to a more comfortable position. "Let's go set up camp. We need to see to the young and the old. Walking all night with no food or rest had to be hard on them."

Yuma nodded as he eyed the Gathering, looking for signs of where the New Ones had gone.

"There!" he said, pointing to the west. "They are there!"

Adam didn't get far before Evan caught up. He fell into step beside his brother without talking and when they reached the land where the New Ones were settling in, they left their packs near a small grove of trees and began helping the elderly set up their camps.

Since the death of Stanley Bluejacket, Carver Sees Hawk was now the oldest of the New Ones who'd come with Tyhen. Evan knew the old man would need help. Carver's right hand was missing three fingers and his knees were swollen with arthritis.

Evan moved through the area, helping anyone in need as he went and by the time he found the old man, Johnston Nantay was already there. He began to backtrack, and as he did noticed a lot of strangers among them. So it had begun - the mixing of the old and the new.

He stopped, watching the interaction out of curiosity and then with growing relief. On the surface, it appeared as if they were readily being accepted. He hoped that would be the case. They had come a very long way and at great risk. Failure was not an option. Then he looked for his brother but didn't see him. They needed to talk.

Adam, where are you?

On the north side of camp.

We need to talk.

There is work to be done. Tonight we talk.

Evan sighed. Adam was right. There was much to do. His steps were slow and his heart was heavy as he moved through the camp. He saw Yuma and Tyhen and promptly blocked his thoughts and turned away. She would know something was wrong soon enough, and he wasn't talking about anything until he talked to Adam.

The arrival of the Dove had sent a surge of excitement throughout the entire Gathering. They'd watched in awe as she flew over their heads and then watched from the riverbank as she turned the strangers away. The young warriors were so full of adrenaline and testosterone they felt ready to burst. They wanted to fight. They'd been ready to go to war when she'd pointed out the strangers and then she stopped them flat. It did not set well with any of them and most especially the Comanche, who were, at all times, a fierce force with which to be reckoned. There were three of the Comanche youths moving through their campgrounds in mute frustration, looking for a way to blow off steam.

Walks Tall was young, but already a proven hunter and warrior.

His younger brother, Broken Wing, was his shadow and held Walks Tall in high esteem.

Little Raven had grown up with the brothers while wishing he was as handsome as Broken Wing and as good a hunter as Walks Tall. Whatever they were doing, he wanted to be doing it, too.

The arrival of the Dove had been startling and then exciting. They were unsettled about taking strangers back with them into their tribes, but seeing the Dove flying in the sky and then doing battle with the strangers had been inspiring. They'd seen more magic happen today than they would have believed could happen in their lifetime. They were all full of energy and heckling one of the older women in their tribe, trying to talk her into giving them some dried meat when they saw the young woman walk into their camp. Once they realized she was not of their tribe, their first instincts were to stir up a little innocent trouble.

Suwanee was afraid and confused.

She didn't know if she'd angered the Dove and didn't know what would happen to her if she had. And seeing the conflict that was now between the brothers hurt her heart because she knew they were fighting over her. She had an older brother who'd died during her eighth winter and none had been born after her. She would never have imagined doing anything to cause him pain.

Meeting them had given her much to think about. While she was giving the brothers the food, she'd also seen into their hearts. The one called Adam wanted her, but his feelings were frightening. They were strong and had a violent feel to them, almost as if he didn't know what to do with how he felt.

The one called Evan had a passionate heart. She'd seen that when they had spirit walked together, but today he had blocked his thoughts and so she knew nothing more about him except what had happened between them in her dream.

She wished she'd never had that vision. She should not have spoken out of turn and brought them into her father's lodge. Everything bad that was happening was all her fault. She kept moving through the camp with her head down, walking blindly without a destination other than to make herself scarce, but with so many people, there was no place to hide.

It wasn't until she paused to get her bearings that she realized she was lost. Almost immediately her heart skipped a beat. She'd never been this far north inside the Gathering and didn't recognize any of the tribes around her. Her uneasiness grew when she saw the trio of young warriors coming toward her, and when they began to shout at her and taunt her, she panicked and turned away.

She'd heard of warriors stealing members of other tribes and using them for slaves, or taking a young woman for a mate against her will. It was clear she'd made a bad situation worse by running away and began to retrace her steps, but the Gathering was so big she was unsure of where her people were camped. She heard one of the young warriors cry out like he'd just counted coup, and then heard the sounds of running feet behind her and panicked.

She started running, darting in and out between the lodges, flying past meat cooking over fires, running too close to a fresh hide that had been stretched on a rack and knocking it into the dust, which angered the woman it belonged to.

"I am sorry! I am sorry!" she cried, as she flew past, but the woman yelled angry words at her anyway, and the young warriors were still giving chase.

CHAPTER ELEVEN

Evan continued to make his way through the camp, helping as needed. He helped the older ones put up their tents and cut down small brush to clear others campsites. He had just finished helping Carver Sees Hawk set up his sleeping tent and paused a moment, looking around to see where to go to next when he noticed one of the old women sit down and take off her moccasin. He recognized her as one of the women from Naaki Chava who used to make cloth on the looms in Cayetano's palace, and when he saw the suppurating hole on the side of her foot, he frowned. That looked infected...even bordering on gangrene. He hurried over to where she was sitting and knelt down beside her.

"Keechee, do you remember me?"

She nodded. "Singing Bird called you Evan."

"Yes, yes she did," he said. "Are you in pain? Your foot looks infected!"

"It hurts, but I have no medicine," she said.

He touched her shoulder.

"You wait. I will find a healer for you," he said, and sent a message to Adam as he got up and walked away. Two looking would be faster than just one.

Adam, help me find Myra Begay. Keechee, the weaver from the palace in Naaki Chava, has an infection in her foot.

When Adam didn't immediately respond, Evan frowned. He was getting weary of his brother's behavior. It was no better than a pouting child.

Adam!

I am looking.

Evan sighed.

If you find her, take her to where Keechee rests.

How do I find this Keechee? Adam asked.

Use your powers for something besides being angry. There is a hole in her foot. Focus on her pain and you will find her.

There was a long moment of silence, which made Evan angry. This was so awful and none of his fault.

And stop treating me like I did something wrong.

Adam didn't answer, but he had obviously let down his guard because the moment Evan felt his brother's torment he regretted his anger. However, this wasn't about them right now. It was about Keechee's need for medicine.

He was still thinking about the mess between him and Adam when he felt Suwanee's panic.

Startled, he immediately focused to see what was wrong and when he saw her running and saw some warriors chasing her, a rage washed over him. They were laughing and jeering at her and when he felt the blood lust from the leader he knew what was on their minds. It never crossed his mind as to why he assumed it was his business to interfere. Instead, he tightened his hold on his spear, focused on Suwanee's energy as a means to locate her and started running.

⌒

The New Ones were just getting settled when members of the tribes began coming into their camps carrying winter robes, food, and fuel for fires. The language barriers were minimal because the New Ones had learned so many dialects from each other over their time at Naaki Chava, and their ability to communicate so easily impressed the tribes.

Montford Nantay was cutting down a few bush sprouts with his knife to make a cleaner area to pitch his sleeping tent when he noticed several warriors staring at him from a few yards away. When one of them realized he'd been caught staring, he seemed to take the eye contact as an invitation and boldly walked toward Montford with the others following close behind.

Montford stopped what he was doing, curious about the man

in the lead. He wasn't very tall, but the eagle feathers tied in his hair made him seem taller. There was a long scar down the side of his left cheek and he walked with a swagger, making the rawhide ties on his clothing dance. He stopped in front of Montford and then pointed to the knife he was holding.

"I am Winter Hawk of the Oglala Sioux. I would see this."

"I am Montford Nantay of the Navajo," he said, and handed the little man his knife.

Winter Hawk pulled his own knife from a strip of rawhide at his waist and held them side by side in his hands, comparing them.

Montford eyed the crude weapon with dismay. They were far less advanced than the people of Naaki Chava had been. The little warrior's knife was hardly more than a long sliver of flint that had been worked on each edge to make it sharp. The thick end of the flint was wrapped in rawhide, while Montford's knife had a metal blade and a finely polished wooden hasp held together with metal bands.

"What manner of weapon is this?" Winter Hawk asked, lightly fingering the blade.

"It is a hunting knife and the blade is made of a metal called iron. Be careful. The edge is very sharp," Montford said, cautioning the man not to cut himself.

Winter Hawk heard and understood the warning, but he still had to try it and when he slid the end of his thumb ever so lightly against the edge and drew blood, he didn't seem to care. Now that he'd held such an amazing weapon, the other warriors with him wanted to hold it, too.

"How do you find such a thing?" Winter Hawk asked, watching as the knife was passed from hand to hand.

"I made it," Montford said.

Winter Hawk retrieved the knife and reluctantly returned it to Montford.

"You will show how to make this?" he asked

"Yes. We will teach you many things in the years to come."

The warriors heard and were pleased. The worth of these New Ones had just gone up.

The day was cold and still. Usually on days like this, once the sun had risen fully in the sky it felt warmer. Wearing their heavy winter clothing was too hot and cumbersome for setting up campsites and gathering wood, so a lot of them had already shed the layer of outer wear.

Tyhen was unpacking their sleeping tent and Yuma had already built a fire and was kneeling nearby, looking through their packs for something to eat when Lola and Dakotah showed up with fresh food.

"The people here are very generous. They gave us too much," Lola said, as she handed him some strips of smoked meat and something that looked like the flat bread they used to bake on hot stones in Naaki Chava. "Dakotah wanted to share with you."

Yuma eyed the way the boy sidled up to Tyhen and leaned his head against her belly, as if she was someone he needed to protect. Yuma had been that way with Singing Bird, but that was because of Tyhen. He'd known there was a baby in her belly before anyone else because he'd heard her voice in his head.

And then the moment that thought went through his mind his heart skipped. What if Dakotah's attachment to Tyhen had nothing to do with her and everything to do with the next Windwalker's daughter? He took a deep breath and then stood, his heart pounding and his hands shaking as he stared at her from across the fire. What if that baby was already a fact?

He watched Tyhen's face as she laid a hand on Dakotah's head.

"Yuma and I thank you," she said.

Dakotah spun out of her arms and headed straight for Yuma.

"I could help. Do you need help?"

Yuma hid a smile. Dakotah was so anxious for a yes that he was could barely stand still.

"Why, yes, I do need help." He looked up at Lola. "He can come with me as I check out the campgrounds. I'll bring him back later."

Dakotah's gaze shifted to Lola, waiting now for her approval.

"Then he can go," she said, and laid a hand lightly on the back of Dakotah's head. "Stay safe."

"Yes, yes, I will stay safe," the little boy echoed.

Tyhen smiled. The little boy was always in her shadow, but still seemed to hold himself aloof. He was a child full of secrets.

Yuma checked to make sure his knife was at his belt and was looking around for where he'd put his heavy coat. Lola was about to leave when Tyhen suddenly felt Evan's panic.

"Wait!" she cried. "Something is wrong with Evan."

Everyone stopped as Tyhen sent him a message.

Evan? Is something wrong? Is it Adam?

Adam was the first to answer, and she was surprised by the tone of his voice.

Nothing is wrong with me. Evan is the one who's going to ruin our lives over a girl. I saw her first, but she's going to choose Evan over me. I saw it happening. It isn't fair!

Before Tyhen could comment, Evan shouted back.

I'm not ruining anything! Suwanee is in danger of being kidnapped and raped. I'm trying to find her, but she's on the move and I keep losing her location.

Tyhen was shocked the brothers were fighting, and Adam was shocked all of that was happening and he hadn't picked up on it. Now his personal desires seemed petty compared to what was happening. He sent a quick message to Evan.

What can I do?

Evan was running through the Gathering as fast as he could run, chasing the energy he felt from her fear. He was so upset about the danger she was in that he spoke to Adam without thinking.

Can you fight? Can you outrun three warriors? Do you know how to use a weapon to save her? I don't know, Adam. What can you do?

Adam reeled as if he'd been punched. Evan's words had been harsh. But they'd also been honest and it was another reminder that he didn't belong in a world this primitive. Here everything was always a matter of life or death. He couldn't hunt. He couldn't fight. He couldn't even do women's work. He was useless – even worthless to these people and to himself.

He was like the old people. Someone had to take care of his needs for food and clothing or they wouldn't get done. He sat, staring blankly at the tall grass bent beneath his feet. It was a hard thing to learn you were a burden.

Tyhen was upset the twins were fighting, but the most important thing now was to help Evan which meant changing all their plans.

"Dakotah, you must go back with Lola. Something bad is happening and Yuma and I have to help Evan."

Anxious about the discontent, Lola took Dakotah by the hand and led him away, explaining as they went that there would be time to do this again.

Yuma forgot about his winter coat as he grabbed his spear and reached for Tyhen.

"If you fly, this time I go with you."

His arm slid around her waist and then the wind began to spin around them. She sent a message to Evan as they were rising above the Gathering.

Yuma and I are coming. We will look for her from above.

Yuma was trying not to be a little terrified by how high they were off the ground, and at the same time in awe that this wonderful woman was his. He glanced at her face, felt the tension in her body, and knew something bad was happening.

"What is Evan doing?" Yuma asked.

"Trying to find Suwanee. Three warriors are chasing her. Evan says they intend to kidnap and rape her. He's trying to get to her before that happens."

"How did he know about this?"

"He must have seen it happening in his head. And there's something else. He and Adam are fighting over her."

Yuma felt sick. Everything kept changing and never for the better, but now was not the time to worry about the twins.

"You know this incident could start a war between tribes we will not be able to control," he said.

She nodded. "I'm going lower. Look for a running girl being chased by three men."

Yuma tightened his hold on Tyhen and kept his gaze on the camp below.

Tyhen kept a sharp eye out for something amiss, but

couldn't help thinking about Adam. She'd heard the pain in his voice. As the Windwalker's daughter she could do many things, but changing the heart of a woman who loves was not one of them. All she knew to do was ask the hard questions the brothers seemed bent on ignoring.

Adam?

What?

If you already know this is Evan's destiny then why are you angry with him? That is out of our control. Look at my life! I was given a task I did not choose. This must be what's happening between you and your brother. You are both part of what must happen so that the future is not destroyed, but maybe you do not do it together. Maybe this is what you must both accept as I have had to accept my fate.

There was a lengthy silence, long enough Tyhen thought he was ignoring her, and then she heard what sounded like a soul-weary sigh. She felt sad for him, but it couldn't be helped. Right now she had to stop a disaster before it happened.

Adam thought about what Tyhen said. He was beginning to understand some things were out of his control – a concept he rarely had to face. He was still unsettled by what felt like betrayal and trying not to be mad at Evan. It felt terrible and he didn't want to feel like this anymore.

Remembering he'd been on a mission to find a healer when all of this began, he resumed his search until he finally saw Myra Begay. He quickly told her what was needed, and when she went to get her medicine bag, he focused on the pain Keechee was feeling and took the healer where she needed to go.

Suwanee had made it all the way through the Comanche campgrounds without getting caught and was halfway across the Gathering before she stumbled. By the time she regained her balance her pursuers had drastically closed the gap. In a panic, she glanced over her shoulder then darted to the left just in time to escape the leader's grasp. She heard him grunt in frustration and kept on running, unaware help was closer than she knew.

Evan wished he could fly like Tyhen instead of dodging so many people and their cooking fires and dwellings. He could feel Suwanee's heartbeat as he ran. He knew she was close but had yet to see her. He'd already tried sending her a message but she either didn't have the ability to hear him, or she was too afraid of what was happening to focus.

All of a sudden he caught a glimpse of three young warriors running through the camp. When he sensed their intent he knew it was them, which meant Suwanee had to be close.

Anxious to find her before they caught up, he backtracked through five campsites to get ahead of them and then darted out from between two tipis just as Suwanee ran past. Seeing her still on the move was a relief. He wasn't sure that she'd seen him until he saw her look back, then stumble and fall.

Seconds later the trio ran out from behind a lodge at full speed. Evan stepped out in front of them and held up his spear.

"You stop now!" he shouted.

Suwanee gasped as she scrambled to her feet. Evan had come to save her.

Walks Tall was furious and pulled his knife, ready to do battle for the girl. He charged toward Evan just as Tyhen and Yuma landed beside him.

"Stop!" Tyhen shouted, and pushed Evan aside.

Walks Tall's arm was on a downward arc, the knife held tight in his fist, but Yuma saw the knife and was already moving. Just as it would have pierced Tyhen's stomach, he jumped in front of her, intent on blocking the thrust with his spear.

Instead, the knife pierced Yuma's chest.

The spear fell from his hand as he staggered, then stared down in disbelief. With a tragic expression of apology on his face, he was reaching for Tyhen when he collapsed.

Tyhen saw what happened through a red haze of rage. The scream that came out of her mouth echoed through the entire campsite, bringing everyone to a halt. With one wave of her hand, the men flew backward into the tipi behind them and were still trying to get back to their feet when she spoke. The tone of her voice was as cold as the day.

"Get back to your people. If he dies I will kill you myself."

They turned and ran as she knelt beside Yuma. Evan was on his knees beside him, trying to stop the bleeding.

"Help me," she said.

Evan quickly pulled Yuma upright, watching with tears in his eyes as Tyhen stepped behind Yuma, wrapped her arms around his waist, and went straight up into the air.

Suwanee was horrified. This happened because of her.

"I am so sorry. I did not mean for -"

Evan raised his hand, stopping her apology before she said anything more.

"You were not at fault. It was not your knife that went into my brother's chest. Come with me. I need to get you back to your father."

When he turned, she grabbed onto the back of his clothing and held on as if her life depended on it.

The moment Evan felt her touch he understood why Yuma had done what he'd just done. There was no explanation for what the heart wants and he was through denying it. If he and Adam had not been at odds about her, none of this would have happened. He didn't understand destiny, but he believed in it, else he and Adam would have died with everyone else when Firewalker burned up the earth. He wasn't sure how their relationship would play out, but he knew she was part of his future.

"Is the Eagle going to die?" Suwanee whispered.

Evan sighed.

"Not if Tyhen can help it," he said, and then took her by the hand.

CHAPTER TWELVE

Tyhen flew over the campground in a rage. She saw the New Ones watching the sky. They knew something was wrong because they'd heard her scream, but she wasn't stopping to explain. She had no time to waste.

Yuma was limp in her arms, his eyes closed. If it wasn't for the blood flow still coming from his chest, it would feel like the flight she'd made to the far mountains with Stanley Blue Jacket's body. This was her waking nightmare.

She flew over the ridge where they'd first seen the Gathering, following the river until she saw a flat ledge of table rock beside the river and landed, easing Yuma down on his back as she did. Once before she'd saved his life as he lay dying from a curse, and she'd do it again or quit this place and leave everyone there to live or die on their own.

She wrapped her fingers around the knife in his chest and took a deep breath. Once she pulled it out, the blood was going to flow faster. It was a serious risk, but she had no other options. She looked at his face – so familiar and so beloved, eyeing the arc of dark eyebrows, the strong jut of his jaw, and the sensuous curve of his lips. Then she leaned over and whispered in his ear.

"Yuma, my Yuma, hear my voice. Once again I am giving you life. Take it and come back to me."

Quickly, she shed her coat, grabbed the knife with both hands and pulled straight up. Blood gushed as the weapon came free. Without wasted motion she pushed up the sleeve of her shift and cut a long, deep gash down the length of her left arm. Her hands were shaking as she angled the blood flow onto his chest and into his wound, only his blood was coming out as fast as hers went in, negating any good it might have done.

It felt like forever but it had only been a few moments when she began searching for his heartbeat. When she realized it was growing fainter, she panicked. Frantic, she moved her arm to let more blood flow into the wound.

"Please, Yuma, please. My blood is your blood. Take it and you will be healed."

Her chest hurt in the way it had when she'd bid her mother and Cayetano goodbye. The fear within her was overwhelming. She could not lose Yuma. She waited and waited for the magic to happen, but felt nothing but the blood between her fingers. When she could no longer feel a heartbeat, she grabbed him by both shoulders and began to shake him, her voice thick with unshed tears.

"No! No! You do not leave me! You said I would love you forever, and our forever does not end here. You come back to me! Come back to me!"

He was still – too still - but she wasn't ready to turn him loose. She grabbed the knife and slashed her other arm almost to the bone, letting the fresh flow of her blood run into his mouth only to watch in painful dismay as it oozed back out and down the sides of his neck.

He was no longer breathing.

Nearly blind with tears and fear of what was happening, she kept rubbing her hands all over his chest, as if trying to put all the blood that he'd shed back inside his body.

"Yuma! Please don't leave me! Swallow what is in your mouth," but he wasn't moving.

Now she was covered in both his blood and her own, sobbing uncontrollably and begging the Old Ones to give him back. Unable to face the truth of what was before her she stood up, threw back her head and screamed. The sound sliced through the air on one note and didn't stop. When the New Ones heard they answered with a wail of despair that echoed across the encampment. There could only be one reason for Tyhen's pain. They fell into each other's arms in grief, crying and praying.

Tyhen was in shock and in so much despair she didn't think

about what she was going to do. She just slid her arms beneath
his body, pulled him into her arms, and shot straight up into the
air with him clutched against her chest, only this time the wind
around them was not spinning. It was a straight blast of air
fueled by her rage that was pushing them up into the sky, like
the fire that spewed from the mountain above Naaki Chava.

Up, up, up, she went with Yuma clutched against her chest
until the Gathering was but a small brown dot upon the earth.
Even as it disappeared from sight she was not looking down,
but staring into Yuma's face, waiting for him to open his eyes
and see her, but it did not happen.

When they were so high that the blood had frozen on his
face and the tube of wind in which they were riding was
turning to ice, Tyhen began to cry out.

"Old Ones! Hear me! See me! See my Yuma! He is not
breathing. I want him back. You have to give him back. Hear
me! You cannot have him! He is my heart!"

Tears were frozen on her lashes and her skin was so cold
she could not feel her hands, but she didn't waver as she
continued to press her case.

"You took my free will without asking my permission. You
gave me to our people to save our future and took me away my
home and my family. You owe me this! Give him back! You
have to give him back!"

The drums were faint but she began to have hope. She knew
that she'd been heard, and so she waited – and then waited
some more until all hope was gone. She looked down at the
man in her arms, watching his skin turning gray because there
was no more blood inside him to feed his heart. Fear shot
through her in waves as she began shouting again, talking
louder and louder until every word was a gut-wrenching roar of
rage.

"Give him back! Do you hear me? Give him back or I am
done. I will quit this earth and let the People's future end in the
flames of Firewalker's descent! I will not do this without him!"

The drums were louder but so was she. She spun out of the
icy tube of wind and flew across the heavens with Yuma's
bloody body in her arms, wanting them to see, to understand.
Then she heard words in her head that made her blood run

cold.

You cannot quit. You carry his child. You carry the next Windwalker who will lead the people as you have done.

She was shocked to hear she was with child, but her rage and indignation were for Yuma.

"You give him back to me or I will die with this child inside me."

Windwalkers do not die.

She was sobbing so hard she had blinded herself with tears. Yuma was a dead weight in her arms and she wanted to die with him.

"It would be a gift to my child if she never breathed on this earth. My soul may never die, but I will not give another moment of time to people who do not value life. You give him back to me! I cannot... I will not... do this without him!"

The drums were beating, and then suddenly they went silent.

She looked down at Yuma's lifeless body in despair and then buried her face against his neck.

"Yuma, my Yuma, I cannot bear this. You cannot leave me behind."

She began moving higher and higher into the heavens where there was no oxygen and no gravity and no life between heaven and earth, save for the spirit walkers who passed through on their way to somewhere else. Her arms were shaking from exhaustion. Either she would drop him and fly upward until she ceased to exist, or they would plummet back to the earth together and be no more. Time became a commodity she no longer needed. He was gone and she wasn't going back alone. So they were done and so it would be.

They were still moving into infinity when she felt movement against her cheek. She thought she heard him groan, and then she felt his chest move as he took a deep breath. Before she could cry aloud the joy that was in her heart, there was a huge shift of air within the silence of space and then the deafening sound of thunder.

She raised her head and looked up.

They were surrounded by eagles - massive birds unlike anything she'd seen on earth.

It was the Old Ones.

They flew around her and then below her and when she understood what they intended, she waited until one soared beneath her and landed on a great outstretched wing with Yuma still in her arms.

The eagles' cries were a shriek upon the wind as they circled the heavens, and then all of a sudden they began plummeting toward earth *en masse* in a downward dive.

She felt the eagles' heartbeats beating in rhythm with Yuma's pulse.

She heard the message *It is done*, and knew they'd granted her request.

Yuma lay in her arms as if asleep, unaware of the bed of eagle feathers or that his protection from the cold was the woman who held his heart.

As for Tyhen, all she could see was a cold, gray blur.

The wind in her ears was a high-pitched shriek.

The drumbeat was so loud that it rattled her soul, but it didn't matter. The Old Ones had given him back to her and they were taking them home.

Word was spreading throughout the Gathering about what had happened. The people were afraid, uncertain what it meant for them? Had they ruined their chance to undo great wrong? Had they come all this way at great hardship and then sealed their fate by old behaviors just as they'd been on the verge of great discovery?

Walks Tall, Broken Wing, and Little Raven were brought before their chief, Counts Coup, in dismal shame.

Counts Coup was furious. They had not only angered the Dove, but by all accounts they had killed the Eagle who protected her. He watched them enter his tipi and stand with their heads down, unable to meet his gaze.

"You have brought shame upon our people. What have you to say for yourself?" he asked.

"We did not mean to harm," Walks Tall said.

Counts Coup's frown darkened.

"Were you not present in our village when the medicine

man told of his visions?"

"We heard," Little Raven said.

"Then you heard him say we no longer wage war upon other tribes. You heard him say we do not steal women and children and keep them with us against their will!"

"We heard," Walks Tall said, but he was beginning to shake. He wanted to stay strong, but the truth was he was afraid for his life.

Counts Coup was furious. "You heard, and yet the same day the Dove comes into our midst and saves us from strangers and their disease, you chose to take a girl against her will."

Walks Tall looked up. "I didn't intend to -"

"Do not lie to me!" Counts Coup shouted. "All of you chased her through two camps. I have been told this, is it true?"

Walks Tall lifted his head and then straightened his shoulders. If he was going to die, he would die like a warrior.

"Yes, it is true."

Counts Coup grabbed Walks Tall's weapons and threw them in the fire.

"You are stupid! You do not learn!"

Walks Tall stifled a groan as he watched his wooden spear catching fire and his knife disappearing in the flames and ashes.

Counts Coup waved his hand at all three of them.

"I have decided! You will all pack up your things and leave this place. You will return to our homeland on your own and if you are still alive when we return, you will be prepared to accept the changes we bring with us."

Walks Tall gave his burning weapons one last glance and followed his friends out of the tipi.

They were gone within the hour and the people in their tribe expressed their shame by turning their backs as they walked away.

When the New Ones saw the blast of air and light go straight up from beyond the ridge, they knew it was Tyhen. They didn't know where she'd gone or if she'd ever come back, but they knew Yuma was dead.

They were mourning not only the loss of two friends, but the loss of hope that the Windwalker's daughter had represented. They'd come such a long way, sacrificed so much only to have it end because three warriors who barely qualified as civilized couldn't control their urges? It was not to be born.

The women began grieving in their way by marking their faces with ashes, while Montford and Johnston Nantay began looking for Adam and Evan for guidance in what to do next.

Dakotah paced the camp with tears drying on his face. He could not believe that this was happening. It was nothing like what he'd been shown in his dreams.

Unaware that the New Ones were looking for him and his brother, Evan was in the camp of the Lakota, returning Suwanee to her father's lodge. When she would have disappeared inside without a word, he stopped her with a look, then cupped her face with his hands.

"Do you believe in destiny?" he asked.

"I believe," she said.

"We are strangers," he reminded her.

She laid a hand on his chest.

"Our spirits are not," she said softly.

Evan's pulse kicked. She was referring to what had happened in their dreams.

"When we leave here, I will go with Tyhen. Will you come with me?" he asked.

Suwanee shivered. She was afraid to go, but more afraid to be left behind.

"I will go," she whispered.

He searched her face and saw their future. It was a good one. It was all that mattered.

"Tell your father I would talk with him soon."

"What about your brother? What will he say?"

Evan wouldn't let himself go there.

"I don't know, but it is what it is between us and fate has spoken."

She shivered again and he frowned.

"You need warmer clothing."

She shrugged. "We have none. It was lost crossing a river to come here."

He frowned, took off the jaguar coat that had been made for him back in Boomerang and put it around her shoulders.

She gasped. The gift was a statement on its own.

"But then you will be cold," she whispered, even as she was pulling the fur up around her chin.

"I have another," he said, and then rubbed his thumb across the bottom of her lip and sighed. "I will return," he said, watching the flush rise beneath her skin and the smile come and go on her lips.

It was not a time for joy, and yet there was a part of him that felt like he was walking on air as she slipped into the lodge and out of sight.

Evan's steps were slow as he walked away. He'd set a future in motion without thinking of Adam, and was too distraught about Yuma to think of a future without him in it. He went back to where he'd left his backpack, but instead of setting up camp, he sat down beneath the cedar tree and buried his face in his hands.

Adam found him like that, and without saying a word sat down beside him and slid his arm across Evan's shoulder.

Evan felt his brother's regret. Today's events had ended the antagonism between them, but their reconciliation had come at a terrible loss.

"Did you see?" Adam asked, meaning had Evan 'seen' Tyhen trying to save Yuma's life?

Evan nodded.

"If we lose Yuma, we lose her, too. This isn't turning out like I expected," he muttered.

"We cannot lose them. We are not done," Adam said.

Evan shrugged.

"Tyhen did what she was supposed to do. She got the New Ones to the Gathering. They know what to do. Maybe *she* is done."

"I cannot believe that," Adam said.

Evan was silent for a few moments and then turned to face his brother.

"I asked Suwanee if she would come with me when we leave this place. She said yes. She also asked if you would be okay. She is very sorry for the discord between us."

Adam had regrets, but he'd had a rude awakening today when Suwanee was in danger. He had no skills to help her. In fact he had no skills to save himself should the need arise. He did not belong in this place. If he'd known it sooner, he might have stayed behind in Boomerang. Tyhen's words were still ringing in his ears. Maybe their destinies would take them in different directions, after all.

"She should not worry. It will be okay," Adam said. "We must set up our camp now. If anyone needs us, they will find us."

Evan's shoulders slumped.

"They are already looking for us. They expect us to give them direction as to what to do next," he said.

Adam frowned.

"Then we should get busy. We need a place to sleep tonight, regardless of what else may happen."

Their hearts were heavy as they began setting up camp. Adam was gathering firewood and Evan was putting up the sleeping tent when they began hearing what sounded like distant claps of thunder. When they realized the day was darkening, they stopped what they were doing and looked up, expecting to see gathering storm clouds. Instead, the sky was clear, but when they looked out onto the prairie, they saw a huge dark shadow coming toward them across the tall grass.

Adam was trying not to panic. He could see a shadow on the land but not what was causing it – not even when he tried to 'see' it with his mind.

"What is that?" he muttered.

Evan couldn't get a read on anything either. The sky above was clear, so what was making that ominous shadow?

Then others began to see the encroaching darkness and chaos ensued. Some began screaming while others were running about looking for children to shelter. Others began praying, crying aloud to the Great Sprit to be saved.

Behind the shadow came the thunder, rolling above them in one long continuous roar. When they looked up, to their horror, something massive had moved between them and the sun.

The People at the Gathering were terrified and fell to the

ground, certain they were all about to die.

The New Ones were fearful, but had more life experience and understanding of astrological occurrences. They weren't sure if what was approaching was something like Firewalker or if they might die. Whatever it was, it was coming straight toward them.

It wasn't until the wind began to blow in great rushing torrents that a glimmer of hope returned. For Dakotah, wind meant Tyhen, and he began running.

"Tyhen! It's Tyhen!" he cried.

Then Adam and Evan felt her probing their thoughts and knew Dakotah had been right. Their relief was overwhelming. She was back, but what of the eagle?

What of Yuma?

He lives.

What is this darkness? Is this you?

It is the Old Ones.

What do you mean?

You will see.

And then they did.

The eagles became visible when they pulled out of their dive, and when they began soaring high above the Gathering in ever-widening circles and their high-pitched shrieking cries turned into unmistakable words of warning, the People dropped to their knees. The Old Ones' anger was evident.

The Dove was our gift to you and you betrayed her.

She called us from our sleep with great anger in her voice and the Eagle dead and broken in her arms.

You brought shame to us... to your ancestors.

She asked us for his life and we gave it back.

Betray us again and it is you who will suffer.

Mistreat these people again in any way and it will be your lives that are lost.

There was a great wailing from the people below as they cried out for mercy, begging for forgiveness, promising anything to be spared from the Thunderbirds' wrath.

Then out of their midst came one lone eagle, more massive

than anything they had ever seen. It began circling downward, getting closer to the ground with every spiral. Unable to stand against the wind from its passing, people were forced to their knees to watch its descent.

When the eagle was treetop level, it tilted sideways, one great wing dragging along the grass to unload its passengers.

Tyhen was prepared for the landing and held Yuma that much tighter as they slid down the massive wing and into the prairie grass.

She was flat on her back with Yuma's body still in her arms when the eagle shot upward, taking the drum beat with him. The other eagles followed, disappearing as abruptly as they had come. She rolled over, easing Yuma down onto his back and then sat up. His heart was beating, his eyelids fluttering. He was alive and she would ask for nothing more.

She laid a hand upon his chest, taking comfort in the steady rise and fall, and when he groaned and then began to regain consciousness she quickly wiped away her tears.

Yuma's body ached and so did his head. All he could remember was walking into a ring of gold light, and then being pulled back almost as quickly as he'd come. He opened his eyes to find Tyhen gazing down at him.

"What happened?" he asked.

She touched his face, his chest, his arms, making certain he was as he'd been before, and choked back a sob.

She was crying, which made him begin to focus on her. When he realized the dark stains upon her clothing were actually dried blood, he knew something bad had happened, but what?

"Tyhen?" he said, then winced from the pain.

His chest was hurting but he couldn't remember why. Then when he touched it and his hand came away bloody, he remembered the attack and the knife piercing his clothing and going into his chest. He should be dead. Why wasn't he dead?

All of a sudden an old memory surfaced - of her cutting her wrists to save his life when he was dying from a curse. What had she done to herself this time?

He sat up slowly then reached for her wrist. When she didn't resist, he pushed up the sleeve on her shift. When he saw the gaping wounds that were beginning to close, hair stood up on the back of his neck.

"What did you do?" he whispered. "What in the name of all that is holy did you do?"

Her eyes were dark with a weariness he did not understand and she seemed older – almost as if she'd aged years in one day.

But the expression on her face was one of cold determination, as was the tone of her voice.

"You were dying. I tried to save you, but you died in my arms so I took you to the Old Ones instead. I made them give you back to me," she said, then took his hand and laid it against her cheek. When she spoke again, her voice was trembling. "I made them give you back."

The sun was in her eyes. The air was cold on her face and she could feel the ground vibrating beneath them from the people who were coming to get them. Their time alone was over.

"They are coming," she said, and stood up in the knee-high prairie grass, pulling him with her. Together they turned to face the onslaught of their people.

CHAPTER THIRTEEN

Hours later, Tyhen and Yuma sat naked beside a ceremonial fire as Johnston Nantay's wife, Suzy, and his sister, Lola, cleaned the blood from their bodies.

The wound in Yuma's chest had ceased bleeding and was almost closed although Myra Begay was applying an ointment of buffalo fat and crushed healing herbs on it anyway.

Tyhen's arms were no longer bleeding and the gashes were nearly healed, but the scars would be a reminder of how far she'd been willing to go to save him.

When Myra offered to apply some of her ointment onto the gashes, Tyhen pushed it away.

"Save it for someone who needs it," she said shortly.

Yuma frowned. She was so angry. Being rude wasn't like her. Something else had happened and he didn't want to wait until they were alone to find out. He sent her a message.

Your anger is spilling over onto innocent people.

Tyhen flinched, then looked up. His dark eyes were questioning, but it was the love she saw that pulled her back.

I am sorry.

What's wrong?

Tears pooled in her eyes and rolled silently down her face.

Startled, Yuma reached for her hand.

Whatever it is, we will not speak of it again. Don't cry. You know the sight of your sadness hurts my heart.

When she closed her eyes and looked away, he thought she was shutting down. Instead, she clasped his hand tightly as her thoughts began flowing from her to him so fast that some of them ran together.

I want this over. I want to find a quiet place to live, build a home to keep us warm in this time of cold and frozen, and dry in times of rain. I want to know you will be sleeping beside me every night in the years to come. You died today. It made me realize how easy it is for a mortal to die. I do not want to waste another moment.

He squeezed her hand in return, explaining what he could remember.

I saw my father in the light. I heard you screaming but I couldn't see you. I was so very sad because I thought you were gone, and then I felt your arms around me and the next thing I knew we were in the tall grass.

Tyhen closed her eyes, unwilling to dwell another moment on the horror. He was alive now and it was all she'd asked for. She heard water sloshing as Lola rinsed her cloth in the bowl of water and felt her touch as she began cleaning the drying blood from her other arm. She was making soft noises of distress as she worked and Tyhen knew the woman was upset and worried, but she was tired of being the one who solved all the problems. Instead, she had one more question for Yuma.

Where do we go from here?

She never saw his smile, but it wouldn't have mattered. Whatever he said would be fine with her. Instead, he threw the question back to her.

Where do you want to go?

Answering him was easy.

Wherever you go, I go.

Then, when the Cherokee leave the Gathering, we go with them.

He heard her sigh.

Is it far to the land of the Cherokee?

He squeezed her hand again.

Not as far as it was coming here.

She thought of the baby in her belly and wanted to welcome her into a home, not a campfire somewhere along the trail.

When she felt the weight of a buffalo robe settling across her shoulders she finally looked up.

"Thank you, Myra. I am sorry for my angry words."

The little healer smiled as she smoothed away the hair from

Tyhen's forehead.

"You are like your mother. When she worried, her words were also hot. We have much to be thankful for today. We thought both of you were lost to us, and now you are here. We are grateful."

Lola pulled the edge of the buffalo robe across Yuma's shoulders, too.

"When you both are warm again, we will help you dress," she said.

Yuma looked around the campsite.

"Where are our clothes?" he asked.

"They were taken to the river to wash clean. There was much blood."

Yuma looked at Tyhen. There was still anger on her face, but when she slid her arm around his shoulder to keep the robe from slipping, he leaned forward and brushed a kiss across her mouth. She smiled. It was all he needed to see. Within a few minutes, he had fallen asleep beside the warmth of the fire.

Tyhen stretched out beside him, covering both of them with the heavy robe.

My sister, we are so very happy you found a way to save Yuma's life. You are a strong leader for us all.

Adam's words did not ease her anger. She wanted nothing more to do with leading and she didn't want to talk about herself. Right before Yuma was stabbed, he and Evan had been yelling at each other. There was too much chaos in their lives for brothers to be fighting.

Are you still angry with Evan?

No. I was foolish. Feeling emotion is not easy. I am ashamed.

She sighed.

What of Suwanee?

She is Evan's to love.

Tyhen was waiting for Evan to speak for himself, but when he was silent she did not hesitate to ask.

Evan? Are you and Adam okay?

Yes, my sister, we are okay. What of Yuma?

He sleeps. He will be well soon.

Tyhen still wasn't satisfied.

What of the girl? Do you love her?

I do not know what love means and we are strangers to each other, but I accept she is part of my destiny.

Tyhen wasn't happy with that answer.

Will you love her?

Evan sighed.

She will become my world.

Do you go with her, or do you come with Yuma and with me?

Evan didn't hesitate.

I have already told her I go with you. She chooses to come with me.

Tyhen was relieved and made no attempt to hide it. She was going to grieve the loss of the New Ones and could not face losing her brothers with them.

Thank you. I did not want to lose both of you again.

We do not abandon you, Tyhen. Ever.

The reassurance in Evan's voice eased her worry, but it did not ease her anger. That was still with her, like hands around her throat that were choking back her joy, and she did not know how to let it go.

The all-night march they'd made to save the People's lives seemed like a lifetime time ago. So much had happened since daybreak it was hard to grasp.

She caught a glimpse of some of the New Ones standing guard around where they were lying. It felt good to let someone else stand in the gap. She had taken care of all of them for a very long time.

And so she slept, unaware of the divisive line growing between the New Ones and the Gathering. What the three young warriors had done was the worst possible thing that could have occurred. Trust was lost before it had a chance to form.

The New Ones had set up a perimeter around their campsite. No one came in unannounced, and no one left the safety of their camp unattended.

The People at the Gathering understood why the guards were there and were contrite. Many of their own healers came to offer help and medicines. Drummers had gathered around a ceremonial fire and soon the air was alive with the cries of the singers. It was a valiant effort in praying for the Eagle's healing and asking forgiveness of the Dove.

Evan had taken it upon himself to walk through the camp of the New Ones and tell them about the Lakota losing their belongings in a river crossing. Despite their reluctance to interact with them, they knew what it felt like to be cold without proper clothing. They began gathering up what clothing the New Ones were willing to part with. In the process, he found a winter robe for Suwanee's mother and one for her father, too. After that, a dozen or more of the New Ones gathered up the coats and robes and cured deerskins that were ready to be cut and made into clothing and followed Evan out of their compound and back through the Gathering to Lakota campground.

Chief Matto was standing outside his lodge talking to some of his warriors when Evan and the New Ones walked up. Once he'd seen the fine coat this warrior had given Suwanee, he had been expecting this visit, but not what the warrior brought with him.

Evan took a deep breath and faced Suwanee's father.

"Chief Matto. I am Evan, a warrior with the New Ones. I have come to speak with you."

Matto eyed the group accompanying the young warrior.

"What of these people?" he asked.

"Your daughter told us what happened in your river crossing. We, too, have lost much on our journey to get here and understand your discomfort. We have extra clothing for cold weather and have come to share it with your people."

Matto was at a loss for words as Evan stepped forward and held out a robe for the chief made from cured deerskin. It had a fur-lined hood and made to hang down past a grown man's knees.

"For you, Chief Matto."

Matto took it with as much ceremony as he could muster and promptly threw it over his shoulders. The weight and warmth of it was welcome.

"I thank you," Matto said, then called his wife outside. "Chata! Come!"

She came hurrying out and was startled to see Evan and the people with him.

Evan glanced at the chief for permission and when the chief nodded, he gave Chata the winter robe he'd brought for her.

"For you," he said, and knew from the sadness in her eyes that Suwanee had already told her she was leaving them. Still, she took the winter robe and like Matto, pulled it over her head.

"These are for the Lakota," Matto said. "You and Suwanee will lead them to the people who are in need."

"She is at the river," Chata said. "I will take." Then she motioned to the New Ones to follow her and led them away.

Now Evan and Matto were alone and the chief wasn't making this moment easy.

"Chief Matto, when we leave the Gathering, I have asked Suwanee to come with me. The Dove is my sister and where she goes, I go."

Even though Matto had already seen the fine coat this young warrior had given to Suwanee and he'd understood the man was claiming her as his wife, it hurt Matto's heart to hear this said aloud. In his mind he'd always imagined Suwanee would take one of the Lakota warriors and was puzzled as to why she and this man, who was a stranger to her, would want to be together.

"I do not understand how you have chosen her. You only saw her one time in our lodge."

"I saw her in my dream and she saw me. We were together in the dream."

Matto grunted. Spirit walking was a thing of great magic and not everyone could do it. He had not known his daughter possessed this trait.

"She has many traits," Evan said, forgetting the chief had not spoken that aloud.

Matto's eyes narrowed as he looked at Evan anew.

Evan sighed. He'd inadvertently given himself away, but it didn't matter. In fact, truth was always best.

"Yes, I heard your thoughts," Evan said. "My brother and I are shamans. We were advisors to the great Chief Cayetano of the Mayan people in Naaki Chava, and we now serve the Windwalker's daughter. My brother and I have powers to see the future and we know when people are being truthful or not."

Matto was impressed. Evan was a warrior with power and he had chosen his daughter.

"If my daughter wishes to leave with you, I will not stop her," Matto said.

Evan breathed a sigh of relief.

"I am a good hunter. I will honor her presence in my life and take care of her always."

Matto nodded.

Evan relaxed. It was done.

"I will come for her when it is time for us to leave," he said.

Matto nodded. "I will tell her," he said, and then added, "We, the Lakota, are grateful for the winter robes. They will keep us warm on the long trek home."

Evan nodded, then as he turned around to leave saw Suwanee walking toward them. He glanced once at the chief and then went to meet her. He didn't stop to question the elation he felt at seeing her. He'd already decided this must be what love felt like, and was slightly overwhelmed by it.

"Suwanee!"

She looked up, saw him coming toward her with a smile on his face and in that moment knew everything she was about to do was right. It was a bit frightening to think of leaving what she knew, but with this warrior as her husband, she would be loved and cherished for the rest of her life. It was enough.

Tyhen had been awakened by the drums. She heard and understood the reasons, but she was still angry and had nothing to say. She was holding fast to Yuma and afraid to close her eyes when she felt a slight touch against her bare shoulder as someone lifted the buffalo robe. She knew within seconds it was Dakotah. When the warmth of his skinny body settled against her back, she sighed. It was hard to hold anger with such a gentle heart beside her, and slowly the rage within her began to die and she slept.

Dakotah, worried about the two people most important in his life, had wormed his way through the guards to where they lay sleeping. He snuggled in behind Tyhen and scooted up against her back, as if protecting her vulnerable side, and in doing so, broke the ice around her heart.

All of the New Ones went to bed that night with renewed anxiety. It was obvious their tasks would not be easy, nor would they just be teaching the People about the white men's ways and languages. There were centuries of tribal customs and behaviors that were going to be difficult to change, and after last night's long walk, they slept the sleep of exhaustion and dreamed of Earth as it had been in the days before Firewalker. It was a requiem for all they'd lost.

The tribes were also troubled and uncertain how bringing the New Ones into their world would impact their lives. The New Ones knew nothing about their way of life and they weren't sure they wanted change. But after all they had witnessed and the angry Thunderbirds flying over them and blocking out the sun, there was no mistaking the message they had been given.

Tyhen and Yuma had gone to their own camp before nightfall, grateful that someone had already set everything up. They went inside too weary to eat and quickly fell asleep.

Tyhen was sleeping and dreaming of home. In the dream she was sitting in Singing Bird's lap, watching the monkeys play outside their window as Singing Bird combed the tangles out of her hair. She could feel her mother's fingers on her scalp – even heard the laughter in her voice. And then all of sudden she felt another presence enter her dream and heard a voice say, "Open your eyes," and so she did.

She woke to see the spirit of an old man standing just inside their tent in a circle of light. His face was lined with wrinkles - so many that his eyes almost disappeared within them. Gray braids wrapped with white fur hung down past his waist, and the bits of clothing he wore were all made of a rawhide bleached white by the infinity of sunlight. His legs were bowed. His feet were bare, and he was holding a staff crowned with white dove feathers tied to the top. He didn't move or speak aloud and yet she began to hear his voice.

When the sun sets tomorrow you must all be gone. Tatanka comes with the snow. Anyone who lingers will be frozen or trampled. The Gathering is done.

Tyhen's heart skipped a beat. As large as the Gathering was, and as many people who were here, the numbers of the great wooly buffalo were far more.

I will tell them, and then what? What about me? What am I to do next?

He was silent for so long she thought he would not answer, and then he raised the staff and pointed it straight at her head.

You are the Windwalker's daughter. You already know your path. If you do not see it with your eyes, then follow it with your heart.

He disappeared before her eyes, and then she heard another voice – one she had thought was lost to her forever.

Tyhen? Tyhen? Can you hear me?

Mother! Oh Mother, I feared I would never hear your voice again.

I saw you with the eagles. You are truly Niyol's daughter and I am so proud of the woman you have become.

Tears burned Tyhen's eyes as she listened, taking in the praise and hearing the words of a mother's love.

Mother, I have a baby in my belly.

Are you afraid?

Yes. I would wish you were going to be with me when I give birth.

You have many with you who love you as I do. The twins know about the baby. They knew before you. A child around you also knows, and Yuma knows. It's why he took the knife meant for your chest. He knew you could not die, but the same gift has yet to be given to your daughter. He killed a man to save me when you were still in my belly, and he took the knife meant for you to save his child.

Tyhen sighed. So much was explained now. Why Yuma reacted with such fierceness. Why Dakotah followed her every step! As for the twins, she should have known nothing was a secret around them. But she couldn't understand how Yuma would know and keep that from her? She would ask later.

Thank you, my mother. I am grateful for your presence. I am grateful for your message. Now I have one for you. Tomorrow we all leave the Gathering. Yuma and I will travel with the Cherokee. We are going home, Mother. On the way I think we will travel through land that was Layla Birdsong's home. I will think of you then when we walk through the Oklahoma that was the Muscogee lands of your time. I will say a prayer for you there.

Tyhen thought she heard a sob, and then her mother's voice grew fainter until the sound was just a whisper.

You are loved.

The silence within her was sudden.

Mother! Mother! Are you still there?

But she was gone.

She rolled over, careful not to aggravate the wounds on her arms, and then ran a finger across the curve of Yuma's lips.

His eyes opened instantly.

"You are in need?"

"How did you know of the baby and not tell me?"

The look of love that spread across his face was overwhelming.

"I knew only moments before I jumped," he said. "It was Evan who told me and I quickly understood the baby would die, even if you did not." Then leaned over and kissed her.

Every emotion Yuma was feeling went through her. When he pulled away, she was blind from unshed tears.

"I have something to tell you, but I am afraid you will be angry with me," she said.

He frowned and shook his head.

"Never."

"I did not know the baby was in my belly until today when the Old Ones told me. I was begging them to save your life. I told them I would not finish this journey without you. I told them I would find a way to end what I am if they did not."

Yuma heard the hurt and fear in her voice and could only imagine what she'd been feeling.

"I am so sorry, my little whirlwind. I did not intend to leave you all alone."

She swallowed around the knot in her throat and then closed her eyes. She did not want to see the shock on his face when she confessed the rest.

"They told me I could not end my life because I was with child. I was so scared and so mad that I didn't want anything without you and told them I didn't care. I told them that I would end both our lives before I'd let her be born with such a burden as the one given to me because it is nothing but sacrifice and pain. I told them I would be doing her a favor if she never drew breath." Her voice was shaking now and hardly more than a whisper. "Are you angry I would let her die after you died trying to save her?"

Yuma cupped her face as her tears rolled beneath his fingers.

"Please don't cry. I understand why you would feel that way. Everything including free will was taken away from you before you were born, just as it will be for our child."

Her voice was shaking as she slid her hand across his waist.

"I've told you this so many times, but I will say it again. I cannot do this without you."

"And now you don't have to," he said.

She sighed. "There's one more thing."

"I am listening."

"We have to be gone from here before sunset tomorrow."

His heart started to pound.

"All of us?" he asked.

"Every person and every thing."

"Why? What's happening?"

"Tatanka comes and so does the snow."

"The buffalo? Coming here?" He groaned. "Everyone here

will be trampled."

"Yes."

He frowned.

"How do you know this?"

"He told me," she said.

"Who's He? Who told you this?" he asked.

"I think it was the First One. I think it was the Great Spirit, himself. He was just here."

While Yuma was trying to wrap his head around the fact that the entity his father had called God might have been standing inside this tent, the rest of what she'd said finally sank in.

"By sunset tomorrow?"

She nodded and then pushed the buffalo robe aside and got up on her knees.

"No one is going to be happy, but they have to be told," she muttered.

"It doesn't matter whether they like it or not," he said, and began feeling around for their clothing until he found the pieces that had been washed clean of the blood.

"They aren't all dry," he said, wishing for light inside the tent.

"We've worn them wet plenty of times," Tyhen said. "Can you find my shift?"

"Just give me a few minutes to sort all this out," he said.

She could just see the shape of his body as he knelt beside her.

"You are well?" she asked, as she laid a hand on his back, making sure she felt no fever.

He paused, then turned around and found her mouth in the darkness as surely as a moth flies straight to the only light. The kiss was brief but it raised the wind around them, lifting the hair from her back and feeding the hunger for him in her belly. The power with which he kissed her was telling. He was back to his old self.

"I am well. The Old Ones gave me back in fighting shape," he said.

"Then it is enough," she said, and began to get dressed.

Suwanee was dreaming of Evan when she began hearing what she thought was someone shouting. It wasn't until she sat up that she realized it was the Dove calling everyone to awaken.

They spilled out of their lodges and their sleeping tents and looked up into the air. The sky was overcast, hiding the shy quarter moon. They could barely see Tyhen, but they heard her loud and clear.

"Tomorrow evening great herds of the wooly beasts you call Tatanka will arrive in this valley and with them comes a storm. Much snow will fall, trapping them here. We have to be gone before that happens."

Except for an undertone of panic, the people did not question what she said. The New Ones were used to reacting to Tyhen's warnings at a moment's notice and immediately began putting out smoldering campfires and repacking the things they had unpacked yesterday morning.

The tribes who'd been waiting at the Gathering gladly obeyed. They had been waiting on the arrival of the Dove so that they could return to their homelands, and now their wait was over.

Tyhen flew back over the New Ones, her heart aching with the knowledge that she would never see these people again. They were already packing. The ache in her chest was so sharp that it hurt to draw breath.

She thought of Montford and Susie, and of Johnston who made the best knives and jerky. She thought of the healer, Myra Begay, and of Keechee, the weaver from Cayetano's palace. She knew somewhere down there Lola and Aaron were packing up thinking Dakotah would go with them, but she knew now that he would not. Because of the baby she carried, Dakotah would go with her.

She thought of the New Ones she'd grown up with, the ones

she'd played ball with back in Naaki Chava. They had shared so many memories together, and now those times were coming to an end.

She hovered over the campsite as the sky lightened in the East, and when the sun was rising over the prairie, she circled the New Ones with her arms outstretched, her dark hair flying out around her face. She was the Windwalker's daughter, but it was Tyhen who had come to say goodbye.

"My heart is heavy. We are the New Ones for only a few moments more. One journey is over but another one is beginning. You go to change history. You must not fail. My quest was to get you to the Gathering. That is done. I leave here with Yuma's people, the Cherokee, and I leave here with his baby in my belly. The next Windwalker for the People is already waiting to be born."

A great roar of jubilation rose up, vibrating the air around her. She searched the crowd below her for Yuma's face and then heard him first.

I am here below you. Look down.

And so she did, straight into his gaze. He was smiling.

Then she saw Dakotah standing beside him. With a trembling voice, she continued her goodbye.

"Walk into your new life knowing that my daughter already has her own eagle. He is waiting for her to be born. See Dakotah! See the boy who stands with my Yuma. She will love him forever and he will protect her with his life."

Then she heard Adam and Evan's voices.

He knows her name. He said she already told him.

At that moment, Tyhen felt the weight of centuries upon her back.

Does he tell you what it is? she asked.

Walela.

Tyhen was speaking slowly as she tried out the word.

Wah – lee' – la, she said, accenting the second syllable, then she heard Evan chuckle.

Yes. It is the Cherokee word for butterfly, which is most fitting. It begins as one thing and turns into another, just as the baby will do. She will be as others for a while until she turns into a Windwalker like you.

Tyhen sighed. Not once had she made a decision of her own. Even her own baby was already named before it was born.

CHAPTER FOURTEEN

Sadness and an air of inevitability hung over the New Ones' campsite as they hastily packed. They tried to pretend it was just another camp to break, but it was doubtful they would ever see each other again. Their shared tragedies had been brutal, but they were leaving with people who had no knowledge of their time. Their past would cease to exist in order to make certain their people's future would thrive. It was a heartbreaking moment that had been long in coming.

If they'd stayed true to plan, Lola and Aaron would have gone with the Navajo back to their homelands, but in the end she had been unable to leave Dakotah behind, so while the rest of the Nantay family and dozens of others went with the Navajo, Lola and Aaron stayed with the contingent of New Ones attached to the Cherokee tribe. Now they were waiting for a chief called Small Foot, so named because one foot was much smaller than the other. Although there were six other chiefs from the seven clans of the Cherokee with them, it would be by his order when the march began.

Yuma's excitement was obvious. He was talking and laughing as he walked among the tribe, knowing he was going to be instrumental in helping his father's people.

Tyhen was standing at the end of a journey her mother had begun and didn't know how to feel. Whatever happened after this was out of her control.

The wind was sharp today, a forerunner of the storm of cold and frozen. The hood on her winter coat had slipped off her head, giving the wind easy access to the long tangled locks around her face before rudely whipping them across her eyes.

The baby she carried still didn't seem real. She had not heard her voice. She had not felt her move, and yet she knew the Old Ones did not lie. All of her thoughts were as tangled as her hair and she had no idea of how to put either one of them back in place. With a sigh, she turned to look at what was left of the Gathering.

The tall grass was trampled as far as the eye could see, and the places where cooking fires had been were absent of grass altogether. A tiny tendril of smoke spiraled up from cooling ashes nearby. She absently stomped it with her foot as Dakotah moved into her line of vision.

He was wrapped in the winter robe Lola had made for him long before the weather got cold. His moccasins were rabbit skin turned inside out so that the fur was against his bare feet, and the rabbit fur leggings went all the way up his deerskin pants to his knees. The hood on his robe was lined with the same fur as his leggings, and his knife was tied to a rawhide belt around his waist. He was a miniature version of every warrior on the plains and the intensity on his face was almost frightening.

As their gazes met, he pointed at her arms.

"You are well?"

She smiled.

"Almost, my little warrior."

He nodded, satisfied with the answer.

"I have a question. Do you have an answer?" she asked.

His eyes suddenly narrowed.

"What is the question?" he asked.

"How did you know about my baby?"

He shrugged.

"They showed me everything in a dream."

She frowned.

"Who are they?"

"The spirits who know the future. They showed it to me after my mother and father were no more."

She brushed the back of her hand against his chin. The skin was still soft and smooth like a child, but he was far from one.

"Did they tell you why you were chosen?" she asked.

He thought a moment. "They said I was brave when the

rocks rolled down from the mountain. We ran, but the rocks caught my father. After that my mother told me to run and don't look back, so I did as she asked. When I stopped running there was no one behind me. That night I could not rest. My heart was hurting so the Old Ones came to me and helped me sleep, then showed me the story in a dream."

Tyhen's heart was pounding. She had not even known him at that time and yet he was already becoming a vital part of her life.

"What did you see in the dream, little warrior?"

"I saw you holding a baby. You told me her name was Walela and you told me what it meant."

Her smile was sudden and pleased. "I told you?"

He nodded.

So she *had* named the baby. He'd just seen her future. It was a small thing, but it made her feel better.

"What else did you see in the dream?" she asked.

"You told me I was a brave warrior. You said I faced the wolves and lived. You said that when your daughter was born, I would be her forever guardian, like Yuma is yours. You said that I would protect her with my life and she would love me forever."

She was stunned.

"You saw all that in your dream?"

"It was what they showed me."

"How do you feel about that?" she asked. "Were you angry that you had been given no choices?"

"No."

She frowned. "Why not?"

"Because I no longer had any family and I was happy that I would be part of yours."

Tyhen's heart melted. She dropped to her knees.

"I am happy, too," she whispered as she wrapped her arms around him.

The shy smile that broke across his face hurt her heart. Like Yuma, he had already lost so much. She made a silent vow to make sure he would never feel abandoned again.

Lola suddenly called out from a short distance away.

"Dakotah! We go!"

Tyhen stood, a little startled that the tribe was already on the move.

"Go back to Lola now. She loves you very much... so much that she gave up her own people to stay with you."

His eyes widened as he turned and looked at the woman who'd been his caretaker for all these months.

"I did not know," he said softly, and ran back to her.

Tyhen saw Lola pull the hood up closer around his face so that the cold would not burn his skin. So two women would love him more than most, and it was good to know his heart would not be empty.

She glanced behind her, knowing she would never see this many people on the move again. Great masses of people were leaving in all directions, except into the west, because that was the direction from which the Tatanka and the snow would come. The tribes that would have been going in that direction now had to make very wide detours.

She caught glimpses of familiar faces as one by one the New Ones began looking back – waving - calling out a goodbye one last time to others who were doing the same, while others just covered their eyes and wept.

It had taken a race through the desert to outrun Firewalker, then more years of living – and some dying - in a time they had never dreamed of, along with a long miserable trek from Naaki Chava to here and this moment just to be separated forever. Today was the end of the New Ones and the beginning of the First Nation.

Then suddenly she was no longer alone. Yuma was by her side and slipped an arm around her waist.

"It is done, my little whirlwind. It is done. Come walk with me. We are on the way to the rest of our life."

His words made her weep. She was too moved to speak, but then from the look on his face there was no need. She leaned into his kiss as the cold touch of his lips began to warm her. Just as the wind around them began to spin he pulled back and took her by the hand.

"I will build you a home with strong walls and a roof that shelters you from the rain and the wind. It will have a floor to walk on and a fireplace to keep us warm. But first we have to get there."

"I am ready," she said.

They took their first steps in unison away from the site of the Gathering and never looked back.

Tyhen wasn't the only one struggling with her feelings. The ache in Suwanee's chest was so great it was hard to breathe. She wanted to cry but was afraid if she did she might never stop.

The parting between her and her father had been silent. He had touched her head then her shoulder, gripping it so firmly that for a moment she wondered if he'd changed his mind about letting her go, and then suddenly he dropped his hand and she was free.

Her heart was pounding as she ran her fingers down the side of his cheek, setting the shape of it into her memory before she turned to her mother.

Although there was a muscle jerking near Chata's eye, she stood motionless, holding a bundle in her arms as a gift for her only daughter. Suwanee would not know until later that it contained the few treasured tools they had managed to save from the river that almost swallowed them whole.

At this point, Suwanee was numb. She had dreamed all night and each dream began with a fear and ended with Evan standing between her and danger, or lying naked beneath him.

She was sad about leaving her people, and even sadder at leaving her mother and father, but the thought of never seeing Evan again was far worse. She knew their destinies were linked and was accepting of what sacrifices she had to make to stay with him.

So she took her mother's gift with tears running down her face, and turned to Evan who was waiting for her to say her goodbyes. She walked toward him with the bundle still in her arms, but his face was a blur. When she stopped before him, he slid an arm across her shoulders and pulled her close. Emotionally exhausted, she leaned into his strength. And when he took her by the hand to lead her away, she matched her stride to his so she would not fall behind. She would remember it always as the death of one life and the birth of another.

Adam watched from a distance. He saw her tears and then looked away, but it did no good. He still felt her sadness. He also knew his brother was torn between causing her grief and fulfilling his duty to Tyhen. The way to the Cherokee lands was long. Adam had seen many rivers and many mountains between that land and this, and wondered how many more times their sister would be tested before peace came into her life.

It seemed like a slap in the face that some of the tribes would have to cross the river of the Gathering before their journey could begin and the Cherokee were among them.

Once they left the campsite, they moved south along the riverbank until they found a place where the river was very wide and the water not so deep. Without hesitation people began stepping into the thigh-deep water, moving as one through the flow while making sure no one fell or was swept away.

The Cherokee moved into line behind the others, waiting their turns to ford the river. Once they stepped into the swiftly moving water, it seeped through their clothing, chilling them all the way to their bones. Some stumbled, others cried out for help when they became too cold to move, but every time that happened, someone would step up to give them a helping hand until finally they were out.

As soon as the last one stepped onto dry ground they began to run to catch up with the others. With no time to build fires and warm up or dry out, they used the rapid beat of their hearts to heat their bodies from the inside out.

Tyhen could have easily flown over the river, but she couldn't fly everyone over and quietly refused Yuma's urging to go on her own.

He remembered all too well how cold he'd been after crossing it to get to her. He didn't want her suffering that.

"You are the Windwalker's daughter. You carry our child.

No one would expect you to take to the water when you could easily cross in the air."

"I am still the Windwalker's daughter, but today I am walking with the Cherokee."

His heart swelled with pride and he said no more.

As they stepped into water up to their waists, he watched her eyes dilate with shock. The cold and the deadly pull of the undercurrents made it impossible to hurry, and by the time they came out on the other side Tyhen was holding tight to Yuma's hand.

"Are you alright?" he asked.

She was shaking so hard she couldn't speak, and nodded instead.

"We run now," Yuma said. "It will warm us quicker."

She turned loose of his hand and willed her feet to move, telling herself that if all the people who'd forded the river ahead of them could do it, then she could, too.

Suwanee was small and the water, which was thigh to waist deep on most of them, would have been up to her chin. When they reached the riverbank, she paused and looked down at the beautiful coat Evan had given her. He'd told her it was made from the skins of a spotted cat and she regretted that it was going to get wet.

"I cannot swim," she said softly and looked down, shamed that she was already causing trouble.

Evan felt her shame and fear and quickly took her hands.

"Look at me," he said.

She lifted her head.

"Do you fear me?" he asked.

"No."

"Then why does your heart beat so fast? Why do you look away from me?"

"I do not want to shame you."

He dropped his backpack and took her in his arms.

"I am so sorry this is happening. I know you are sad to leave your people, but I am forever grateful you chose to come with me. We are both stumbling through the new times. We know nothing of what is ahead of us, but know I will do everything in my power to make you happy and keep you safe."

When he hugged her, she leaned against him. He could feel her trembling. Part of it was because she was afraid of the water, and part of it was because she was in his arms.

His only option was to carry her across but he needed help, and was grateful he didn't have to ask. Within moments Adam was with them. He said nothing as he shouldered Evan's backpack while Evan helped Suwanee tie her bundle into the pack she was carrying on her back. Then he knelt.

"Climb onto my back, wrap your arms around my neck and your legs around my waist and hold on," he said.

She gave Adam a nervous look, but he was already in the water, so she did as Evan asked.

"Whatever you do, don't let go of me," he said, as he stood up, then into the water they went.

He gasped from the cold and heard Suwanee moan as she pressed her face against the back of his neck. He knew her eyes were closed, and that she trusted him with her life. Despite the current, the water wasn't quite up to his waist. Being tall had merits and this was one of them. He made the crossing with sure, steady, strides. He wouldn't let himself think of the cold and thought instead of the heat of the jungle in Naaki Chava, and the playful monkeys in the trees outside Cayetano's palace.

Once out of the water, Adam handed over the backpack and they began to run to catch up with the others. Having heavy winter clothing and robes soaking wet made it difficult to move at first, but the longer they ran, the easier it became. By the time the sun was moving toward mid-day, their clothing had begun to dry and their bodies were warm.

Dakotah had ridden across the river on Aaron's shoulders, giving him a better than average view of the masses of people making the crossing with them and wondered how many of them would die like his mother and father had before they could return to their homes.

He saw Tyhen and Yuma in the distance ahead of them, then saw the twins and the Lakota girl who was going with them. He had not realized the New Ones would be divided up and leaving with other tribes. It made him terribly sad to think of the friends he would no longer see, and then remembered his task. There would be a new Windwalker and she would be his to protect. It gave him purpose and a sense of pride that he would matter in this world after all.

Hours later:

The sun was hiding behind a cold gray sky – a warning of the building storm behind them, but it was the faint line of green rising on the horizon that held their focus. It was forest. And since most of the other trees had lost their leaves, they had to be some kind of evergreens, maybe cedar or pines.

Chief Small Foot wants to set up camp inside the trees.

Adam's voice was so abrupt it startled her, and then Evan added more information.

But he does not know if there will be room to set up their dwellings. He wants to ask you to help, but doesn't know how to approach you.

Thank you, my brothers. Tell him I go now to see what is there so I can answer his question.

She stopped and began taking off her backpack.

"What's wrong?" Yuma asked.

"The Chief needs to know if there's room to set up camp within those distant trees. I will be back."

Yuma could see her lips moving but did not hear the chant because the sound of the wind spinning around her was already drowning out her words. And when she went straight up into the air and then flew into the East, he ignored the startled gasps of those around him as he picked up her backpack and kept on walking.

Tyhen knew her destination, but what she had not expected was the sudden difference in temperature as she rose into the sky. The air above was far colder than the ground below and within seconds her eyelashes were tinged with frost and her face was burning. She didn't know the proper name for what was happening, but she felt truly cold and frozen.

Faster and faster she flew until she was so close she could see the massive limbs on the tall trees. If it had not been for the cold, it would have made her think of the jungle in which she'd grown up because she could not see an immediate end to the growth.

As she flew closer, she was startled to see that the entire southern side of the forest looked as if a great beast had leaned down and taken a huge bite out of the trees. But it was the blackened ground without any sign of new growth that told her a fire had happened there, and not so very long ago. While it was unfortunate for the forest, it was good news for the Cherokee. The massive space sheltered on three sides would serve their purpose well.

After a quick circle of the area, she flew back into the wind, and because of the cold, she flew lower to the ground.

As she did, she saw two piles of upturned earth and recognized them as what the New Ones called graves. The Mayans had not buried their dead in this way, but according to the teachings of her mother, the white men did. No grass had grown back, so they had to be fairly new and she guessed it was some of the soldiers she had confronted who died from the sickness they had carried. Seeing those graves was a stark reminder that they were traveling a very dangerous road.

Upon her return, she looked for Chief Small Foot and when she saw a man with long gray hair and a black buffalo robe over his shoulders, she knew it was him.

As she landed, her sudden appearance startled him because he stopped and took a quick step back. Upon second look, she saw a man of stature, both in behavior and height. He made her think of Cayetano and so she gave him the respect deserving of a leader by waiting for him to speak first.

"What do you have to tell me?" Chief Small Foot asked.

"I have seen a place inside the trees with room to make camp. Not long ago there was a great fire. Many trees have burned away and others fell over onto the ground. There will be dead wood for your fires and space for the lodges."

The chief nodded, obviously pleased with the news.

"The Cherokee thank the Dove for this news. It is good."

"What do you want your people to know and I will tell them," Tyhen said.

"Tell them they must lengthen their strides. The snow comes faster. Tell them there is a place inside the woods for us to camp."

"It is done," Tyhen said, and quickly took to the air and relayed the chief's message.

It seemed to give the tribe new focus as they picked up the pace. They were all anxious about the snow and relieved to know there was a campsite ahead.

As she circled the marchers, one warrior let out a loud cry. It was not a word, but a sound... yiyiyiyiyiyi... a cry of celebration and of thanks. Traveling home with the Dove at their side was their talisman.

By the time she found Yuma and set down beside him, there were ice crystals in her eyelashes and throughout her hair.

Yuma took one look at her and pulled her into his arms then turned to shelter her so that it was his back that was to the wind.

"You are too cold," he said sharply.

She did not argue.

He took her face in his hands, kissing her long and hard until he felt her skin warming beneath the palms of his hands and didn't stop until he heard her moan.

Her eyelids were closed, her mouth slightly parted as he reluctantly pulled back.

"We need to go now," he said softly.

Tyhen slowly opened her eyes.

"We will do this again?"

He ran a finger along the underside of her bottom lip.

"We will do this again," he promised.

She picked up her backpack and settled it into a comfortable position.

Once again Adam's voice was in her head.

The storm will be bad.

And again, Evan added information.

But it will not stay long on the ground.

Thank you, my brothers. Then walk faster. It will take far longer for you to get there than it did for me to fly.

CHAPTER FIFTEEN

It took longer to reach the campsite than it did for the Cherokee women to set up camp. It was an eye-opening experience for the New Ones to realize that task was considered women's work. Yuma could tell by the look on Lola's face that Aaron wasn't going to get off so easy, and neither would he.

It was also something of a shock to the Cherokee warriors seeing the men doing most of the heavy work in the New Ones camps. Yuma smiled and nudged Tyhen when he saw the warriors nervously eyeing their own women, who were taking in the differences in their lifestyles.

"Already the changes are being noted," he said.

Tyhen stared at the size of the lodge poles the women were dragging, and the skill with which they set them up before unrolling the skins that made up the outer shell of the tipis they called lodges.

"And none too soon," she muttered. "Look at how small some of those women are and yet they are expected to set up those up alone?"

"I see women helping each other, but I do not see men helping with this in any way," Yuma said.

"Then you can show them," Tyhen said.

Yuma laughed.

A shiver of longing moved through her, making her ache to be with him. She waited for the day when she could live life for herself – with Yuma – and with their child.

Then a cold gust of wind slapped her in the face, reminding her of why they were here and what needed to be done, and she returned to the task of unpacking.

And then Chief Small Foot walked up, saw the condition of the small tents they were unpacking, and called them together.

He was not a large man, but his demeanor was regal. The force of his voice accentuated his words as he pointed at the tents they were beginning to erect.

"These are too thin. They are too small. The snow will make them fall on you. You will die from the cold."

"It is all we have," Yuma said.

"Then you will share our lodges until you are able to make one of your own. Wait here. People will come for you."

The New Ones looked at each other and then shrugged as the Chief walked away. A short time later more than a half dozen warriors came to them and led them through the campgrounds, depositing a New One here and two New Ones there, until all who'd come were bedded down inside lodges.

Tyhen and Yuma were in a lodge with a woman called Willow. Her husband had died at the Gathering while waiting for the New Ones to come. Willow was as grateful for the company as she was having a warrior at her fire. Yuma would become the hunter, the one who provided, and she would no longer be one of the lonely women who looked to the charity of others for the food she would eat.

Willow nervously received the Dove into her lodge but did not know how to talk to her until she realized Tyhen was suffering from the cold. At that point she spread a buffalo robe near the cooking fire in the center, then laid another stick onto the fire.

"You sit. Be warm," Willow said.

Tyhen sat, grateful to be off her feet and near the fire. The conical shape of a tipi was a perfect shelter – protection from the wind and cold – large enough inside for a small cooking fire and a small opening in the top for the smoke to go through. Both the silence and the warmth overcame her as she lay down and curled up. She felt Yuma's touch as a cover was pulled over her shoulders and the last thing she heard was Yuma telling Willow he was going to get more wood.

Because Adam and Evan looked alike, it was assumed they would stay together, but with room for only two in the next lodge, it was about to cause a problem.

Adam felt Evan's immediate confusion and quickly spoke.

"She goes with him," Adam said, resisting the urge to even touch Suwanee's shoulder as he pointed her out. Touching her would have tuned him into everything she was feeling. It was difficult enough to accept she would never belong to him without experiencing how she felt about his brother.

He moved on with the others without looking back, relieving them of the need to feel guilty, but Evan felt it just the same. Their separation was inevitable, yet he couldn't help feeling he'd betrayed him.

Suwanee did not know how to relate what she was feeling. Although Evan seemed satisfied, she could tell he was bothered, and when she slipped her hand into his, she heard his thoughts. It was something she'd always been able to do once she touched anyone, but she never spoke of it. Now she was wondering if she should keep it a secret from Evan, too.

He glanced at her.

"I think you are like Adam and like me. Whether you tell me or not, I will always know," he said softly.

She saw the truth in his dark eyes. And so it would be.

Wolf Cries, the warrior who took them into his lodge, pointed at his wife.

"I am Wolf Cries. She is Red Wing," he said.

"I am called Evan. This is my woman. Her name is Suwanee."

Suwanee's pulse kicked. He called her his woman. She glanced up, caught him watching her and realized he felt what she was feeling. The desire to be naked with him was great, but there was no place for them to be alone.

Evan wanted to be with Suwanee. He wanted to experience in the flesh that which he had experienced in spirit. He wanted to be inside her when his body took flight. But they were not alone and he knew they were not entirely welcome here. He could hear their thoughts and knew they were uneasy about sleeping among strangers.

In the long run, it was Suwanee's gentle nature and quick smile that warmed Red Wing's heart, and in doing so also eased their fears. When Wolf Cries announced he was going into the forest to hunt, Evan went with him.

They left dressed for the cold and carrying their spears. The walk through the campground was short, and once inside the trees, everything seemed to come alive. They could hear a high-pitched whistle as the wind moved across the long grass, and when it reached the forested area and began moving through the needled branches of the pines, its voice turned into whispers and moans, warning of the impending storm.

They were not the only ones on the hunt and what game might have been close had already been scared away. It was a while before they found a deer trail, and once Evan saw the tracks and tuned in, he was able to lead the way to a small herd of deer.

Wolf Cries was impressed with the light-skinned warrior's hunting and tracking skills and was rethinking his reluctance to welcome them into his lodge. He tapped Evan on the shoulder then pointed, indicating his target. Evan nodded, then pointed to the deer he intended to take.

They were downwind from the herd and sure-footed, moving silently through the trees until they were close enough. They stepped out of cover at the same time, took aim and threw.

Evan's aim was sure and deadly. The deer stumbled a few yards and dropped.

Wolf Cries spear found its mark, but he had to chase his deer several hundred yards before its heart finally stopped and then it fell.

Evan dropped to one knee, wasting no time as he quickly field dressed his kill, then he threw the deer carcass over his shoulder and went to find his hunting partner.

Wolf Cries was struggling to bleed and gut the deer, wishing he'd brought the knife made of bone when Evan tapped him on the shoulder.

"I share this with you," Evan said, and handed over his knife. "It is very sharp. You must be careful of that blade."

Wolf Cries was elated, and at the same time in awe of how

easily it cut through skin and flesh. In no time he had bled and gutted his kill, wrapped up the heart and liver and put them in his hunting pouch. He cleaned the blade and then reluctantly handed the knife back to Evan.

"It is good," he said gruffly.

Evan nodded, slipped the knife back through his belt and shouldered his kill.

They were on the way back when Wolf Cries curiosity got the best of him.

"How do you know our language?" he asked.

Evan thought of all the hours Singing Bird had spent teaching them when they were younger, and how all of the New Ones in Naaki Chava had learned each other's words and how to say them.

"We know many languages," he said. "It was part of our preparation before we came to you."

Wolf Cries heard, but his curiosity was not yet satisfied.

"You are not as we are," he said, pointing to Evan's paler skin.

"No. My brother and I had no family and so we were raised with your people."

Wolf Cries understood that concept. They often raised children from other tribes, sometimes stealing them to give to their women who had either lost a child or were barren. He started to comment and then remembered being told that the old ways had to change. No warring with other tribes. No stealing their women or children. The new way was strange.

Evan also took advantage of Wolf Cries' distraction to check him out. The warrior was of average height with dark skin and a gray wolf's tail hanging from his belt.. He had heard Wolf Cries' earlier thoughts and knew the man was envious of the knife and a little embarrassed that his kill had not been as clean as Evan's.

When they arrived back into the encampment, Wolf Cries began looking for certain lodges until he found one he was looking for and called out.

An old woman emerged smiling, obviously pleased to see the hunters. Wolf Cries pulled out the heart he'd cut from the deer and gave it to her.

As she took the meat wrapped in leaves and disappeared into her lodge, Evan realized the woman had no man.

"One more," Wolf Cries said, and began a second search through the camp until he saw a lodge with the image of three deer painted on the hides.

Again he called out, and yet another old woman emerged, received the liver he gave her with great ceremony, and ducked back into her lodge out of the cold.

"They have no hunters in their lodges?" Evan asked.

"The first woman is Red Wing's mother. Her father died on the walk to the Gathering. This woman is my mother. She has been alone for two winters."

Evan's general opinion of Wolf Cries was growing. Not only had he been willing to take two strangers into his lodge, but he was also taking care of two more women. It was something for the New Ones to remember as they assimilated themselves into this tribe. These people might be less that civilized in appearance, but their culture already knew about taking care of others.

While Evan was returning to Wolf Cries' lodge with fresh meat, Adam was sitting by the fire of Dull Knife and Cloud Woman, painfully aware of their opinion of him. He carried no weapons and there was little food in his pack for them to share. While it shamed him to ask, he sent a panicked message to Evan.

You are hunting?

Yes, with good luck. We took two deer.

I have nothing to give these people.

I will gladly share, brother. Tell them I am in camp and I bring food. They won't care where it comes from.

Again, Adam was made painfully aware of how useless he was in this place.

I thank you.

Evan seemed angry at his brother's defeated behavior.

You are my brother. You are not useless and you are as needed as I am, but for different reasons.

Adam looked up at the warrior and his woman who were staring at him from across the small fire burning in the center of the lodge.

"My brother brings fresh meat. He will be here soon to share with you."

The scowl on Dull Knife's face lifted.

Cloud Woman grabbed a leather water pouch and ran out to fill it from the creek nearby.

Adam linked into the warrior's thoughts and began to relax. The man wasn't angry. He was trying to hide his fear of the tall man with the pale skin.

Adam leaned forward and spoke Cherokee in a soft, rhythmic tone.

"I have no weapons, but I can help. I will bring in more firewood."

Dull Knife frowned.

"Woman's work," he muttered.

Adam shook his head.

"Not anymore," he said shortly, and stood, well aware that by stature alone he was looming over the man.

Dull Knife blinked.

Adam ducked down and left him sitting.

Things were already changing for both of them, whether they liked it or not.

Lola, Aaron, and Dakotah were in the lodge belonging to Rabbit Runs. He was old and withered, a small man with long white flyaway hair. He might have been able to run like a rabbit once upon a time, but now he walked with a limp. And because he had no woman in his tipi, there was no cooking fire burning inside it.

Dakotah looked around at the few things hanging from the lodge poles and then sat down near where Lola was busy building a fire. He wasn't afraid of the old man, but his clothing was torn and stained and he seemed to not know what was happening. He heard Lola whispering to Aaron in the English language. He heard her say the word, senile, but he didn't know what it meant.

Rabbit Runs seemed excited about the possibility of a fire and began pushing the small pile of twigs and leaves toward where Lola was sitting.

Aaron hesitated to leave Lola alone with the old man, but they were going to need wood and food.

"Dakotah, come with me. You will bring wood to this lodge. I go to hunt food."

Lola nodded and then smiled at the boy, who looked a bit concerned about leaving her behind.

"I will be fine," she said.

Dakotah wasn't so sure, but the sooner he came back with the firewood the better.

And so the evening went. The New Ones were settling in, and the Cherokee adjusting to the strangers in their midst.

It was still daylight and the smoke of many fires was rising above the treetops when the first flakes of snow began to fall. Within in an hour, it was a white-out.

The smoke holes in the Cherokee lodges were pulled shut to keep out the snow. Small fires inside were fed slowly throughout the night while the glowing embers lit the cone-shaped interiors with a faint smoky glow.

The snow was blowing sideways out on the prairie, but the campsite was sheltered within the forest and protected from the brunt of the storm's fury.

Tyhen couldn't sleep. The force of the wind outside was stirring senses she didn't know she possessed. When she closed her eyes it felt as if she was part of the storm, flying like an arrow through the cold and frozen with no destination in sight. The thunder of her heartbeat drowned out the wind's piercing shriek. Instead of being afraid, it was familiar, like being at home.

Yuma woke between one breath and another, sensing something was wrong. He lay without moving, listening to Willow's soft snores and the howl of the wind. He could feel the weight of Tyhen's breast against the back of his hand and the steady thump of her heartbeat beneath his palm.

It wasn't until he focused on the dimly lit interior and saw the spinning smoke above their heads that he knew something was happening with Tyhen. Either she was dreaming or -

He gasped.

Without moving a muscle, he knew they were floating. The buffalo robe that had covered them was now on the floor beneath them. He didn't know what was happening but he had to stop her now before she accidentally tore down the old woman's lodge.

Tyhen! No!

Tyhen jerked as Yuma's voice broke the vision.

They dropped back onto the buffalo robe with a faint thump.

Willow snorted in her sleep and then rolled over.

Tyhen's heart was pounding as she rolled over into Yuma's arms and felt the warmth of his breath upon her face.

"What happened?" she whispered.

He lowered his voice to a husky whisper.

"You tell me. We were floating."

"I was in the wind," she said.

He frowned. "What do you mean... were you dreaming?"

"I don't think so."

"Then what?"

"I felt... it seemed to... I don't know how to explain. It has never happened to me before."

Yuma was getting worried.

"What never happened before?"

He felt her shiver and then the warmth of her breath as she whispered near his ear.

"I was in it."

He frowned.

"In what, Tyhen?"

"The wind... the storm... I was part of the storm. The wind is in me. I am the wind. I cannot explain."

The hair crawled on the back of Yuma's neck. They had never considered her not being in control of the power she'd been given. What could this mean? Was she losing the human part of herself? Was she becoming what her father had been, taking human form only when it mattered?

He tightened his hold, his voice a reflection of his fear.

"You belong to me. Do you hear me? You belong to me."

She slid her arms around his neck.

"I am afraid," she whispered.

Horror enveloped him. "No, no, no! You are not the wind. You control it, but it is not you! Do you hear me! Do you understand?"

He didn't know he was shouting now, or that Willow was awake and cowering on the far side of the lodge with her skinning knife held tight within her grasp.

Tyhen winced beneath the pain of his grip.

"Yuma, don't! You are hurting me!"

He flinched as if he'd been slapped, then turned her loose and sat up. His hands were shaking as he pulled down the sides of her shift and then kissed the places where he'd gripped her too tightly.

"I am sorry. I am so sorry," he said.

Tyhen got up and crawled into his lap as he wrapped his arms around her.

"Don't lose yourself, little whirlwind. It was written before you were born that you belong to me."

In the aftermath of his fright, Yuma realized how they had frightened the old woman.

"You have nothing to fear," he said. "Come, come close to the fire and be warm."

"You were shouting," she said.

"It was from fear for my woman. She had a vision. I did not like it and that was my reaction. I am sorry. All is well."

Willow shook her head as she crawled back beneath her buffalo robe, but she took the skinning knife with her.

Yuma sighed. Life was complicated enough without living it under the nose of strangers. He lay back down, taking Tyhen with him, and pulled the cover up over them once more. Satisfied that she was safe and warm within his arms, he soon fell back to sleep.

But Tyhen couldn't sleep. Something was happening to her that was almost frightening. She had floated above the ground without conscious thought. No chant. No focus on moving up.

How would she sleep if she could not trust her own body to stay put?

It is the child within you creating the chaos.

Even though she didn't fully understand, it was the calm manner in Adam's voice that stilled her panic.

The child? How can this be?

Something more was given to you by the Old Ones when Yuma died and, in turn, it was given to her, too.

I don't understand.

Remember how your father died giving you his powers?

She thought about the heartbreak of seeing his face, what it felt like to be held in his arms, and then never seeing him again.

I remember.

So, the Old Ones have already given the child her power. You need not die for her to be who she was born to be, and it will be so from this day forward.

Oh no.

What's wrong? You should be happy you do not have to die.

But I don't want to live forever. I don't want to live without my Yuma.

I have no answer for that. But I do know that you are in no danger of disappearing. When the baby is born, you will settle back into yourself.

Her heart hurt as she closed her eyes. Just when she thought life was becoming less complicated.

CHAPTER SIXTEEN

When it was too dark within Wolf Cries lodge for Red Wing to see what she was doing, she laid aside the moccasin she was making, banked the fire, slipped out of her shift, and crawled beneath the covers of the buffalo robe as naked as the day she'd been born.

Wolf Cries watched, grunting slightly as he watched his wife undress, and when she lay down, he quickly removed his clothing and joined her without care for the fact that they had company.

Evan could see nothing, but it was obvious what they were doing beneath the heavy robe and it made him ache to be with Suwanee in the same way.

Embers from the fire lit the interior of the lodge just enough for him to see that Suwanee was already removing her shift. But instead of crawling into their bedding, she stood instead, giving him full view of her body.

Now Evan understood the meaning of Wolf Cries' grunt because it was the only sound he could make. Suwanee's hair was hanging almost to her waist. Her breasts were full, her belly slightly rounded. Her legs were shapely and when he thought about lying with her he grew hard.

When she held out her hand, he began taking off clothing as rapidly as he could manage, completely oblivious to the writhing bodies beneath the buffalo robe on the other side of the fire.

He was fully erect when he came out of his pants and leggings and even the dimness inside the tipi could not disguise his size. Suwanee shivered as her knees went weak. She wanted that inside of her. She wanted to feel the weight of his body atop her. She wanted him to come apart in her arms. It was the only power a woman had and she didn't intend to lose it.

In two steps she was in front of him and then he was pulling her down onto their blankets. His hands were shaking as he pulled their covering up over them. When he turned to face her in the darkness he used his hands to map the contours of her body. And when he slid his hand between her legs, she rolled over on her back to make room for him to come in.

Within seconds he was on top of her, sliding into the warm, wet depths of her and thought he would die from the pleasure.

Dull Knife's belly was full from the meat Adam's brother had given them. He was curled up beneath their winter robes with Cloud Woman's butt against his lap. Every time she shifted against him in her sleep he grew a little bit harder until finally he awoke fully erect. Without moving, he took her from behind, satisfying his urges without fuss or bother.

On the other side of their fire, Adam lay with his eyes wide open, listening to their heavy breathing and occasional grunts beneath their covers while staring at the smoke from their dying fire swirling about his head. With the smoke hole closed, it had nowhere else to go.

The sound of the wind was, in his mind, like the roar of a bear just before it attacked. The cured hides that made the cover for the tipi had dipped slightly inward between the lodge poles on the west side - most likely from the wind and the weight of the snow. He wondered if it would cave in on top of them and glanced across the banked embers. They didn't seem concerned. Maybe he shouldn't either.

He wondered how Evan and Suwanee had fared with their hosts and the moment he thought of them, he was in Evan's head, feeling Suwanee beneath him, feeling the lust of an erection and the wet warmth of being inside her body. The erotic sensations he had never before experienced were overwhelming. He couldn't control a thought or create an emotional block. Every move of Evan's body was his. Every gasp of pleasure Evan gave was Adam's torture. He had the need but no way to relieve it. He hated this thing called emotion. He didn't want to feel because feeling hurt. He didn't want to care, but he did. He wanted to touch himself but was afraid he would die. All of a sudden there was a wash of heat throughout his body then he felt it gathering, gathering until there was nothing in his thought but the blood rushing toward his erection. Nearly out of his mind, he heard a moan and when he realized it was coming from his own mouth, he panicked. Frantic not to wake the couple and embarrass himself even more than he already had, he rolled over onto his belly, buried his face against his arm and rode Evan's climax all the way to the end, spilling his own seed onto his covers as Evan came undone in his sweet woman's arms.

Lola and Aaron slept facing each other with Dakotah between them. The fire she'd built earlier was now the source of heat keeping the lodge warm.

Earlier, Aaron had come back from hunting with six rabbits – enough for food for all four of them and a little to eat tomorrow in case the snow was too deep in which to hunt.

She had gladly prepared the meat but yearned for vegetables and fruit. As she slept, she dreamed of a roof over their heads and food growing in her garden. In the dream she was planting the seeds she had been carrying from Naaki Chava for all these long months. She carried them through fording the rivers and the hot, dry desert - through the rain and the cold. Even when they believed they might die in the prairie fire, she had not tossed them aside to lighten her load. They were more valuable to her now than any amount of money could have ever been from the land before Firewalker, and in her dream she was planting them in the ground.

They slept without concern, thankful to be in this lodge and not in the small tent in the middle of the storm. They didn't know that Rabbit Runs was awake or that he was packing his things. In the old man's troubled mind he didn't know where his woman was and he needed to find her. It wasn't the first time he'd done this. The people in his tribe knew his spirit was lost and tried to watch out for him, but it was a survival of the fittest life in which they lived and there was a limit to their charity and concern.

Rabbit Runs was muttering to himself as he stuffed random things into his hunting pouch, then he picked up his spear and stepped over Aaron's feet as he moved toward the exit.

It was the blast of cold air on Dakotah's face that woke him. He opened his eyes just as the old man slipped out of the tipi. Within moments swirling snow was inside the tipi and the temperature took a drastic drop.

Dakotah cried out.

"Stop him! He will die!"

Aaron was awake and trying to figure out what was happening and Lola woke with confusion, thinking something was happening to Dakotah.

"He went out! The old man went outside!" Dakotah cried. "I saw him."

Lola and Aaron began putting on their cold weather clothing as Dakotah ran to pull down the flap to keep out the cold and snow.

Aaron was frantically wrapping leggings over his deerskin pants, desperate to get to Rabbit Runs before the old man was lost.

Lola was shaking from the cold as she knelt at the smoldering fire and added a few small sticks.

All of a sudden Adam's voice was in Dakotah's head.

Tell Aaron the old man is but a few steps outside the lodge. He is already dead. It was his heart.

"Aaron! Stop! Adam said he is already dead."

Both Lola and Aaron turned and stared at the boy.

"What do you mean, Adam told you?"

"I heard his voice in my head. He said, 'tell Aaron the old man is just outside.' He said he is dead. He said it was his heart."

Aaron frowned.

"Has this ever happened to you before? Hearing voices, I mean?"

Dakotah shrugged.

"Sometimes the Old Ones talk to me in my sleep."

Lola was trying not to panic and accept yet another facet of this strange boy she'd come to love.

Aaron wrapped the buffalo robe around him, tied it tight at the waist so it would not fly away in the wind.

"Just outside the tent, he said?"

Dakotah nodded.

Lola didn't want him to leave.

"You might get lost, too. What if you don't find your way back?"

Aaron accepted the possibility and dug through his pack until he pulled out a rope made of long grass and rawhide braided together which he then tied to his wrist. He handed the other end to Lola.

"So you will hold onto me then, okay?"

She nodded, satisfied to know that if he got turned around he could follow the rope back to her.

Tell Aaron to count ten steps forward from the doorway. He is there in the snow.

"Adam says count ten steps forward from the doorway. He is there in the snow."

Aaron nodded, then bent down and untied the flap, crawled out into the darkness and was immediately swallowed by the storm.

Lola knelt in the low opening, thinking she would be able to see Aaron, but it was impossible. The snow was swirling in around her as the bitter cold once again swept through the lodge. The new fire crackled once behind her as she fed out the rope while praying that the fire did not die.

Suddenly the rope was no longer moving!

"He must have found him," Lola said, but her fingers were now numb and she couldn't quit shaking.

The moments lengthened and she was on the point of panic when she felt two tugs on the rope and swallowed on a sob.

Aaron had him! They were coming back. Then he tugged twice again and Lola moaned. She didn't understand.

"He wants you to pull it," Dakotah cried. "He cannot see where to go. He needs you to pull so he can follow."

She gave the boy a frantic glance and then nodded.

"Yes, yes, I will pull him in."

"Not too hard. It must not break," Dakotah said.

Lola was so cold she wasn't thinking clearly and when Dakotah appeared behind her and began pulling in the rope hand over hand, she crawled back toward the fire and put on a larger piece of wood. Within moments Aaron was crawling in the doorway, dragging the old man's body with him.

As soon as he was inside Dakotah pulled the flap shut and tied it off, then followed Aaron to the fire and untied the rope from his wrist. He rolled it back up again and stowed it in his pack while Aaron was trying to get warm. He hadn't moved since he reached the heat and he couldn't talk because his lips were frozen together.

Lola was crying as she rubbed his face and hands, trying to warm them while Dakotah sat with his legs crossed, his gaze fixed on Rabbit Runs' eyes. One had frozen open and the other was frozen shut. It looked like he was winking.

Dakotah wondered if his father and mother had seen their death coming in this way, then pulled his knees up to his chin and hid his face. He didn't want to see this anymore.

Is everyone okay?

Dakotah nodded, then realized Adam couldn't see him. He wondered if he thought his answer would Adam hear it.

Yes. Aaron is very cold. Rabbit Runs is dead.

It was his fate. You did good, Dakotah. You heard my words. You did good.

Lola was still crying and Aaron was beginning to shake.

Dakotah wanted to cry, too, but it would serve no purpose so he covered the old man with a sleeping robe so he wouldn't have to see him again.

The snow stopped sometime the next morning. By midday the sun was out and forming a thin icy crust on more than three feet of accumulated snow.

Adam's night from hell had ended with a death. In his mind it could have not been any worse. Even though Dull Knife and

Cloud Woman were sleeping soundly just a few feet away, he had never felt so alone. When the inside of the tipi began to get cold, he moved to the fire, stirred a few embers and added a small piece of wood. Once it caught, he added one more and then sat and watched them burn while thinking of Naaki Chava.

As soon as he knew Tyhen was awake he sent her the message.

Yuma was outside the tipi removing snow from the west side of the teepee to keep it from falling inward from the weight.

Tyhen was trying to apologize to Willow for upsetting her last night, but Willow was still bothered by their loud shouts in the middle of the night and was having none of it. When she heard Adam's voice in her head she was actually relieved.

Tyhen. You have a duty.

To do what, my brother?

A man died last night. His name is Rabbit Runs. Lola and her family were put in his lodge but his mind was not right. He left the lodge during the storm and Dakotah saw him leave. Aaron found him a few feet from the lodge. You need to tell Chief Small Foot that the old man did not die from the cold. His heart quit before he froze. It will matter to him to know this. I think the old man was somehow related to him.

I will tell him now.

Dress warmly. The snow is deep. Don't walk. Fly.

Tyhen was so bothered by the news that she missed the despondent note in Adam's voice.

When she began putting on all of her furs and leggings Willow stopped what she was doing.

"What is happening? Where are you going?" she asked.

"To tell Chief Small Foot of a death last night.

Willow frowned.

"How do you know this?

"My brothers are shamans. They talk to the spirits. They see the future. They see the past. I hear their voices in my head."

Willow's eyes widened. It was a stark reminder that the guests in her lodge were most unusual and her attitude shifted.

"Did he say who it was that died?"

"An old man named Rabbit Runs."

Willow frowned as she pointed to her head.

"He was a man with no spirit. It left him when his woman died. He did not know what he was doing and now his suffering has ended."

Tyhen absorbed the matter-of-fact manner in which Willow received the news and hoped the chief took it the same way.

When she stepped out of the lodge, the bitter cold began to bite her face, making it tingle and burn.

Yuma saw her immediately and stomped his way through the snow to her.

"What are you doing? It's too cold to be outside."

"You are here," she said, and then began to explain. "Adam told me an old man died last night. It was the lodge where Lola and her family slept. I have to go tell the chief."

Yuma quickly unwrapped the rabbit skins from the lower half of his face and wrapped them around her instead until all he could see was her eyes and forehead.

"Hurry back," he said.

She was already chanting and when she lifted her arms, went straight up.

The wind was sharper above the ground and so she wasted no time.

Adam. Evan. Can one of you tell me which lodge belongs to Chief Small Foot?

Evan's voice was suddenly in her ear.

Dull Knife said it is the largest lodge facing the rising sun. It has the image of an eagle near the top of the smoke hole.

Yes, I see it.

Moments later she landed a few yards from the front entrance and called out.

"Chief Small Foot! I am Tyhen. I bring a message."

Moments later a woman stepped out into the cold, holding the flap aside so that Tyhen could enter.

The chief was sitting cross-legged in a nest of many robes and blankets made of many kinds of skins. Their cooking fire was alive and the smoke hole opened enough to let out most of the smoke.

"What is this message?" he asked.

She pulled the fur down from around her mouth.

"One of my brothers tells me one of the Cherokee is no more. His spirit left him last night during the storm."

The chief frowned.

"What name did he wear?"

Tyhen glanced at the chief's woman. She didn't know how, but she knew the old man was somehow connected to her.

"Rabbit Runs."

The woman dropped to her knees and began to wail.

"I am sorry," Tyhen said.

Chief Small Foot nodded.

"His spirit was lost. He had been waiting for it to find him again."

"My brother said the old man ran out into the storm. New Ones were staying with him and one of them ran out after him. He was already gone before he found him."

The Chief was on his feet.

"He went into the storm after Rabbit Runs?"

She nodded.

He grunted softly.

"A brave warrior. He could have lost his own life for one who was already gone."

Tyhen shrugged.

"It is how we live," she said.

The chief heard her words and was silent for a few moments before he finally nodded.

"It is good," he said. "Tell your people some will come to prepare his body, but that they will no longer be able to stay there."

Tyhen didn't question the decision.

"I will tell them," she said, then glanced at the weeping woman one last time and left.

She stood for a few moments outside the chief's lodge to gather her emotions, and then she sent her brothers one last message.

Adam! Evan! Can Dakotah hear you?

They answered in unison.

Yes. We already told him the Chief is sending someone for the body.

She sighed, grateful for their presence.

Thank you.

They didn't answer, but it didn't matter. The situation was no longer her problem.

She pulled the rabbit furs back up around her face and then took to the sky. She saw Yuma watching for her outside the lodge and when she landed the snow spun up around her.

"Come inside quickly. Willow has hot food," Yuma said, and then watched her eyes narrow.

"What's wrong?" he asked.

She shrugged.

"Willow does not like me."

"But I do," Yuma said, then pulled the fur down to her chin and kissed her.

She kissed him back with quick abandon and then slipped inside the lodge with Yuma right behind her.

Willow was kneeling by the fire. She looked up, frowning as the cold came in with them.

Tyhen went straight to the fire to warm, and when Willow saw her fingers trembling from the cold and the red burn to her cheeks, her expression softened.

"I think much of your life is given to others."

Quick tears burned Tyhen's eyes but she blinked them away.

"It is why I was born," she said, but she was thinking of Dakotah in the tipi with a dead man and wondering how he fared.

She let Yuma unwind the furs from her face and neck, and then sat with the heavy robe still around her shoulders until the lodge felt warm again.

It was a sobering way to begin a day.

⚭

Lola, Aaron, and Dakotah were sitting quietly within Rabbit Runs' lodge when four women entered, followed by the chief and his wife.

The moment they entered, the trio stood, their gazes looking down in respect to the grieving family.

Chief Small Foot eyed the body beneath the buffalo robe, then looked at the New Ones standing before him.

"There is a warrior waiting for you outside of this lodge. He will take you to the lodge of White Hawk. His leg is crooked and he can no longer hunt. You will feed him and he will shelter you. It is a fair trade."

"We thank you," Aaron said.

Small Foot walked closer, staring straight into Aaron's eyes.

"What are you called?"

"I am Aaron."

Small Foot said the name, but it sounded strange on his tongue.

"You went out into the storm for the old one?"

Aaron nodded, then pointed to the boy. "If it had not been for Dakotah, we might not have known he was gone."

The chief then looked at the boy between them.

"This is your son."

Before they could answer, Dakotah lifted his head.

"I am Dakotah, the son of Michael Chavez."

Chief Small Foot frowned. In their culture, children did not speak for themselves unless asked, but these were the New Ones and it would seem this was no longer so.

"Where is your father?" he asked.

Dakotah's chin quivered once, but his gaze never wavered.

"He died running from the mountain that came undone."

Lola put a hand on the back of his head.

"Many died that day, including both of his parents. He was alone. We have cared for him for many months."

The chief grunted, curious about such a boy.

"You saw Rabbit Runs leave his lodge?"

Dakotah nodded.

"The cold air woke me up."

Small Foot pointed at his wife.

"She is Little Wren, my wife. Rabbit Runs was her father."

Dakotah's eyes widened. Without hesitation he pulled out of Lola's grasp and went straight toward her.

"Dakotah! No!" Lola said, embarrassed that he was not behaving properly in front of the chief.

But the chief held up his hand, curious as to what this small boy would do next.

Dakotah heard Lola, but the woman's cries were louder and they hurt his heart. Within seconds he was beside her. When he touched her shoulder, he felt her flinch.

"My father died, too. I am sorry for your sadness," he said softly.

It was the sudden appearance of a New One that stopped her tears, and the fact that it was a child trying to give her comfort was even more of a curiosity.

Her face was still streaked with tears, but there was a look of wonder in her eyes.

"What is your name, boy?" she asked.

"I am called Dakotah."

"Your father is no more?"

He nodded, then squatted down beside her, curious as to what the four women were doing.

"What are they doing?" he asked.

Little Wren took a deep breath and then wiped the tears from her face.

"They are preparing his body. It is part of our burial custom."

"You do it every time?"

She nodded.

The frown between his eyes deepened.

"What happens if you do not prepare?"

She answered without thinking.

"Then he would not be able to find his way to the Great Spirit."

Dakotah rocked back on his heels. There was a pain in the middle of his chest and it was getting bigger with every breath. He pressed a hand against his heart, trying to stop the ache, but it did no good. When the tears began rolling silently down his cheeks, Little Wren thought he was crying because of the dead body before him.

"Do not be afraid of death. It is part of life," she said.

Dakotah just shook his head as the tears continued to roll.

Lola ran to him, then knelt and took him into her arms.

"Why do you cry?" she whispered.

"We did not prepare their bodies. They cannot find their

way to the Great Spirit," he wailed.

Little Wren looked horrified. She had not realized the consequences of what she'd said.

"I am sorry," she said, and then looked to her husband for an answer.

Chief Small Foot did not like it when women and children cried, especially for reasons such as this. He called out abruptly.

"Dakotah!"

The demanding tone of the chief's voice got his attention.

He wiped his tears and crawled out of Lola's arms.

"Yes, Chief?"

"My wife did not tell you of all the traditions. What they are doing here is only when the body of the dead can be found. When they cannot, we have another ceremony to help them find the right path. We will say the name Michael Chavez aloud in that ceremony so that the Old Ones will know he is coming."

Dakotah wiped snot with the back of his hand.

"And my mother... you will say Julie Chavez, too?"

Small Foot pointed at him.

"You will say the names. You will tell the Old Ones they are coming. Because you are their son, their spirits will hear your voice and will be lost no more."

A slow smile broke across Dakotah's face.

"I can do that?"

Small Foot would not look at his people because they knew he had made all that up.

"You can do that. These people who care for you. They will bring you to the ceremony for Rabbit Runs and then your sadness will be over. Yes?"

Dakotah nodded.

"Good. Then it is done. Go with the warrior outside now. He will come for you when it time for the ceremony to begin."

Dakotah gave Lola a hug and then ran to Aaron and hugged him, too.

"We are having a ceremony!" he cried.

"I heard," Aaron said. "That is good, but we have to leave now. Get your pack."

Dakotah picked it up and dashed out of the lodge without looking back.

"Thank you," Lola said.

Small Foot shrugged as he laid a hand on the back of his wife's head.

"She does not cry anymore," he said gruffly.

And that's when Lola got it. Dakotah had done for Little Wren what the chief could not. It was the mutual suffering Little Wren had seen in the boy and clung to. He'd found a way to ease her heart.

They followed Dakotah from the lodge and then followed the warrior to yet another Cherokee willing to share space.

"I am called White Hawk," the warrior said.

They saw the crooked leg and the staggering limp and then looked away.

"I am called Aaron. We are grateful for your kindness."

Lola began to unpack their things on the other side of the lodge then realized she had not spoken to their new host.

"I am called Lola. This boy is Dakotah. We look after him. Do you have a woman?"

"She is no more," White Hawk said.

"Then I am permitted to keep your fire and cook the food?"

"It will be appreciated," White Hawk said.

"I will hunt for food," Aaron said.

"Snow is too deep. Animals not come out," White Hawk said. "We have enough for now."

And so it went as the trio settled yet again.

Like many of the others, Aaron plowed through the snow long enough to gather firewood from the abundance of dead wood while Lola kept Dakotah occupied enough that he did not bother the warrior willing to share his home.

CHAPTER SEVENTEEN

Because of the rapidly changing weather and the urgency to get back to their tribal land, the Cherokee could not honor Rabbit Runs death in their traditional ways. All they could do was bury him.

So while the women were preparing his body and gathering the best of his weapons and amulets to bury with him, warriors were inside his lodge, digging the grave beneath the smoke hole where the cooking fire had been.

When they were ready, Chief Small Foot sent two warriors - one for the Dove, because she was the one who brought the message of his passing, and one for the boy called Dakotah who had ghosts to put to rest.

The twins warned Tyhen what was about to occur, so she and Yuma hurried to make themselves presentable. It had been so long since she'd cared about personal appearance that it felt strange to be spending time doing it.

She was trying to get tangles out of her hair with her fingers while bemoaning the fact she'd lost her comb somewhere between the prairie fire and the wolf attack on Dakotah.

At that point Yuma tried to help, and then the first time he accidentally pulled her hair, Willow got up from her seat near the fire, waving her hands and talking so fast neither one of them could understand her.

She pushed Yuma aside, ordered Tyhen to sit down, and then proceeded to remove every tangle out of Tyhen's hair with what looked like the pointed end of a deer antler.

For Willow, the fact that a Windwalker's daughter was human enough to have tangles in her hair had brought her down to a level that the little woman could understand.

Willow muttered and fussed as she picked out the knots, while Yuma slipped to the other side of the tent and stretched out on their bedding to watch Tyhen's face.

As thin as she was and as tumbled and tangled as her long dark hair had become, to him she was the most beautiful woman he'd ever seen. The simple act of watching her eyes flash when Willow pulled at a knot made him want her - the way she jutted her chin in mute disapproval as Willow muttered behind her back made him smile. Being snowed in inside a Cherokee lodge with her would have been ideal if it wasn't for the awkward presence of another woman. So he watched her with love in his heart, dreaming of their future and happier times.

Tyhen felt like the prey Yuma hunted. He was following her every movement without moving a muscle, almost as if he was waiting to pounce. His eyelids were nearly closed and his mouth was slightly parted. She knew he was thinking about making love to her and the feeling was mutual, but there was Willow behind them and a body that needed burying.

A few minutes later Willow grunted and laid the aged bone aside. She was through.

Breathing a sigh of relief that it was over, Tyhen impulsively grabbed Willow's hands and gave them a quick squeeze.

"Thank you," she said.

Willow tried to pretend it didn't matter that the Windwalker's daughter was pleased with her, but she was smiling as she resumed her seat by the fire.

Within minutes they began to hear the steady crunch of snow. Footsteps! And when the footsteps ceased and then a voice called out, they knew the warrior had come to take them to the burial. She followed Yuma out of the lodge, leaving the old woman behind to tend the fire.

After the dim and smoky interior, the glittering reflection of sun on snow was blinding. They were still blinking to adjust their vision as the warrior led them away.

At first Yuma was focused only on Tyhen and getting her out of the cold, but as they walked through the camp he began noticing people coming out of their lodges and then standing in silence as they moved past. He had already guessed the deep snow was going to limit any kind of ceremony for Rabbit Runs, passing, but instead of staying in where it was warm, they were coming out to stand witness as a gesture of respect.

Tyhen saw them and remembered leaving Naaki Chava without the ceremony they had expected because the downpour of rain was so heavy. And now the weather made it difficult for the people to get to the ceremony, so they had come to stand witness so the family would know they cared.

Some were crying; others stared mutely as they watched them pass. She thought about all of the people they'd lost since their exit from Naaki Chava, remembering them with sadness. The Cherokee must be feeling the same way in losing theirs. These people had left their villages for her, to hear the message she would bring, and she could only imagine how many were wondering if it was worth it.

She was still lost in thought when the trek ended abruptly at a lodge. She looked at Yuma.

"I thought he was taking us to the burial," she whispered.

"You will see," Yuma said.

"You wait," the warrior said, and disappeared inside the lodge.

When they heard footsteps behind them, they turned to see who was coming and when they saw Lola, Aaron, and Dakotah approaching, led by another warrior, they were surprised. They had been guests in Rabbit Runs' lodge, but only for one night. She wondered why they were here when the rest of the village was not, but before she could ask what was happening they were summoned to enter.

Tyhen glanced at Yuma.

Is there a ceremony before the burial? Is that why we are here?

Yuma shook his head.

I think this is where they will bury him.

"Chief Small Foot waits," the warrior said, urging them

inside.

Yuma ducked down and led the way inside with Tyhen right behind him. It was very dim and cold without the fire and there was a shallow grave where the fire would have been burning. Yuma was right, she thought. Here is where he will be buried.

All of a sudden Evan's voice was in her ear.

Dakotah is there because he has a mission to fulfill. It will help him deal with the grief of his parents deaths.

She was startled. Unaware the boy was still grieving, she felt guilty for not knowing it.

Yuma moved up beside her and put his hand at her waist, but said nothing. His gaze was focused on the boy, wondering if he was upset by this death, but could tell nothing from Dakotah's behavior. He was as still and stone-faced as the chief standing at the foot of the grave.

The chief's wife, Little Wren, was kneeling beside her father's body, quietly weeping.

Tyhen glanced at her briefly before looking down at the old man and immediately thought of Stanley Blue Jacket. He had been small and withered like this.

Rabbit Runs had been laid out on the buffalo robe under which he used to sleep, and they had dressed him in what must have been his best. His long white hair hung in two braids over his shoulders, and there was an eagle feather tied into his hair. A bear-tooth necklace spanned half the breadth of his chest and a design made of porcupine quills had been sewn into the tops of his moccasins. It was as close to the warrior he had once been as they could make him look.

Tyhen wasn't the only one looking at how he had been laid out. Dakotah was remembering him as he'd been when Aaron dragged him back into the lodge and was most grateful for the fact both of his eyes were closed and that he was going to the Great Spirit with a warm buffalo robe.

The warriors cautiously side-stepped the chief's woman as they picked up the ends of the buffalo robe to carry body to the grave.

In the distance drums began to beat, and then a singer from the tribe began singing the death song, letting the Old Ones know that a warrior called Rabbit Runs was walking the path to the Great Spirit.

Dakotah was holding his breath, watching everything Chief Small Foot was doing, taking in every tiny detail of how they placed the body, how they straightened out the robe and then covered the body with a deerskin before they began to bury him. He heard the words the chief was saying and then glanced at the chief's wife. She had been crying yesterday when he'd spoken to her and she was crying now. He wondered if she had ever stopped.

Even though he knew the old man was dead, when the first handfuls of dirt they tossed in hit the deerskin with a thump it made him jump. After that, all he could think about was that Rabbit Runs could not breathe with dirt in his face, but they kept throwing in dirt until it was mounded over the body.

Little Wren was still crying when the chief waved the warriors out of the lodge. There was a brief moment as they left when Dakotah believed Chief Small Foot had forgotten his promise. Dakotah was trying not to cry when the chief suddenly turned and pointed at him.

"The drummers are still drumming. The singer is still singing the death song. It is time now for you. Tell the Old Ones that two more will be walking the path. Say their names aloud. Say them twice. Once so the spirits of your parents will hear your voice and know where to go, and once so the Great Spirit will know that they come."

Dakotah stepped forward, standing just outside the circle where the cooking fire had been, and looked up through the smoke hole to the small circle of sky and shouted.

"Michael Chavez! This is your son, Dakotah! Hear the drums! Hear the death song! They are singing it for you."

Tyhen's heart skipped a beat. The look on the little boy's face broke her heart.

Dakotah took a deep breath and then continued, speaking loudly as he'd been instructed to do.

"Julie Chavez. This is your son, Dakotah. Hear the drums! Hear the death song! They are singing it for you."

Tyhen was so moved it hurt to breathe. Until now she had not known he had been saddened that they had left his parents among the rocks in the landslide, but she felt it now, and it was so strong within her heart she wondered if this was what it felt like to die.

Tears were rolling down Dakotah's face, but he didn't falter as he loudly repeated the message - this time to the Old Ones.

"Michael Chavez is walking the path. I ask the Old Ones to show him the way to the Great Spirit."

His voice quavered, and for a second Tyhen thought he was going to break down. Instead, he lifted his chin and spoke louder.

"Julie Chavez is walking the path. I ask the Old Ones to show her the way to the Great Spirit."

He was soldier straight and stoic as he looked at Chief Small Foot for confirmation that he'd said everything right.

The chief nodded.

"It is done," he said. "You are a good son. Their spirits are no longer lost. They are on their way home."

Dakotah nodded, then it seemed as if all the air left his body. His shoulders slumped as he turned and instead of walking to Lola, he went straight to Tyhen and wrapped his arms around her, his cheek resting just beneath her breasts.

Tyhen was in shock. She couldn't look at Lola for fear she would see disappointment on her face. Today was for Dakotah and what he needed, so she held him without moving until the chief led the way out of the lodge and walked back to their lodge with his wife at his side.

Outside, the sun was still shining and the glare on the snow was still blinding, but the symbolism of walking from a dark tipi into light was not lost on any of them.

Dakotah looked up at Tyhen and then put a hand on her belly.

"The baby cried for me," he said softly, and then fell into line behind Aaron and Lola as they followed the trail back to White Hawk's lodge.

Tyhen ran a hand over her belly as she watched him walking away, then turned as she felt Yuma's arm on the back of her arm.

"Did you hear what he said to me?"

"No."

"He said the baby cried for him."

Yuma put his hand on top of hers.

"He means our baby?" he asked.

She nodded. "He laid his head against me. I thought it was for me to comfort him, but he was listening to her. How is he so connected to her when I am not? Why can't I hear her yet? I don't understand this."

Yuma cupped her face.

"They are as we were – as we are now. Is it not true that we are complete only when we are together?"

Her expression shifted from envy to understanding.

"Yes."

"From the time you were small, you sought only my company. You trailed after me and not your mother or Cayetano."

Her shoulders slumped.

"My mother must surely have felt abandoned."

"She understood the need for our bond, and she had Cayetano, just like now you have me. The baby will need Dakotah in the years to come."

"I know this is so. I didn't think," she muttered.

"So, that is in the future. Now it is time to go back to Willow's lodge. It is too cold out here."

He led the way back, walking single-file and following the path they made when they came.

Tyhen was concentrating on putting one foot in front of the other in the narrow trail when she heard Evan's voice.

A chinook will come. The snow will be gone by morning.

She stopped.

"Yuma, what is a Chinook?"

He turned around.

"It is a warm wind. Why do you ask?"

"Evan said one will come tonight and in the morning the snow will be gone."

He squinted against the glare of the snow and thought about the fire in Willow's lodge.

"Good. The sooner we can get south of this place the better. I don't know how the seasons are at this time in this world, but in our time, south meant warm."

Tyhen smiled.

"I like warm."

He laughed.

"No cold and frozen for you, little whirlwind. You might be the Windwalker's daughter, but you have Cayetano's love of the Mayan jungle in your blood."

The wind came before sundown, expressing displeasure at the snow blanketing the land by blowing all night at a steady blast.

The Cherokee fell asleep to the sound of dripping water and woke up in a meadow full of mud. Breaking camp was not only messy but slow. When Chief Small Foot finally gave the signal to resume their march it was with no small sense of relief.

But as they moved forward, they shared a single thought - the early snow had been but a warning of how short their time before the real winter set in. They walked with haste, intent to be back in their villages before the endless nights of cold turned their world inward like a bear in its den.

As the last of them were moving over a rise in the land, one of them stopped to look back.

He saw the prairie of long grass, broken from the weight of the snow, and the large swath of blackened land in the middle of the forest – and one lone tipi that had been left standing – the one belonging to the warrior called Rabbit Runs who was, like the Cherokee moving East, already gone.

Four days later:

It was nearing midday when Chief Small Foot suddenly called a halt. A scout he'd sent ahead earlier that morning was coming back through the trees and brush on the run.

The chief walked a distance away from the others, frowning as he went.

"What news do you bring?" he asked, as the scout came to a halt.

"There is a dead man ahead. He wears the clothing of the strangers who came to the Gathering to make us sick. Some of the bones are not there because his body was left unprepared."

Small Foot frowned. It was obvious the scout feared a lingering spirit and he knew if this wasn't handled properly, every bad thing that happened from here to their village would be blamed on the angry spirit of the man's dishonored body.

His tribal medicine man had died on the trip to the Gathering. There were other probably other medicine men within the other clans on this march, but he didn't know them and without one to make strong medicine for protection, they had no one to chase away bad spirits. Then he thought of the Dove and her brothers who were said to be shamans. He was about to send a runner back through the People to bring them forward when they walked out of the waiting crowd around him.

He grunted in surprise as they approached.

"How do you come before I have even sent for you?" he asked.

Tyhen waved to the men standing on either side of her.

"My brothers knew your needs and heard your thoughts. What must we do?"

Chief Small Foot couldn't decide whether to be upset that they had heard his thoughts, or grateful they were there to help. He settled for the help and began to explain.

"The strangers you chased away from the Gathering have also run away from their duties. One of them died. His body is a distance ahead and they did not honor his body with a burial. My scout tells me the body has been disturbed and some of his bones are not there. If we walk past him without respecting the dead, I do not want my people to think we have dishonored this man. It will not be good for them to believe they could be cursed."

Tyhen looked at her brothers.

"What do we do?"

Adam's immediate thought was how to satisfy their beliefs, rather than try to explain it would not matter, and so he was the first to speak.

"Since the Cherokee believe a body must be whole before it

is buried, burying the body as it was discovered will not relieve their worries," he said.

She frowned.

"Then what do we do? Surely you do not mean for us to look for the lost bones? What if they were eaten or dragged away long distances?"

When Evan's eyes narrowed, she knew he was seeing not only the problem, but the solution.

"Cover the bones with rocks so that the animals cannot scatter them further. Tell them that will keep the spirit satisfied and in place, and we can pass without fear of it attaching itself to us in any way."

Adam quickly added.

"We stop here so that each one can find a rock. They are to get one as big as they can carry with ease, and then we will march. As we pass the bones, each one will lay their rock upon the bones until all are covered and we have passed without harm.

Chief Small Foot was pleased and it showed.

"I will tell them," Tyhen said, as her brothers disappeared back into the crowd.

When the chief nodded his approval, she took to the sky to deliver the message.

Within moments people were scattering in all directions to search for such a rock to suit their needs as Tyhen landed beside Yuma, who had already been told a body had been found.

"Is it one of the soldiers?"

She nodded.

"Are they still contagious? Would touching their bones cause any sickness?" he asked.

She shook her head. "I do not think so because it was the twins who devised this plan."

"Then it is good. Our things are with Willow. I told her to stay here and I will bring a rock for her."

She glanced at the old woman who was sitting motionless with her eyes closed.

"She is very tired," Tyhen said.

"She is old and the trip to the Gathering was difficult for

her. Going home is going to be worse because of the cold. So we should go rock hunting."

"I saw a rocky outcrop from above."

"Show me," he said, and she did.

The body was in a clearing near the banks of a dry creek. The entire tribe was apprehensive about walking up on the body until they saw it. The soldier had been frightening sitting high on the animal that ran so fast. He was not frightening anymore. The thing he had worn on his head was askew on the skull. Most of the flesh was gone and the clothing had been torn away, obviously by animals. Parts of both legs were missing. His boots were a short distance away with the feet still inside them.

Now that their fear was gone, they began covering the boots, then an arm lying a short distance from the boots, and then the body. They did not toss their rocks, but bent down and placed them gently, taking care not to dislodge what was left of the Spanish soldier's bones.

About halfway through their passing one of the singers began singing the death song, telling the Old Ones that a stranger's spirit was lost in this land and to help him find his way.

The hair rose on the back of Yuma's neck as the song sank into his bones. He had witnessed Dakotah's ritual with an ache in his heart, reminded all too vividly of his own father's death at the Navajo reservation while waiting for Firewalker.

The drummers had drummed for his father. The singers had sung the death song for him, and then they had buried him beside their truck and Yuma remembered almost nothing of the ceremony – only that he had awakened the next day on top of his father's grave. All he remembered after that were hours of fear, the scorching heat and then being in the canyon with the others, running for their lives with Layla Birdsong in the lead.

His muse was interrupted when Tyhen paused beside him to place her rock upon the corpse. He laid his rock beside hers and then looked behind them to make sure Willow was still following. The old woman paused only long enough to place her stone and quickly fell into step. The warrior beside her was dragging her belongings, as was their habit. When the Cherokee traveled long distances, they took down their lodges, and using the lodge poles and the coverings as a kind of sled, they tied on everything else they would need and dragged them behind them.

All he knew was that the fierce-faced warrior pulling Willow's belongings was a family member, and only one of thousands traveling the same way.

Satisfied that Willow was holding up, Yuma turned around.

"Is everything okay?" Tyhen asked.

He nodded. "I think water is ahead. Are you thirsty? We can fill our water pouches."

She frowned. "I should go see. I can fly more easily than Chief Small Foot's scouts can run."

Before Yuma could answer he saw her expression go still.

It was Evan's voice was in her ear.

Adam is walking with the Chief. He already told him the water is to the south. We will reach it before long.

Will we have to be in that water to cross it?

No, my sister. We will walk beside it, not through it.

Good.

Focus shifted when Evan was gone.

"Adam is already walking with the chief to lead the way to water," she said.

Yuma dug through his pack, pulled out a piece from one of the rabbits Willow had cooked last night and turned around to look for Willow. She was even farther behind them than the last time he'd looked and so he backtracked to give her the food.

"You should eat," he said, and handed her the meat.

Her dark eyes flashed with surprise as she accepted the food.

"I thank you," she said, and bit off a piece from the bone.

The warrior beside her seemed taken aback. Since the Eagle had returned from the dead, most of the tribe was afraid of him, and yet here he was offering food to an old woman.

Yuma didn't want to antagonize the man and nodded once

by way of a greeting.

"We come to water soon," he said, and started to return to Tyhen when the warrior spoke.

"I am called Wolf Moon, Chief of the Paint Clan. This woman is the sister of my mother."

"I am Yuma. I am the Eagle who watches over the Dove."

Wolf Moon nodded. He already knew who Yuma was, but the official trading of names was like permission to speak to each other whenever they wished.

"You are good to feed my mother's sister."

Yuma smiled.

"She is good to shelter us in her lodge," he said, and then jogged back to Tyhen, dug another piece of meat from his pack and handed it to her.

Always hungry, Tyhen took a bite without thinking and then realized Yuma wasn't eating and tried to give it back.

"No, this is for you. Eat it," he said.

She frowned. "You fed Willow and you are feeding me, but you do not eat."

"I am not so hungry and you are. Remember, now you eat for yourself and our baby."

Without thinking, she brushed her hand across the coat covering her belly, as if making sure it was fastened to keep away the cold.

"I didn't think. I am sorry," she said, and took another bite, a smaller one that she chewed more slowly.

Yuma brown eyes darkened. "You do not apologize for anything, my little whirlwind... just eat."

She continued to nibble on the meat until there was nothing left but the bones then dropped them onto the ground where they disappeared beneath the dead leaves and grass.

CHAPTER EIGHTEEN

Weeks later:

Daylight was becoming a rare commodity as winter closed in. Once they reached the mountains, which Yuma said in his time had been called The Appalachians, the different clans within the tribe began to separate from the whole, anxious to return to nearby tribal lands.

Tyhen watched with trepidation as the a-ni-tsi-s-kwa, which Yuma called the Bird clan, departed early one morning, moving down the mountain in a different direction. A few days later, the a-ni-ka-wi, also known as the Deer clan in Yuma's time, were gone before sunrise.

The amount of daylight was shorter in the mountains because the peaks began cutting off the sunlight long before it reached the true horizon. Besides the impending danger of being stranded by the weather, they had more wild animals to contend with. The bears had already taken to their winter dens, but they saw the big cats with long teeth almost daily. The wapiti, which the New Ones called elk, were more plentiful than their smaller cousins, the deer. Huge wolves, gray, black, and now and then a rare white, would be seen slipping through the trees before sundown on their way to a hunt. They howled throughout the night, keeping everyone on edge and had it not been for the great number of them on the march, they would have been in danger of attack on a regular basis.

The trip was wearing on everyone. They camped under the stars because there was no time to do otherwise. They slept close to each other and close to fires that were fed throughout the night to keep wild animals away.

Warriors took turns guarding the perimeters, making certain the elderly, the women, and the children who would have been the easiest and most vulnerable prey, were bedded down within the center of the camp each night.

Children were taught at an early age not to cry because crying would have alerted old enemies to their whereabouts, but this trek was pushing everyone to their limits. More than one child crawled beneath their sleeping robes in tears, tired of the cold and of being hungry.

On yet another morning when clouds had fallen onto the earth making it impossible to see more than a few steps away, and the dead leaves on the forest floor were white with frost, the a-ni-waya, which Tyhen learned meant Wolf Clan, separated from the tribe and, like their totem, walked into the heavy fog and disappeared.

Each day, large groups of hunters were sent ahead to bring down game, and wherever they caught up with the hunters is where they camped for the night. No matter how many elk they brought down, or deer that they killed, there was never enough food for them all. There was no time to stay put for a few days so that food could be replaced. It was either go hungry now, or freeze to death later. So they walked with empty bellies and weary souls.

A few days later as they broke camp for the new day's march, Tyhen witnessed two more clans saying their goodbyes.

"More are leaving," she said, as Yuma was rolling up their bedding.

He paused and looked up.

"It is the a-ni-sa-ho-ni, the Blue Clan, and the a-ni-gi-lo-hi, the Long Hair."

She frowned. "Do they never see each other again?"

He hated the fear in her eyes and the uncertainty in her voice. It was so unlike her, but then she had never had a baby in her belly before, or lost everyone from her childhood but for him and the twins. He dropped what he was doing and held her, feeling the cold silk of her hair against his cheek and the rapid thunder of her heart.

"Yes, they see. They do not marry within their clan so there are times when they are together."

"When do we leave?" she asked.

He hesitated to answer, not wanting to upset her any more. His clan was the Wolf and they had already parted from the group, but because of Tyhen's desire to live where it was warmest, they would continue to travel with the clan that was going closest to the coast.

"We will be with the last group. They live closest to the coast."

"Near big water? Like the place where my mother and Cayetano live?"

"Yes, like Boomerang."

"What is this clan called?"

"The a-ni-wo-di. The Paint Clan."

"What does that mean? Why are they different from the others?"

"It is the clan of conjurers, the place of great medicine. Among other things, they make the red paint for war."

"There is to be no more war," she said.

"Maybe with the strangers there will be war," he said.

She thought about it a few moments and then nodded. That was a likely possibility.

"There are only two clans left now. The Paint Clan, and the a-ni-ga-togi-we, the Wild Potato Clan. They are the food gatherers, the farmers, like the people of Naaki Chava who grew food down in the valley where we lived."

She nodded, satisfied for the moment that they would not be living in the high mountains, and a few days later when the Wild Potato Clan left, Chief Small Foot left with them.

Tyhen was confused all over again as she watched them go.

"Who is chief now that Small Foot is gone?"

"He wasn't chief over all of the Cherokee."

"But I thought he was."

Yuma shook his head. "There is no one main chief – only seven with equal power, unless there was a war and then one would become the main War Chief."

She sighed. So much to absorb.

"Who speaks for us now?"

"The chief of the Paint Clan."

"Do we know him?"

Yuma nodded. "His name is Wolf Moon. He is the son of Willow's sister."

Her eyes widened in surprise.

"The warrior who was pulling the sled with her belongings is a chief?"

Yuma nodded. "He could have ordered others, but it was his choice. She is family.'"

"I do not understand so much separation. I do not think I like this."

He lifted her hand to his lips and kissed the palm and then kissed her until she groaned.

"Don't think of what you don't know. Think of what you do. This is not so much different from Naaki Chava or the different rulers in the different cities. These mountains are like the jungle. Just higher and colder. The tribal villages are like the cities that were there, and the clan chiefs are like the rulers within those cities."

"I guess. It's just so different."

She wrapped her arms around his waist and laid her face against the rough surface of his winter coat.

It smelled of wood smoke and pine and she longed for the warm waters of the healing pool in Naaki Chava. Her body was changing and she had no one to consult as to why it was happening or if it would ever be the same. She missed her mother and she missed the familiarity of the old life.

"I am the same," Yuma said softly, and held her close, rubbing the continuous ache of her lower back until he felt her relax against him.

And so the moment passed and the march resumed.

That night, as Yuma curled up behind Tyhen's back and pulled her close against him, he hurt for the fact that he could feel her ribs. Her body was feeding the baby and taking away the nourishment for herself. The cold wind moaned as it blew through the treetops and he was afraid to sleep for fear she would fly away in his arms. Earlier Lola's family had made camp beside them and it felt good to be sleeping beside people they knew.

The quarter moon had sailed halfway across the sky when Yuma suddenly woke. He lay without moving, trying to figure out what had awakened him. And then he realized Tyhen's body was beginning to tremble and his heart jumped in fear. Once again the wind was calling her. She was about to float off of the ground.

Just as he was about to wake her, Dakotah crawled out from under the covers where he'd been sleeping next to Aaron and quickly slipped beneath the covers next to Tyhen.

Aaron roused just in time to see where he went, realized Yuma was awake and thought Dakotah had caused it.

"I am sorry," Aaron said softly, and reached for the robe. "Dakotah, what are you doing?"

The little boy peeked out from under it, as a turtle pokes its head from the shell.

"If I sleep beside the crying baby she will be quiet and then her mother will not fly," he said.

Yuma was in shock. Tyhen was trying to fly because the baby was crying? All this time she thought she was only hearing the wind, but she had been hearing her baby. She had not been trying to fly away from him. She had been trying to get to the baby.

Yuma's relief was huge.

"No, Aaron, let him be. If this will calm Tyhen's sleep I would appreciate it," he said.

Aaron frowned. "But if it does not, Dakotah will come back to me."

Dakotah heard, but he already knew it would work and ducked back beneath the buffalo robe, snuggling his backside into the curve of Tyhen's body warmth.

When he felt a pat upon his head, he knew it was Yuma, then he heard the baby cry once more.

I am Dakotah, and I am here.

The crying ceased almost instantly.

He smiled, and in moments was asleep.

❧

Tyhen woke before morning with her arms around Dakotah's waist and her chin on the top of his head. Yuma was behind her, holding both of them. Her first instinct was pure joy because she was so warm. Whatever had sparked this, it had given her the best night's sleep she had enjoyed in many months.

She felt Yuma beginning to wake, but didn't move, choosing to enjoy daybreak in silence.

The mountains on which they slept loomed dark against a sky that was already greeting the new day, and she wondered what it would bring.

Yesterday she'd heard Evan talking to Suwanee about how much farther they had to go and she suspected Suwanee was suffering both loneliness and exhaustion. Tyhen remembered how lost she'd felt when they'd left her family behind in Naaki Chava and now Suwanee was experiencing the same thing. The sting of loss is sharp, no matter who is trying to help soothe the pain.

She knew Evan was at peace with his woman and could tell from the look in his eyes that he loved her. But she worried for Adam. She had been trying to connect with him for days, but each time she tried he shut her out.

Maybe while he was sleeping she could get a read on what was happening, so she closed her eyes to concentrate and was troubled by what she saw.

Adam was not in his bed. She concentrated more until she saw him standing alone on an outcrop of rock a short distance away from his camp, staring out into the valley below.

My brother! Why do you not sleep?

For a few moments she feared he would not answer, and then she felt him drop his guard and was battered by the slam of unbearable grief.

Adam! What is wrong? How can I help you?

It is nothing and I do not need help, my sister. How do you feel? Does the baby speak to you yet?

No. Only to Dakotah.

It was the same for you. Yuma knew everything about you before anyone saw your face. It will happen in its time and you and your daughter will be fast friends.

The message made her feel better. It was only after he'd shut himself off and she'd lost the connection that she realized he'd given her news about herself so she would not push him for further answers. There was a pain in her chest that kept growing. It was one more part of the change. They were losing him and she didn't know how to stop it from happening.

Evan woke up just as Adam let down his guard and, like Tyhen, he felt his brother's sadness with every fiber of his being. When he heard Adam lie to her, it hurt even more because he knew the truth. Everything was wrong for Adam. He felt ostracized by his inability to provide even the simplest of things for himself. He could set up a tent. He could build a fire, and he could see into the future and into people's hearts – none of which would be enough to keep him alive. It was a sad statement for a man in this part of the world.

Evan was still dealing with the guilt of being with a woman his brother had wanted too when Suwanee stirred within his arms. Had it not been for the fact that they were asleep within the eyes and ears of many, he would have made love to her again and again. She was like a fever in his blood and he couldn't get enough.

A simple glance or smile and it felt as if his heart might burst. Watching her on her knees tending their fire, or roasting the grouse he had killed, or the rabbit he had caught to feed them made him weak. His love for her was both a blessing and a curse.

And while he did not know how to soothe his brother's heart, what he did know was that Suwanee was with child. She had yet to affirm it by missing her monthly bleed, but he had known it within hours after his seed had taken root within her. He also knew that once Adam learned this news, the distance between them would be cold and final. Fate had taken control of their lives and they were helpless to change how it would play out.

Dakotah woke needing to pee and slipped out of Tyhen's

arms to wake Aaron. After his solitary jaunt weeks earlier and nearly being killed by wolves, he was under orders not to go in the dark alone again. Moments later they were both slipping through the camp to some nearby bushes.

As he left her, Tyhen rolled over beneath the buffalo robe and woke Yuma with a kiss.

"Good morning, my Yuma," she whispered.

He groaned beneath his breath as her hands moved across his body. She wanted him, and this was no place to act upon it. Instead of telling her no, he told her something that he knew would immediately shift her focus.

"I know why you are trying to fly in your sleep," he said.

He heard her sharp intake of breath and then her whisper.

"Why?"

"You are hearing the baby cry. It is instinct that makes you want to go to her, but you do not wake and so you fly, trying to follow the sound."

A shudder rolled through her, followed by a relief so strong it brought tears to her eyes.

"How do you know this?"

"Dakotah. Last night we both woke just as you were about to float up into the air. He slipped out of his bed and into ours and within seconds you were no longer trembling."

"How did he know?" she asked.

"He said he can hear the baby crying, so when he gets close to you she knows him, and it is enough to satisfy her discomfort, I suppose."

"I wonder why I do not hear her when I am awake?" Tyhen asked.

"Maybe because she is not crying. Maybe she does not feel unsettled when you are moving. Maybe it's only when you are still that she feels she is alone. Who knows? But Dakotah's connection to her helped you, and for me, that is good news."

She shifted closer to him, using his arm for a pillow, and when she did, he pulled her close.

"Don't dwell on what you cannot change. It will come when it is time," he said.

"I just don't understand why I cannot hear her voice."

At that moment Dakotah flopped down on top of their

buffalo robe and patted her shoulder so she would know he was there. When she pushed the robe aside he leaned forward, his elbows on his knees.

"I know why you cannot hear her."

Tyhen sat up.

"Why?"

"Because she does not yet know how to speak."

Tyhen's eyes widened, then she threw back her head and laughed.

The sound rang out around the campsite and then into the air and across the mountain and echoed back, spreading her moment of joy across every weary soul. It was a sound they had not heard in a very long time and it was still ringing in their hearts as they struck camp.

It was almost two moons since they had left the Gathering. The Wild Potato Clan had been gone from them for three sleeps. The sky was gray and the air felt both damp and cold.

They had just topped a ridge when Wolf Moon suddenly stopped to look down into the valley below. The air was cool, but it was not cold, and when the wind blew the hair away from his face, he smelled the ocean.

Smoke was rising through the trees. Smoke meant cooking fires and, from the valley and the shoreline beyond, he knew exactly where they were.

"A-ni-wo-di!" he shouted, letting out a cry of joy that echoed from ridge to ridge and into the valley.

Yuma was ecstatic. It was all he could do to stand still.

"When we make camp tonight, there will be no more moving the next day. We did it, my little whirlwind! We did it! We are in the land of the Paint Clan, in the place without snow."

The smile on her face was worth all the nights of turmoil. Here she would have rest and food and once again, comfort.

Tyhen sat down. Her belly was rounder now and her back often ached.

"I need to talk with Wolf Moon," he said.

"I will wait here," she said, and then watched him take off through the crowd with a spring in his step.

She was out of the wind with the sunlight on her face. She closed her eyes without thinking, willing to get rest anytime she could take it.

Her thoughts drifted as time passed and she was almost asleep when she heard a soft voice.

I am here.

Her eyes flew open as she sat up and grabbed her belly.

Is this my daughter's voice?

Yes.

Oh little girl, I have been longing for this moment.

There were a few moments of silence and she thought it was over, and then the tiny voice was in her head again.

I see through your eyes. Show me the sky.

Within seconds Tyhen was on her feet.

Yuma, when you look up I will be flying. Nothing is wrong. Our daughter just wants to see the sky.

Without an explanation to anyone she went airborne, startling the people around her who then stared in mute fascination at the woman who knew how to fly.

And just like that, the earthbound shackles that had kept her feet to the ground had been shattered. She went up with her eyes wide open and the wind in her face then turned sideways to circle the mountain below.

The slopes were lush and green, populated with pine and cedar trees standing straight and the tips as narrow as a finger pointing straight for the stars.

From this height, the freshwater lakes appeared as splashes of blue, and the narrow spirals of smoke from below smelled of pine cones and buck brush.

She could see the lodges and beaten paths throughout the forest, all leading down to the shore. Beyond, the endless ocean was in constant movement, abounding with creatures such as she had never seen. This would be her daughter's world - the world in which the people must change so that the purity of what she saw would not be destroyed.

She saw a shadow on the land below and looked up at the underside of a bird so large that it did not seem real. The wingspan was massive and it was flying so close to her that at first she felt fear, then she heard the calm in Evan's voice.

It is called a Condor. It will not hurt you. It knows you are a daughter of the wind. It flies to protect you.

Then she heard a high, piercing shriek as another bird suddenly appeared in the sky with the wingspan of four men and the white crown of the eagle she knew so well.

It flew over the condor with a shriek of disapproval and then slipped beneath her, spread out its great wings, and soared.

Yuma stood beside Wolf Moon with a mixture of pride and a little panic that two such massive birds were matching her every move. When she dipped, they flew in tandem, and when she circled, they were there beside her.

The people of the Paint Clan knew magic. They knew how to conjure spirits and speak to the Old Ones, but they had never seen magic such as this.

They stared in mute wonder as the Windwalker's daughter sailed through the sky and in that moment understood the true power within her.

Tyhen was ecstatic feeling the release of earthly burdens that did not exist up in the sky. She was light and pain free and for the moment unburdened by the sadness yet to come.

Do you see this, my child? It is our world. It as much our domain as the ground on which we walk.

She heard a giggle and then a squeal and then silence until Evan spoke once more.

She sleeps, rocked in her mother's arms in a heavenly embrace.

It was time to return.

CHAPTER NINETEEN

Adam stood alone from the clan, watching Tyhen fly among the aerial giants with an ache in his throat. She would thrive here, and so would the baby. The sight above him was so beautiful he had to turn away before he shamed himself with tears. Warriors didn't cry. But then he wasn't a warrior. He was barely a man.

He scanned the crowd for sight of his brother – never thinking as he searched the faces that he didn't think about looking for Evan. He was always looking for himself.

And then he saw him, a head above most of the men around him, laughing and pointing as their little sister sealed her fate forever in the Cherokee hearts.

Off to the right and standing among the women, he saw Suwanee. She was looking up in open-mouth amazement and he couldn't blame her. People weren't meant to fly – unless you were a Windwalker's daughter. Sunlight bathed her face with a warm glow. She was proudly wearing the jaguar coat that Singing Bird had made for Evan and beaming as the women around her seemed to be exclaiming over the hides with which it had been made. They had never seen an animal with a coat such as this, and they had never seen men such as the twins. There was already gossip about how they would fit into a clan known for spells and potions and conjuring up spirits.

Suddenly Adam felt as if he was being watched and when he looked, Evan was staring straight at him. Adam sighed. Fine. So now he knew he'd been staring at his woman. It didn't hurt to look and he'd purposefully kept his distance.

His heart was cold as he turned away without acknowledging his brother and began searching the crowd for Yuma. He was the other brother – the little one who, as a child, had let them into his tribe of one with generosity and open arms. Adam didn't quite know how to talk to him now. Yuma stood with one foot in the land of reality and the other in the spirit world with Tyhen. He had died and been resurrected by the Old Ones and there were times when Adam saw Yuma that he fancied the man had a glow, like an aura made of gold. He didn't know what that meant, but Yuma had changed, too.

Everyone was changing and growing except him. He didn't want to go down into the village of the Paint Clan and live his life on the perimeter of happiness, always seeing it in others but never in himself. He was broken in so many ways. So broken.

And then he saw Tyhen coming down from the sky with a smile on her face. She was too thin but the walk was ending. She would soon be healthy again.

He took a shaky breath as he gazed upon the crowd, seeing the joy on their faces and feeling the delight within their hearts. They had something to be happy about. They were home.

He watched Evan separate himself from the men and go to his woman, saw the tender way in which he greeted her and then they picked up their packs. Instead of going with them, he stayed where he was and watched as they began winding their way through the trees to the village below.

When they were finally out of sight, he set their tent on the ground beneath a tree, pulled out the letter he'd written to them all on a piece of deer skin, laid it on his rolled up tent then put a rock on it so it would not blow away.

He then moved to the small promontory of table rock with the backpack in his hand, pulled out the spinning cube and began trying to balance it on the rock. It took four tries before the cube began to spin, and the faster it turned, the brighter the light became around it. Adam's heart was pounding so hard that he felt it would surely burst. Faster and faster it turned, becoming brighter and brighter until finally the portal opened. In one hand he held a pocket knife that had come from the future. It was the key he needed to get from here to there.

Without a backward glance, he grabbed the cube in one hand, the knife in the other, and leaped into the light.

Yuma held Tyhen's hand all the way down the mountain, talking with excitement in his voice as he spoke of the future.

Chief Wolf Moon had seemed more than interested about the log home Yuma wanted to build, so Yuma's first project upon arrival was to begin cutting down trees suitable for a cabin. In the meantime, they still had permission to stay with Willow until their own home was built.

Evan was equally elated, so ready to get into his own home. Everything about this journey was coming to an end. It was time to rebuild their lives. He was high on happiness, his gaze fixed adoringly at the woman who carried his child, and never once gave a thought to his brother's whereabouts.

They entered the village to shouts of welcome from the old ones who had stayed behind. Within a short while, lodges were going up, cooking fires were built and hunters disappeared into the forest with their stone hatchets and their spears.

Yuma helped Willow and Tyhen set up their tipi then left to hunt for fresh meat.

Wolf Cries and Red Wing, who had offered their lodge to Evan and Suwanee, had separated earlier with the Long Hair Clan, which left Evan and Suwanee without shelter.

As soon as Chief Wolf Moon resumed his duties as principal Chief, he found them shelter with an old man named Sees With One, named so because he had one dead eye and one that could still see.

After making certain that Suwanee would be safe with him, Evan also took to the woods. Without the hunters in the village, even the old people who'd stayed behind were getting hungry and tired of eating fish, which was the only thing they could still catch.

Because White Hawk had left the tribe with the Deer Clan, Lola and her family were also homeless. Wolf Moon sent them to the lodge of Fish Woman, a widow, and then went through the rest of the New Ones who needed shelter until he was done.

Then he took three of his best warriors into the forest and sent three women to the shore with their fish baskets. There were no stores of food and everyone was verging on starvation.

Unwilling to sit and do nothing, Tyhen went with the women to fish, leaving Willow gathering wood for a fire.

Evan had taken his bow and arrow into the woods and after an hour had two large grouse in his hunting pouch. He was moving quietly through the woods when he flushed another. He raised the bow with the arrow already notched, led the bird's flight path just enough and let fly. It was a perfect shot. The bird dropped a short distance away and as he jogged over to pick it up, he thought about Adam, wondering where they'd put him. Assuming they would need food wherever he was, he sent him a quick message.

Brother, I have grouse. Where are you now?

The fact that Adam didn't immediately answer wasn't surprising. He was distant and touchy and Evan was doing all he could to not make matters worse, but when a few minutes passed without an answer, Evan frowned.

Adam! Where are you? Whose lodge do you share so that I may bring food?

Disgusted, Evan opened himself to the entire village. Knowing he could easily hone in on Adam's whereabouts, instead he was hit with a sense of being empty. He couldn't sense him. He couldn't feel him. He couldn't hear him because Adam wasn't there.

He frowned, trying to remember the last time he'd seen him and then knew it was up on the mountain. Surely he had not stayed up on there. Surely he would have come down with the others.

And searched again, this time closing his eyes for more focus and scanned the area for a sign.

It wasn't until he swept the sight through a second time that he saw the tent leaning up against a tree. His heart started to pound. He was so scared he broke out in a cold sweat and sent a frantic message to Tyhen.

Tyhen was standing motionless in the shallows with a woven fish net in her hands. The water was cold, but not cold like frozen, and the white fish with yellow stripes were swimming closer and closer. She was so hungry for something different to eat that she was determined to bring at least one of them home.

The fading sun was at her back. The ebb and flow of the tide pulled at her feet, threatening her balance. She could see the other women from the corner of her eye but, like her, they were moving slowly or not at all, waiting for a chance to throw their nets.

Tyhen held her breath, watching as the school of fish swam closer and closer, and when they were almost at her feet she threw the net and then yanked the cord, gathering it up into a snare. She was almost dancing as she hauled the net into shore with her catch still flopping and knelt down to see how many she'd caught.

Four! She'd caught four! Delighted with her success she dumped them in her hunting pouch and was going back for more when she heard Evan's frantic voice.

I can't find Adam.

And just like that, the knot in Tyhen's stomach was back.

Do you mean he's not answering you or -

He didn't answer me. I looked for him. He is not in the village. He is not on the mountain. I do not feel him anywhere.

The last time I saw him was when you were flying. I am on my way up to where I saw him last.

On the mountain? Why? Do you think he's been hurt?

Evan's voice was shaking and she could tell he was near tears.

In my vision I saw his tent beneath a tree but he is not there.

I will fly there. I'm sure we will find him.

She ran to the women and gave them back their net.

"I have to help a friend," she said, and flew up into the air and back to the village.

Willow was outside when she landed, and she handed her

the fish.

"I'm sorry I can't help clean them. A friend is in trouble," she said, and opened her arms, let the wind lift her up and flew toward the mountain.

She saw Evan running up the path and felt his panic, which made her anxious, too. She reached the ridge where Wolf Moon had stopped, then flew a circle over the area, going lower and lower with each lap to make sure he had not injured himself in a fall. By the time she was certain he wasn't in any ravine, she circled back and landed just as Evan came running over the ridge.

He gave her a frantic glance and then ran for the trees. She was right behind him when they saw the tent. Evan was the first to reach it and the first to see the note Adam had left on top.

The moment he touched it, he stumbled backward in shock. He didn't have to read it to know what he'd done.

"What?" Tyhen said.

Evan was mute and shaking, his face expressionless.

She grabbed the deer skin, saw the writing, then read the words.

I do not belong in this world. I cannot reconcile myself with the utter lack of civilization and I am useless to everyone, including myself. I love you all, my brother most, and wish him a long and happy life. I am gone from this place and I will not be back. I have to know for myself if all this sacrifice was worth it.

Tyhen's heart was breaking. They both knew what he had done. He'd taken the spinning cube and gone to the future, so if in the years to come they happened to mess this up, he was already dead.

Evan was in torment, blinded with tears and a need to make the world suffer as he suffered now. This wasn't fair. It wasn't fair. Their lives had been a mad man's experiment almost gone wrong. They had nothing but each other until the woman who came between them. He needed to blame. He needed to hurt. He needed to know everyone was suffering as he suffered.

Tyhen started to go to him, trying to think of something consoling when Evan turned in a tear-filled rage and threw the tent over the cliff. Then he began walking in circles, muttering to himself as he repeatedly hammered both sides of his legs with his fists. Then suddenly he dropped to his knees, threw back his head and let out a most shattering shriek of despair.

The sound echoed down into the village – sent the animals in the forest into hiding – startled the warriors on the hunt – frightened the women down at the shore – shattering Tyhen. The first person she thought of was the man who loved her most.

Yuma! Adam is gone.

There were a few seconds of silence when she knew he was trying to absorb what she'd said, and then the reply, eerily similar to the one she'd given Adam.

What do you mean, he's gone?

He left a note. He took the spinning cube and leaped into the future. He won't be back and Evan is going crazy.

Where are you?

On the ridge above the village where Wolf Moon stopped.

I'm on my way.

Suwanee was gathering firewood when she heard the sound. It was a shriek of pain and rage unlike anything she had ever heard, and yet the moment she heard it she knew that it was Evan. She'd seen him go up the mountain on the run and whatever had happened to him there, had suffered him a mortal blow. The moment that went through her mind she knew it had to do with Adam, which scared her. If anything happened to his brother, he would hate her forever.

"No, oh no, oh no," she cried, dropped the firewood and began to run.

Chief Wolf Moon heard the scream, turned to the mountain and closed his eyes. He saw Evan's face and then saw his face again.

The brother! Something had happened to his brother.

He took his spear and four warriors and headed up the mountain, thinking a wild animal had attacked him or maybe he had fallen down the mountain. Familiar with the trail, they moved quickly, and when they reached the overlook and saw the Dove holding onto her brother, using every ounce of strength she had to keep him from throwing himself off the ridge, they ran to help.

But Yuma was ahead of them. He came flying out of the trees from above and saw Tyhen in a struggle with Evan and leaped for the both of them.

"I have him," he said. "Turn loose before he hurts you."

Tyhen let go, then rolled over and scrambled to her feet as Yuma took him down.

Now Evan was belly down and screaming and Wolf Moon didn't know what to do. It was not good luck that the new shamans were already causing trouble.

His frown deepened as he strode over to Tyhen.

"What is wrong with him?" Wolf Moon asked.

Tyhen was shaking, too sad to let go and cry for fear she'd never stop.

"His brother is gone."

Wolf Moon's frown deepened.

"He did not want to stay with the Paint Clan? He did not want to stay with his brother?"

Tyhen shoved shaky fingers through her hair, trying to figure out how to explain what happened.

"It is not that. He felt he could not stay. He took his spinning cube and went into the future. He will not be back."

Wolf Moon's eyes narrowed.

"He went into the future? How does this happen? What is a spinning cube?"

"It is a thing that lets people move from the past to the future and back again. He was sad. He felt he did not belong. He left. Evan is..." Tyhen sighed, and then pointed. "You see how he is. It matters not where Adam went. What matters is that for Evan, his brother just died.

Wolf Moon had seen weeping many times in his life and witnessed much sadness, but he had never seen a brother try to take his own life to follow a family member on the path to the Great Spirit.

He frowned. "He is weak without his brother?"

Tyhen turned on him in anger.

"It is not weakness. He has just lost half of himself. They were one in their mother's belly and then they turned into two. They were the same in everything always and now Evan is no longer whole."

At that moment Suwanee came over the ridge, breathless and holding her side from the pain of running too far, too fast. Evan saw her and then looked right through her. That's when she knew Adam was dead and he blamed her for the distance it had put between them.

She ran to him, desperate to see the love in his eyes and saw nothing but despair.

"Evan, my heart, what has happened?" she cried.

Yuma let him up, thinking Suwanee's appearance would calm him down, but Evan leaped to his feet in anger.

"Adam is gone. He killed himself and it is my fault. He wanted you and I knew it and took you for myself."

Suwanee reeled as if she'd been slapped. Her head dropped as her heart broke. It was as she feared. He hated himself, which meant he would also hate her now.

Tyhen heard this and was enraged. This was not the brother she knew, lashing out at innocent people without care for how it hurt them.

She walked away from Wolf Moon, grabbed Evan by the shoulders, and shook him where he stood.

"Stop talking!" she cried. "You talk crazy from the grief. You have both used the spinning cube more than once without harming yourselves. You have no way of knowing if anything has happened to him. You are not in charge of what your heart feels, and you do not sacrifice yourself just because your brother's world did not turn as he would like."

"Turn loose of me," Evan said, and pushed out of her arms.

"Then grow up!" Tyhen shouted.

He glared.

She glared back.

Yuma was stuck between them without knowing what to

say without making it all worse.

But it was Suwanee who finally brought him to his senses. Broken in spirit she turned away, took three steps and fainted.

Everyone jumped to catch her, but it was too late. She hit the ground with a thud.

The sound hit Evan like a blow to the gut. What had he done? What if she lost the baby? That would be his fault, too.

He picked her up in his arms.

"Do you have a healer?" he asked.

"We have many," Wolf Moon said.

"Send one of them to the lodge of Sees With One."

Tyhen felt for Suwanee's heartbeat. It was steady.

"She is okay. She just fainted," Tyhen said.

"She has a baby in her belly," Evan said. "I need to make sure she is okay."

"Let me have her," Tyhen said. "I can get her down faster."

Evan hesitated, then handed her over and started running, intent on getting there as fast as he could.

Tyhen went straight up and then flew down to the village with the tiny woman in her arms and straight to the lodge where Evan had been sent.

The old man was standing outside when they arrived.

"What happened?" he asked.

"She fainted."

The old man frowned. "I do not know that word."

"She got upset and fell to the ground and did not get up," Tyhen muttered.

The old man felt of her forehead and then frowned.

"She will wake up soon I think."

"Do you know a healer?" she asked.

"I am one," he said. "Come inside."

Tyhen carried the tiny woman inside the lodge and gently laid her down on the sleeping robes.

A few minutes later Evan entered the lodge too out of breath to speak, and with Yuma at his heels.

Tyhen glared at Evan.

"Sit down and do not talk until you have something wise to say, and when she wakes up you apologize, and then you do it again every day for the rest of your life. She has left everything she knows for you. She will grow big with your baby inside her with no one to explain what is happening to her body. If we do not mess this up, nothing is wrong with Adam other than the fact that he chose to live a life out of your shadow."

Evan was more than ten years older than her, but right now he felt like a child who had done something foolish – something bad – and was afraid he would not be able to make it right.

"I will. I promise. I am sorry. It was a shock."

She took a deep breath and then shook her head.

"I can only imagine how you feel," she said softly. "I am so sorry that he chose this, but you have to honor the fact that it was his choice."

Evan nodded, but he was already focusing on Sees With One who was tending to his woman.

"She is not injured?"

"No."

"Why doesn't she wake up?"

"Maybe she does not want to," the old man said, then walked out of the lodge.

"Now's your time to start talking," Tyhen said. "Give her a reason to wake up."

She turned around and walked into Yuma's arms, so heartbroken that another one was missing from what was left of her family. He led her out of the lodge, leaving Evan alone to make his peace.

Evan didn't waste a moment as he took her by the hand and held it to his cheek.

"My love, I am so sorry. I spoke harsh words to you that you did not deserve. I was wrong to be angry. Wake up. Please wake up. You are my life."

He watched her eyelids flutter and breathed a slow sigh of relief. He sat motionless, waiting for her eyes to open, and when they finally did, he saw his reflection in her gaze.

"Are you alright? Do you hurt? I am so sorry."

Suwanee lifted her arms.

He pulled her into his lap and then rocked her where they sat, telling her over and over of his regret until she had heard enough and put her hand over his mouth to stop his talking.

"I did not sleep just because you hurt my feelings. I think it happened because I carry your child and I ran all the way up the mountain. The world began to spin and I fell asleep."

He held her that much tighter.

"I know about the baby. I am so happy."

She nodded. "So am I. We will have a fine strong son like you. I know."

Evan sighed. "One I hope who has more patience and a calmer heart."

"I am so sorry your brother left," she whispered.

Evan shrugged. "I knew he was unhappy, and you were only part of it. He did not know how to hunt. He knew nothing about living this life. He felt like he was useless."

She sighed. "This life is hard but he could have learned."

Evan shook his head.

"He didn't want to and now he's gone. It is as Tyhen said. It was his choice."

"We will have a baby," Suwanee said.

Evan smiled. "Yes, we will."

She snuggled closer within his embrace, grateful that the hate was gone from his face. She never wanted to see that again.

CHAPTER TWENTY

Spring had come to the village. The forest around them was alive with new growth. Baby-green leaves trembled and shook from the incoming sea breezes, the air was warm - the cloudless sky a shade of true blue.

The sea was churning with froth on the lips of the waves - a sign of an incoming storm. The chains of small islands beyond the bay were wreathed in swarms of the sea birds that roosted there.

More than a third of the villagers were now living in cabins and grateful for the solid walls and a roof that did not sway in the wind or leak rain. The introduction of furniture was yet another innovation that had yet to catch on, except for the beds. While the women liked the comfort of a table to prepare the food, they still chose to sit on the floor cross-legged to eat and visit. But they did enjoy what the New Ones called beds, and sleeping off the floor on a surface piled high with warm skins and furs.

Children over the age of five summers went to school for half a day. They were learning what the New Ones called math. The concept of numbers was interesting, even to the adults, and they were learning along with their children. But they didn't understand the need for learning the languages of strangers that may never come to their shores.

It wasn't until Evan told them that the languages were a powerful tool, a kind of magic. That if they knew what was being said, then the strangers would never be able to overpower them, or use deceit to take what was theirs. After that, even the adults came to sit in on the classes.

The women were taught that by crushing shells that littered their beaches by the thousands to mix with the mud and grass they used to chink between the logs that it would turn the chinking into a kind of cement, making it less receptive to being washed away by the rains.

Lola longed for a place to plant a garden, but quickly accepted that with the abundance of deer and elk, it would most likely be eaten before it could be harvested. She tried not to dwell on those precious seeds she'd sheltered for so many months on their march.

Aaron, who was thriving in a fishing environment, had put on weight to the point he was nearly back to his former size. He kept his long hair tied back at the nape of his neck and his body was getting brown again from long days in the sun.

Yet while he was satisfied with the place they had settled in this world, he felt bad for Lola and wanted to see her happy. He thought for several days as to how she could make her garden before he remembered greenhouses. While they had no way to replicate the plastic or windows that had been on them in the days before Firewalker, he got an idea of how to adapt it, and with a few friends, they went to work.

As trees were cut down to build new houses, they began reclaiming the land around it until he had a large, fully cleared field close to their cabin. They dug out tree stumps and carried out rocks until it was ready to till and plant.

After that he began building what looked like the walls of a log cabin, but much longer with much slimmer, taller trees, and without chinking the spaces between. To the New Ones, it resembled a fence made of welded pipe, like the ranchers used to pen their animals before Firewalker.

Aaron made it high so that deer and elk could not lean over it to eat what was growing, and wide and long to accommodate more than one garden.

Lola was ecstatic and often worked hand in hand with the men carrying logs and setting them in place. She put Dakotah at work lopping off the tiny branches and twigs Aaron left on the fencing just so nothing would be tempted to come eat off the leaves. She went to bed each night thinking about what she would plant first and where she would plant it.

Like all of the other children, Dakotah went to the school, and when he wasn't helping Aaron in the afternoon, he made himself available to Tyhen so that he could be closer to the baby. He was still the single source of instant comfort to the child and wondered about the day when he would see her face.

Everyone was in a state of change, including Tyhen. Her body was big and her steps were slower. She hadn't flown in weeks and was patiently awaiting her baby's birth.

At night Yuma held her in his arms and listened to her talk about her day and wondering about the New Ones who'd gone with other tribes, wondering how they fared.

He heard the fear in her voice when she spoke of having the baby without her mother at her side. He had not forgotten what she'd said to Evan the day Adam disappeared, and how she'd confronted him about putting any of the blame onto his wife, reminding him that she'd left everything she knew to be with him and for him to never forget that fact.

It had touched him deeply, knowing that she was talking about herself when she'd said it. Because he could not bear to see her sad, every night when he kissed her goodnight and then wrapped her up in his arms with his hand on her belly, he promised both his wife and his daughter that they would not face this journey on their own.

Content with her life and the man who had been given back to her, she welcomed each day, believing that the worst was over.

Tyhen stood in the doorway of their two room log cabin, watching how the morning sunlight turned the ocean into sparkling gold and letting the wind have its way with her hair.

She wore a loose deerskin shift, her feet were bare, her hair unfettered and hanging down the middle of her back. Her belly was heavy, her movements slow and methodical. Although spring had come to the village, she felt like a bear waking up from its winter sleep, wanting to roar from a hungry belly and yet cranky because it was awake.

The baby was kicking. She had been kicking for days now.

Tyhen thought she must be trying to kick her way out. She laid a hand on her belly, absently rubbing in a slow, steady circle, as if trying to calm the constant turmoil within, and then laughed aloud as a little foot suddenly kicked hard against her palm.

"Ow, little girl. That almost hurt. What are you trying to tell me."

I see what you see. What is it?

"Do you mean the ocean?"

It moves. Is it alive?

Tyhen narrowed her eyes against the sun's glare, trying to look at it as her daughter saw without understanding what it was, and then realized she was right. With the constant motion of ebb and flow, the birds diving to pluck a fish from beneath the surface and the dolphins swimming just offshore, it did look alive.

"The ocean is water, which is not alive, but it is alive with what is in it."

I am ready.

Tyhen's heart skipped a beat.

"To be born?"

Will it hurt?

Tyhen rubbed her belly more, wishing she could touch her to reassure her she would be fine.

"You leave the work to me. All you have to do is keep moving and then it will be over."

A storm comes.

"I know. The sea looks angry."

I am the wind. I come with it tonight.

Tyhen shivered with anxious anticipation.

"I will be ready," she promised, and kept rubbing her belly until the baby settled and she kicked her no more.

Satisfied that her days of waiting would be over, she walked outside a few steps until she could see Yuma down at the beach.

The men of the village were building yet another boat to go with the two they'd built during the winter. The lives of the Paint Clan were changing and, by tomorrow, another Windwalker would be born.

Suwanee moved slowly, burdened by the huge weight of her belly. Being small, she knew this would not be easy, but she had not been prepared for Evan's news. Two moons ago he said there were two babies inside her belly and that she must lie down often and let him worry about doing what needed to be done. He even talked a girl older than Dakotah to come a few hours every day, and do for Suwanee what she could no longer do for herself. In exchange, he would pay her with the hide of his next elk.

It made Suwanee the talk of the village. Not only was she going to have two babies, but she had someone doing her daily chores, and the woman doing it was going to get a most prized hide for her trouble.

It was, quite likely, the first instance of 'hired help' in this new world, but it would not be the last.

Yuma glanced up from the beach and saw Tyhen watching them from above. He stopped and lifted an arm in greeting, but either she didn't see or she was lost in thought. Either way, her stillness made him uneasy and after a quick glance at the angle of the sun, he called a halt to their work.

"I think a storm is coming," he said, as he picked up his tools to carry back to the cabin. "I say this is enough work on the new boat for today. I will hunt later."

The men didn't argue. Physical work every day was an anomaly for warriors. They used to spend their time making new spears or shaping stones for new axes. All the rest had been women's work. Now they were hot and tired each day and ready for something to eat.

Yuma started up the path toward home with haste, anxious to see if Tyhen was well.

He felt pride as he glanced up at their cabin. They had done a lot of work in a short time. The small area around the house had been cleared of rocks and brush and he had built a roofed porch over the front door so that she could sit out and watch the ocean, even if it rained. He remembered the flowers in his mother's garden and made a point to look for flowering bushes in the forest so that he could transplant them around the porch. It would look pretty and be as near to the floral Eden of Naaki Chava that he could create.

As he neared the house he felt the wind behind him push harder than before. He turned to look at the sky. It was changing. More clouds were there now and in the far distance across the water he could see darkness. It was the storm. It would likely take a few hours to get here, but tonight it would rain and the wind would blow and he was most grateful not to be riding it out beneath lodge poles and deerskin.

In a hurry, he ran the last few yards to the house, laid his work tools on the porch, and then leaped the steps and went inside.

Tyhen was going through the things she had been preparing for the baby. When she heard his footsteps, she turned with a smile.

"I saw you at the beach. That will be another fine boat when it is done."

He went to her, laid a hand on her belly, slid the other beneath her hair and pulled her to him, feeling the race of her blood against one hand and the kick of the baby with the other.

He leaned in and kissed her slowly, with a lingering ache. It had been a long time since they had been together, although he didn't mind. It was but a passing thing in their lives. Right now, the baby was more important than soothing his lust.

"She wants out," he said.

Tyhen laid her hands over his. They held the child together, but it would be the last time there was a barrier between them.

"The baby comes with the wind," she said.

Yuma's heart skipped a beat as his thoughts slid to Tyhen. As powerful as she was, she would still suffer as all women suffered, bringing a child into the world. Suddenly he was a little bit afraid.

"Are you ready? Is there anything you need for me to do?"

She smiled. "We will eat something now. Afterward you

will tell Lola and Willow. Tell them to come before the storm begins so neither will get wet."

Yuma's heart was pounding.

"I should tell them now," he said.

"I do not want them underfoot until they are needed," she said.

"I want this time to myself. Right now, we eat. There is meat from what we roasted in the fireplace last night. I made bread this morning after you left."

She pointed to the circles of baked flat bread. The Cherokee made flour from wild potatoes, pounding them into a kind of flour and then mixing it with water and baking it on a stone. Yesterday Dakotah had brought her a handful of small black berries. He told her they were mostly sweet, which made her laugh. She could tell by the purple stains on his fingers and lips that they had been sweet enough for him to eat.

She had stirred them into the flour this morning before she baked the bread and was delightfully surprised by the taste.

Now she smiled again, watching the surprised expression on Yuma's face as he bit into the bread.

"This is good! What did you put in it?"

"Some black berries Dakotah gave me yesterday. He ate many, I think. This was what was left by the time he got to me."

Yuma laughed and took another bite.

"I will thank him when I see him. You sit," he said, pointing to the bench at the table. "I will bring the food to you."

"I don't want much. My hunger is small today."

He nodded, but when she wasn't looking gave her another nervous glance. She seemed far calmer than he felt. He so wished this day was already over.

Wind-tossed waves higher than Yuma's head crashed against the shore. He watched from their front porch to be certain the village boats were both secure and high enough from the water not to be swept away. Once he was certain they were safe, he turned his face to the wind and closed his eyes.

Lola and Willow were inside and had been for hours. They'd made him leave a short while ago. Yuma wanted to be with her. He would wait, but in the end, he would be there. He wasn't a man to break a promise.

He didn't hear any sounds from inside, but that could be partly due to the din the wind was making. Suddenly the first drops of rain were blown against his face. He opened his eyes just as the roar of thunder rolled across the bay, followed by a spear of lightning that struck out on the water.

The storm was upon them, and no matter what those women said, he was going back inside.

Wind and rain blew in as he opened the door. Before anyone could yell at him, he shut it fast behind him. Tyhen was pacing back and forth, her face wreathed with sweat, her hands beneath her belly, as if she was trying to hold onto the child to keep it from being born. Even though it was a subconscious act, it struck Yuma as most poignant. Even now as the baby was in the act of being born, Tyhen was still trying to keep her safe from what awaited in the years to come.

Willow frowned.

"You do not belong here."

His chin came up and his eyes narrowed as he returned the frown.

"I helped make this happen. I do not leave her to suffer it alone."

Willow was taken aback. She had never heard words like that come out of warrior's mouth before.

Lola smiled. When it came to protecting Tyhen, Yuma was first in line.

Tyhen reached for him in mute desperation as another contraction rippled across her back and belly. She leaned her forehead against his chest, her fingers digging into his forearms as she shuddered and then groaned.

As soon as the contraction passed, she began to walk again, and so he walked with her, whispering sweet things meant only for her ear. He was shocked when the next contraction came so fast on the heels of the other.

"Lola! The pains are so close together. How long has this been happening?"

"A while," she said.

Suddenly, Tyhen's moan turned into a high-pitched keen.

Willow grabbed bedding from off their bed, threw it down on the floor and made Tyhen squat.

Yuma knelt behind her and slid his arms beneath her shoulders.

She leaned back against his strength as another pain rolled from her back to the middle of her belly. The moan in her throat rolled out as a scream when the baby's head was crowning.

Willow and Lola were there, ready to catch the baby.

"I see her!" Lola cried. "Push, Tyhen, push!"

"So tired," Tyhen muttered, and then as another wave of pain rolled through her, she threw her head back on Yuma's shoulders, rode through the pain with a long, guttural groan and did as Lola asked - pushing, pushing without taking a breath or losing focus.

All of a sudden there was a cry, and Tyhen drew breath on a sob.

She was here!

Yuma could see nothing but the back of Tyhen's head and her bare knees. He smelled the blood and when Tyhen collapsed against him, he held her tighter.

Then he heard the cry. It was a tiny one as baby cries go, but it was a sign that she drew breath. He could tell by the smiles on the women's faces that the baby was whole, and when she cried again, it was a little louder with more indignation and he smiled.

When they cut the cord and wiped her clean, he could only stare at her in mute astonishment. That's what he and Tyhen had made. That perfect child is what came from their love. The room blurred and then the women took charge.

When he sat down on the bench, still shaking in very muscle, Lola suddenly thrust the baby into his arms.

"Hold her."

And so he did.

She was wailing to the walls and the wind blasting against the cabin, expressing her indignation at such a rude entrance into this world and it so reminded him of when he'd first seen

Tyhen that it made him laugh, and then he was laughing through tears.

He opened up the covering to look upon his child and knew she would be tall like her mother. Her little body was long, as were her legs and feet. The little fingers that curled around his thumb held hard and fast. She would be stubborn, also like her mother. She already bore a full head of black hair.

He rubbed a finger along the side of her cheek he felt the softness of newborn skin and laughed again from total joy. It was the second bout of laughter that stilled the baby's cries.

"There you are," Yuma said, watching as her eyes began to follow the sound of his voice. He seemed to remember learning in the time before Firewalker that babies could not see when they were first born, but he didn't believe that was true. Not with this one. Another Windwalker had been born.

Eyes so dark they appeared to be black looked up at him from a tiny face that would one day become a beauty. Her nose was barely there, her tiny mouth opened and shut, as if instinctively searching for the nourishment she would get at her mother's breasts.

"I am Yuma. I am your father and I am the Eagle who looks after the Dove. Welcome to this world little girl and know that you are loved."

He watched her blink, and then she was done with the introduction to her father as she let out another wail that brought Lola running.

"Tyhen is ready now," she said. "I will take her to her mother."

Yuma stood.

"I will carry her," he said softly. "It is the first time, but it will not be the last that she is in my arms."

He crossed the room and went into their bedroom.

Tyhen was propped up in the bed, waiting for the moment to hold her daughter in her arms. When she saw Yuma walk in carrying the baby, a wave of emotion swept through her. She had loved him as a boy. She loved him as a man. But she had never known she would love him more as he bent down and placed their baby in her arms.

"She is angry with me," Yuma said, as the baby continued

to wail. "I am sadly failing in what she needs."

Tyhen lowered the cover over her breast and cradled the baby against her.

"Hello, my daughter. Open your eyes and see your mother."

It was the voice – the voice she'd heard all the months she'd been waiting to be born. The crying trickled off into little more than a mouse squeak.

Yuma laughed, which made Tyhen smile.

"Good girl. Now hear your name, my baby, so that you will know when you are called. You are Walela, the butterfly. Born as one thing that turns into another. You are a Windwalker and you are loved."

Dakotah sat at the open window of their cabin, feeling the rain on his face and the wind in his hair. There was a trembling within him that he could not control.

She was here!

She would love him forever and he would protect her with his life.

EPILOGUE

Three months later…

It was late afternoon and had it not been for the sea breeze, the heat of the day would have been unbearable.

Suwanee was miserable and with no way to ease her burden by lying down, she got up to move to the porch. Evan had built what he called a rocking chair and put it on the porch for her alone.

The girl who helped her was gone for the day and Evan would be home at any moment. He had been hunting all day and was down in the village sharing meat they didn't need with the widows who no longer had a man who hunted for them.

It was cooler on the porch, but it did not ease her misery. She saw the dark shade beneath the trees in the forest a short distance away and had a sudden longing to feel the dirt beneath her feet.

Evan would disapprove, but he would get over it, she thought, and was smiling to herself as she eased down the steps and headed for the shade.

It felt good to be doing something positive. She was so tired of staying still and not tending to her man. She would be glad when these babies were out of her belly so that she could live a normal life again.

The dirt was hot beneath her feet but the shade soon cooled them. She moved her toes back and forth in the dirt and then laughed. She could not see her feet because her belly was in the way.

The forest beckoned. For a child who'd grown up in the

north, there were always trees and the vast valleys between the mountains in which she'd played. She moved a few steps farther, seeing a bush with tiny flowers, then seeing another bush heavy with some kind of berry. But the simple fact that no animal had been eating there was her warning to leave them alone. If an animal or bird wouldn't eat them, they had to be poison.

Ignoring the burgeoning bush, she began following what appeared to be a deer path just because she could, and the next time she looked up, she could not see the cabin. On the heels of that reality came a pain so fierce across her back that she thought she would die, and then she panicked.

The babies! It was time and she was not where she should be.

The pain began to fade and when it did, she headed back down the deer path as fast as she could move. Fear was in her heart and something within her – some kind of self-preservation, told her trouble was only starting. Another wave of pain was so great she doubled over as water gushed from inside her and ran down her legs. Unable to stand, she dropped to her hands and knees and rode it out.

She thought about screaming for help, but again, instinct told her to stay quiet, and as soon as she could, she pushed herself up and began moving again, this time faster and faster.

She was running when the next wave of pain struck and she grabbed onto the limbs of a tree and held on in horror as she felt a baby sliding out of her body. Frantic, she tore off her shift and caught the baby in it just before it hit the ground. The baby was not moving, and she was so afraid she could not breathe. She turned it over in her arms and thumped the tiny back until she felt something move and realized it had taken a breath. It wasn't until she turned him over that Evan's prediction about a boy proved to be true.

Her heart was pounding now because what she'd sensed behind her, she could now hear. The shuffling grunt and the rustling of leaves told her it was a bear and from the blood she had shed it was on her trail. Without hesitation she bit the cord in two, separating herself from the child, rolled it up in her shift and began to run again.

She had only gone a short distance down the path when she heard the bear again. It was closer and pains were rolling through her and the second baby was falling out between her legs. She caught it with one hand and clutched it against her too, then holding them tight against her breasts, she began to run.

She was screaming now, praying to the Great Spirit to lend strength and speed to her legs, but she could hear it coming faster and faster down the trail. With only seconds to make the decision, she jumped off the path long enough to hide the first baby beneath heavy brush next to some pines, and then took off running down the path, hoping that the bear would follow her instead. There was no time to separate herself from the second child and so she ran, faster than she would have believed she could run while blood poured from her body, screaming Evan's name as she went.

Evan was on his way back to the cabin when a vision flashed before him. All he saw was Suwanee on her hands and knees in the woods and his heart nearly stopped. He couldn't believe she'd done it, but he knew she was out of the cabin and giving birth in the woods. He began to run.

His first instinct was to send a message to his brother, then remembered he was no longer in their world and sent a message instead to Tyhen.

I need help. Suwanee is in the woods. The babies are coming and she is in trouble.

Tyhen's voice in his ear was an immediate relief. Someone was going to come help.

Where is she? What kind of trouble?

I think on the deer path straight behind the cabin. I feel more than pain from the birth. I feel danger.

We are on the way.

It was all he needed to hear and lengthened his stride.

Tyhen dumped the baby in Dakotah's arms.

"Take care of her for me. Something is happening to Suwanee."

Dakotah's eyes widened and then he clutched her close. It was his first time to protect her and he had no notion that he would fail.

Tyhen ran out of the house calling Yuma's name. He came running from the back where he'd been cutting up firewood, still holding the precious axe from before Firewalker in his hand.

"What's wrong?" he cried, picking up his spear with his other hand as he ran toward her.

She threw her arms around him and within seconds they were in the air.

"Something is happening to Suwanee. She is on the mountain behind their cabin. Evan said the babies are coming but she is in danger. Help me watch for her below."

His hands tightened on his weapons as he began scanning the area. They flew over the cabin and then Tyhen went lower until they were so close to the treetops he could almost feel them.

Suddenly he saw movement and yelled.

"Down there! I think I see her running!"

Tyhen swooped lower.

"I see her!" Yuma cried.

And then Tyhen did, too. She was completely naked and running for her life with a baby clasped against her breast, and only a short distance behind her, they saw the bear.

"Put me down! Put me down!" Yuma yelled.

And so she did, crashing through treetops, scattering leaves from the rush of the wind in which they flew. By the time they had landed, Suwanee and the bear were already farther down the trail.

They were running when they heard a roar and then a scream, and then they took a turn in the trail and saw them.

The bear was already on top of her. Yuma didn't miss a stride. Still running, he pulled back his spear and leaped. The spear went through the bear's back as he landed on top and then he swung his axe with his other hand, severing the bear's head from its spine with one blow.

The bear fell sideways just as Evan reached the scene. He saw Suwanee face down in the dirt, and although he knew she was dead, began screaming and tugging at the bear, trying to drag it off of her lifeless body.

Finally, it was Tyhen and the power of the wind that lifted the bear up and flung it against a nearby tree.

Evan was on his knees, shaking and mumbling as he grasped Suwanee's shoulder and turned her over, then rocked back on his heels. The baby was still clutched to her chest, still connected to her by the life cord.

Evan couldn't move. He couldn't breathe. He couldn't think.

Then Tyhen pushed him aside and grabbed the tiny child from Suwanee's arms and felt for a pulse. There was none.

She blew in its mouth in the way her mother had taught her, and then pushed on the tiny chest with two fingers, then breathed again, and then again, until the blue tinge beneath the skin turned pink and she heard it cry.

"He lives, he lives," Yuma said, and at Tyhen's instruction, cut the cord and cleared the baby's mouth.

Evan was sobbing as they placed his son in his arms. He saw Adam's face on a baby with brown skin and thought, Adam came back in the only way that he could.

Then Tyhen gasped, and the fear behind it made his blood run cold.

"She's already had the other baby. That's why she has no clothes. She wrapped it up in her shift. Think Evan, think! Where is your son? He might still be alive."

Evan shuddered as the shock of what she said rolled through him. He thrust the baby into Yuma's arms and closed his eyes and heard a cry.

"I hear him," Evan mumbled, and started walking back up the path, and the farther he walked, the louder grew the cry.

Tyhen could hear nothing, but she didn't doubt his word. They followed Evan up the mountain, leaving Suwanee's poor battered body behind. She didn't need them anymore, but her son did, and if it was the last thing they could do for her, they didn't intend to let her down.

Evan was still moving, but the cries were getting weaker which scared him, so he began to run. If the cries stopped, he would not find the baby in time.

It was instinct that made him stop. So he stood on the path without moving, listening, listening, and finally heard what his heart had been feeling.

Something was moving in the brush. He stumbled off the path, following instinct rather than sound as he shoved aside the brush beneath a tall stately pine.

First he saw a foot and then a tiny leg poking out from beneath the folds of Suwanee's shift. He bent down and picked the bundle up, then held it close against his chest.

Tyhen and Yuma arrived just as Evan began to unwrap the folds.

"You found him!" Yuma cried. "Is he alright? Has he been harmed?"

Evan was staring down into another version of his brother's face. Same eyes. Same nose. Same warm brown skin. And not only was he was breathing, he was also trying to get his fist into his mouth.

When he turned to face them, tears were rolling down his face.

"He is alive and unharmed. Suwanee saved them. She sacrificed her life to save them!" His voice was shaking as he held the baby close. "How am I going to live without her? How am I going to raise them alone?"

Tyhen hugged her brother as Yuma put an arm across his shoulder. They looked at the matching babies in awe and in disbelief. How can something so rare and beautiful come from such a tragedy such as this?

Tyhen was doing everything not to break down and sob. Her thoughts were nothing but anger and confusion.

First Adam and now this? What were the Old Ones doing, putting him through such a loss?

Then she focused her thoughts. Her brother needed her. He needed Yuma.

"Look at us, Evan. We are your family. As long as you have us, you are never alone."

He lifted his head, first looking at the naked baby Yuma was holding then knelt with the child he'd just found and unwrapped the shift.

"Give him to me," Evan said.

Yuma put the baby in his hands and in turn, Evan laid him back down beside his brother. Almost instantly their bodies curled into one another. They knew it was how they had lived in their mother's belly, curled up in each other's arms.

Evan's heart was breaking as he wrapped them up and then stood with them close against his chest.

"I need to go home," he said, and started walking down the path.

"Walk with him," Tyhen said. "I'm going to get Suwanee."

"What are you going to do with her?" he asked.

"I am going to take her home, too. There is a place to bury her behind their cabin. In time, he will need someone to talk to and it should be her."

Yuma nodded and then ran to catch up as Tyhen flew straight up and then down the path ahead of them.

Tyhen's hands were trembling and she was crying as she worked, removing the afterbirth and most of the blood from Suwanee's body with handfuls of leaves. Finally, she picked the body up in her arms. It was evident how tiny she had been, but how she died had been proof of what a mighty spirit she had within her. Then Tyhen took to the sky with the body against her chest and flew down toward the village.

The sun was about to set and the shadows were moving across the trees and rooftops, and across the lodges standing tall. Smoke was spiraling up through smoke holes. The news of her death had yet to be told.

She circled the cabin and then came down in front of the porch.

Lola saw her and saw the body she was carrying and let out a heartfelt wail as she came running.

Tyhen's heart was breaking and the story of Suwanee's death had yet to be told, but at this moment, she knew she'd finally learned life's first real truth.

The saddest part of life will never be about you, but about someone else's death.

The End

THE HERITAGE
Prophecy Series
Book Four

EXCERPT

Adam came through the portal in a blinding flash of light, unaware that every moment of it happening had just been caught on tape. He had the spinning cube in one hand, the pocket knife and backpack in the other, and only seconds to assess his surroundings before he darted off into the shadows of a city.

He didn't know where he was or what daylight would bring, but he needed different clothes and a place to hide, and to find them he turned on every psychic trait he possessed.

He found the clothing first, folded in the backseat of a truck. It had been so long since he'd seen a vehicle of any kind he'd almost forgotten what to call it.

The pants were made of what was called denim. That much he remembered, and the sleeves in the shirt were too short. He rolled them up and then tossed the clothing he'd worn into the truck, telling himself he hadn't really stolen anything. It was just a trade.

The air was warm - the night dark save for the street lights at every corner. Unless things had drastically changed he was going to need money, too, but first things, first.

What he needed now was a safe place to hide.

ABOUT THE AUTHOR

Sharon Sala is a long-time member of RWA, as well as a member of OKRWA. She has 100 plus books in print, published in five different genres – Romance, Young Adult, Western, Fiction, and Women's Fiction. First published in 1991, she's an eight-time RITA finalist, winner of the Janet Dailey Award, five-time Career Achievement winner from RT Magazine, five time winner of the National Reader's Choice Award, and five time winner of the Colorado Romance Writer's Award of Excellence, winner of the Heart of Excellence Award, as well as winner of the Booksellers Best Award. In 2011 she was named RWA's recipient of the Nora Roberts Lifetime Achievement Award. Her books are New York Times , USA Today, Publisher's Weekly best-sellers. Writing changed her life, her world, and her fate.